ONLY LOVE CAN MELT THE VENGEFUL HEART

It seemed the most natural thing in the world when Adam lowered his lips to hers. He pulled her even closer, molding her body against his. Time seemed suspended, sensation reduced to the pleasure of his lips, the enticement of his tongue, and the promise of delight to follow.

He hesitated, his chest heaving as he fought to breathe. Letitia stared up at him, trying to understand the emotion in his eyes. Before she could speak, his head lowered again. If the first kiss had been arousing, the second was devastating. Desire flamed within her. With a little moan, she tore her lips from his and buried her head in the hollow of his shoulder. She knew what was happening to her, knew what she wanted, but she didn't know what to do about it.

SWEET REVENGE

JEAN STRIBLING

HarperPaperbacks
A Division of HarperCollinsPublishers

This is a work of fiction. The characters, incidents, and
dialogues are products of the author's imagination and
are not to be construed as real. Any resemblance to
actual events or persons, living or dead, is entirely
coincidental.

HarperPaperbacks *A Division of* HarperCollins*Publishers*
       10 East 53rd Street, New York, N.Y. 10022

Cover illustration by Diane Sivavec

First printing: August 1993

Printed in the United States of America

HarperPaperbacks, HarperMonogram, and colophon are
trademarks of HarperCollins*Publishers*

10 9 8 7 6 5 4 3 2 1

To Mom,
with love from Annie
and
to Dawn Carroll Boese,
from the bottom of my heart—
thanks, pal!

Prologue

Willamette River Valley, Oregon, 1867

  Adam McCormick scowled at the fresh, damp earth covering his mother's grave and wondered if there was any purpose to a person's life. There couldn't be; what had been the point of his mother's life? For that matter, what was the purpose of his own? He had always lived by the code of doing the best you can with what you have and never, ever discounting the importance of luck.

  Luck, he thought bitterly. His mother'd never had any. He glanced down at the words on the simple wooden tombstone: Ingrid Bjorklund McCormick. 1816–1866. Native of Sweden. *The wicked is driven away in his wickedness: but the righteous hath hope in his death. Proverbs 14:32.*

  She'd died at fifty. A lifetime of hard work and bad choices had made those years harsh ones. He subtracted in his head—she'd been seventeen when he'd been born. His hands clenched into fists as he stood, fighting back emotions that threatened to overwhelm him.

He reached out and rubbed his hand across the painted name. McCormick. It was her last husband's name. Her first husband's name, her son's real name, had been lost forever when Adam was three, when she married Robert McCormick and forced her son to take his stepfather's name as his own.

"Adam?"

He glanced at his half brother. Swen was at least four inches taller than Adam's scant six feet, but Adam could see his features repeated in the younger man's wheat-blond hair, blue eyes, and long, straight nose, a legacy from their mother.

Swen pointed toward the Willamette River and the ugly mouse-gray clouds building to the south. "It's going to rain again."

Adam nodded and clapped his hat back on his head. He'd been sixteen, his brother's present age, when Robert convinced Ma to leave New York State. The three of them set out west, for Adam couldn't abandon Ma to face Robert's harsh ways alone. Robert had continually touted the Oregon Territory as the land of milk and honey, paradise on earth. After experiencing the Oregon climate firsthand, Adam doubted that paradise could be even one-tenth as wet.

Now Swen's hands moved awkwardly by his sides. "Can you stay?"

Adam hesitated, his thoughts still mired in the past. He'd remained with his mother as long as he could, but a year after they'd reached the Willamette Valley,

Robert decided to prove his manhood one time too many by taking his belt to Adam. And Adam had left Oregon, running away to seek his fortune in the gold-fields of California.

He'd fallen in with an itinerant peddler who, among other things, carried a supply of liquor. It'd been potent stuff, especially to a youngster unused to spirits. Adam remembered how he'd vowed to make his own way, find his fortune, and rescue Ma from Robert's brutality.

His gaze swept over the tragic little cemetery. Instead of seeking his freedom and fortune, maybe he should have stayed and killed his stepfather, the bastard. Adam knew he'd made a mistake, coming here. He'd leave today. He had to get away from this place and all the painful memories it held.

He squared his shoulders, trying to swallow the unexpected lump in his throat. Swen was his brother, but . . . "I'm sorry. I can't stay."

Swen's reply was unexpectedly mature. "I understand. I've kind of gotten used to Ma being gone, but you—" He ducked his head, pulled a letter from his coat pocket, and handed it to Adam. "Ma left you this, made me promise you'd get it. She told me you'd make it through the war."

Adam's chest tightened as he slowly turned the letter over in his hands. He'd never envisioned this. He wasn't prepared for it.

"Ma changed a lot the last couple of years. This preacher came into town and . . ." Swen fidgeted nervously. "She just, uh, changed."

"She always took her religion seriously."

"Yeah, but this . . . this . . ." Swen tried again.

"Preacher Morrison is a hard man. He only preaches the Old Testament. Never the New. And Pa . . . he . . . he didn't make it any easier. When Ma got ill—she was so sick, she knew she was dying—and Pa wouldn't let up on her."

Adam couldn't get rid of his overwhelming sense of guilt. But if he'd stayed, would it have made any difference?

"After Preacher Morrison got ahold of Ma, I couldn't talk to her—I was frightened for her! I couldn't stop the preacher and I couldn't stop Pa." Swen's voice broke. He turned away to hide his tears and then continued. "It was like she'd only listen to her God. And Pa . . . oh God, Adam, it didn't matter when Pa hit me, but when he lit into Ma . . . I . . . I . . ." Swen choked and finished, all in a rush. "I couldn't stand by, and when it was all over, Ma was dead."

Robert McCormick had always solved his problems with his fists. But the realization that he'd actually hit Ma when she was ill swept away all of Adam's guilt and misery, leaving only a cold, burning fury.

He'd find Robert, wherever he was, and give him the beating he deserved. In fact, murder was too good for the bastard.

There was no doubt in Adam's mind that he'd avenge his mother's death. "Where's Robert?" Adam demanded. "Oregon City, or—?"

Swen gulped. "He's dead, too. Morrison wouldn't let me bury him here in the graveyard. And it's just as well Pa is dead, considering the look on your face."

Adam swore, a short, pithy epithet.

Swen tried to explain. "That night after I . . . after

he . . . after Ma died, he took off. I found out later he'd gotten blind drunk, fell, and drowned in a stream."

Adam swore again and again. But all his invective didn't make him feel one whit better.

"Damn it!" he finished. "It's just not fair!"

He looked down at the letter crumpled in his hand. All the ways he'd failed his mother rushed into his thoughts at once. Finally, he tucked her last message carefully inside his shirt. He'd read it later, not now.

There was no way he could bring Ma back, no way he could reach Robert, no way to get any satisfaction out of this hellish situation. A man had to know when to walk away, but God! it was hard.

He thought of one thing he could do for Ma and made up his mind with characteristic swiftness. "I'm heading for San Francisco. Do you want to come with me?"

Swen's eyes widened in astonishment. "Me? I . . . I don't know."

"I wish you would," Adam said softly. "You stood by Ma, I didn't. I admire you for that and I owe you, more than words can say. Besides, brothers ought to stick together."

"I . . . oh. Do you mean it?"

Adam cuffed his brother gently. "Leave you in this watery paradise? Ma'd never forgive me."

Adam waited until he'd gained the privacy of his berth on the *Athena,* a barque sailing to San Francisco. Then, with a sigh, he opened his mother's final letter and began to read.

My dear son,

When you read this I will be gone. Will you grieve for me? I had two sons, but only Swen stood beside me while you, Adam, deserted me.

There is only one thing in my life left undone. If you have any feelings left for me you will undertake this task for me. Just recently I learned a man who calls himself Hunt Ramsey is living on a rancho near San Diego. He dishonored me when I was young and vulnerable to his persuasive ways. He condemned me to a life of eternal sin, and he's the man who destroyed your grandparents and your father.

I know I'm dying and yet I find I can think only of one thing when I should be preparing myself to meet my maker.

"O Lord, thou knowest: remember me, and visit me, and revenge me of my persecutors; take me not away in thy longsuffering; know that for thy sake I have suffered rebuke." Jeremiah 15:15

Adam, you left me, left me with Robert when I needed you the most. Oh, I know you came back and tried to buy my forgiveness with your money. I turned you away then, but now you can right the wrong you did to me by avenging our family. I need you now, Adam, as I have never needed you before.

Adam, God has come to me and promised me that you will be the instrument of His revenge against Hunt Ramsey. By doing what our Lord asks you will redeem yourself in my eyes.

My everlasting life and hope of glory depend on you. My trust rests in you. Prove to me that you are indeed my son. Don't fail me at my time of greatest need. Don't fail me.

Your loving mother

Adam's lips twisted bitterly. An odd expression warmed his eyes. At last, something he could do for Ma. He ran his thumb over Ingrid's letter and vowed, "I won't fail you, Ma. I swear to you, I'll do whatever it takes to avenge my grandparents, my father, and you."

1

Fayette County, Kentucky, 1867

Massive oaks lined each side of the drive, pointing the way to Bellewood Plantation. The bare arms of the trees reached for the crystalline purity of the blue sky, while patches of frost lurked in the shade.

Inside the house, in the second-story master bedroom, Letitia Ramsey Sinclair pulled straight the sheet and blankets covering her grandmother and tucked the edges under the feather mattress. Her blue eyes were shadowed from the sleepless nights she'd spent at her grandmother's bedside, and her shoulders drooped with tiredness. She looked at Bellewood's housekeeper and asked, "Opal, do you think Grandmama will wake up again?"

On the other side of the bed, the massive black woman repeated Letitia's action with the coverings and spoke with deliberate slowness. "Honey, you know what Doctor Shifflette said. It's a miracle Miz Sinclair's lived as long as she has since that fit took her away."

Letitia carried a pitcher across the room to the washstand and emptied the dirty water into the slop jar. "It's just . . . I . . . I don't want Grandmama to die. There's so much I have to say to her. I know I could make her understand if I could just talk to her."

Restlessly, Letitia walked across the room and fingered the glass rings circling the neck of the bottle of cordial resting on Grandmama's dressing table. Opal piled dirty rags in a basket and joined Letitia.

"Honey, don't take this so hard." Opal held her arms out and Letitia gravitated into the shelter of the embrace.

Opal slowly stroked Letitia's brown hair. "I wish I could make this come out right for you." Her hand continued its hypnotic movement. "When you were a child I could bandage your scrapes and give you one of Sally Ann's cookies to make it better. Sometimes, I could even comfort you when Miz Sinclair lit into you."

Letitia looked up and smiled. "You've always made me feel better, especially after one of Grandmama's tirades."

Opal grew serious. "I know it's important to you. I know you got to make some sort of peace with your grandmama. But child, I want you to listen to me real careful. It's more important that you come to peace with yourself."

"How can I? I try to do right—but Grandmama always finds fault. I want to be a good person. But how can I? What if Grandmama is right? What if I'm—"

"You just hush. You're plumb tired out from tending Miz Sinclair and you're not thinking straight. Your grandmama's an old, unhappy woman. How many times I got to tell you Miz Sinclair don't really hate you. She hate herself, that's what's wrong with her."

"If I could only believe that."

"Baby, you wouldn't believe nothing nobody say to you right now. You're just too tired and upset. You go to your room and rest. Opal will let you know if anything happens."

"In a while." Letitia walked to the straight-backed chair placed by Grandmama's bed and sat. "I'll stay, just a little longer, just in case. . . ."

"You're gonna get so wore out you're gonna be the one laid down on your sickbed. And then what are we gonna do?"

"Don't fret. I'll rest, I promise."

"So who's gonna run Bellewood if you get sick?" Opal demanded. "You've been running the place since last year. Miz Sinclair, she just gave up since the war ended. Without you there wouldn't be no Bellewood. You've kept us together."

Letitia thought about what Opal had said. It was true, Grandmama hadn't played an active role in the management of the plantation since they'd heard the news from Appomattox Courthouse, but Bellewood without Grandmama was inconceivable.

"I'll be fine. We'll all be fine." She wished she could believe her own promises.

Opal picked up the slop jar and paused by the door. "I worry 'bout you, honey. You take too much on yourself. The good Lord shouldn't put such a burden on somebody as young and pretty as you are."

"Young, maybe. Even though I do feel about a

thousand years old right now. But I'll never be pretty."
Letitia knew her limitations.

"You're beautiful when you smile. Remember what
I said when I read your palm. You'll know hardship
and suffering, but someday you'll have plenty to smile
about."

Opal shook her head and muttered under her
breath, but Letitia didn't listen as she gazed at Grandmama. Opal left and the old woman's stertorous
breathing filled the room, the sound competing with
the fetid smell of dying. Grandmama's arms lay by her
sides, the position echoed by the pencil-straight place-
ment of the iron gray braids resting on either side of
her face. Even in unconsciousness, her beak of a nose
and her downturned mouth expressed her dissatisfied
nature.

The chair back dug into Letitia's spine. She rose and
walked to the window, staring at the barn that housed
the wealth of Bellewood—its horses. Since Grandmama's collapse, Basil, the head groom, had ordered
his men to lay straw on the drive so the sound of
horse's hooves and wagon wheels wouldn't disturb the
mistress of Bellewood. Letitia glanced back at her
grandmother and feared Doctor Shifflette was right.
Nothing would disturb Grandmama ever again.

Frigid winter air leaked in around the window-
panes, but Letitia didn't move. Her gaze focused on
the near paddock where Basil was working Princess,
their most promising yearling filly, on a lunge line. The
horse tossed her head and kicked up her heels. Her
shrill whinny reached Letitia's ears, but she had to
imagine the sound of Basil's low voice as he soothed
the filly.

Grandmama snorted and started to choke, and Letitia swung around. Her hands tensed with apprehension. Grandmama thrust her head back, and a loud gargling sound filled the room before she gasped an unintelligible word.

Letitia hastened to the bedside, praying that Grandmama could find it in her heart to deal kindly with her only grandchild.

She bent near and asked, "Can you hear me?"

"Melanie?" The voice was weak but recognizable.

"No, Grandmama. It's me, Letitia. Mama's dead."

A disgusted croak and then, "Letitia?"

"Yes. Are you in pain? Can I get you something? A drink of water? Should I call the doctor?"

The old lady's hand shot out and her clawlike fingers fastened around Letitia's slender wrist. "Listen to me."

Her grandmother's grasp tightened, and Letitia gasped. All of Grandmama's old vigor and strength seemed to flow back, and twin spots of color appeared high on her cheekbones.

"I'm dying and so is Bellewood." Her voice was firm.

"When I'm gone there will be nothing here for you. There will be no more Bellewood. Do you understand? I'll give my daughter's bastard a home no longer."

"What?" Letitia gasped. What was Grandmama saying? What did she mean? She'd called her granddaughter terrible things before, accused Letitia of horrible acts, but why this? Had her illness affected her mind? "I know you've never cared for me, but—"

"A bastard, that's what you are," Grandmama interrupted, her words full of burning fury. "Your mother, for I cannot call her my daughter, slept with Clay Jewell. You're the result."

Clay Jewell? But he was a married man, with grown children of his own. Still, if his reputation was to be believed, he had fathered plenty of illegitimate children.

Stunned, Letitia whispered, "But, Hunt Ramsey, my papa . . ."

Grandmama snorted. "Do you think I'd let a Sinclair marry our overseer unless it was the only available course? You know as well as I do that this county is littered with Clay Jewell's by-blows. I forced your mother to marry Hunt Ramsey so that Clay's bastard, you, would never carry the Sinclair name. Oh, I know you married your second cousin Shelly. But it didn't matter to me. He didn't inherit the Sinclair strength."

The ugly words whirled around in Letitia's mind. If what Grandmama said was true, and it must be, it explained so much, explained why she hated her granddaughter so, why Shelly's mother had . . .

"Grandmama," Letitia pleaded. "Wait. I have to make you understand. I have to understand. Why didn't you tell me this before? I've never expected anything from you. All I've ever wanted from you is your love."

"Love!" Grandmama spat out the word. Her color faded and she fought to speak. "You . . . you don't deserve my love."

Silence filled the room.

"Please," Letitia whispered. "Why can't you at least accept me?"

Grandmama wheezed horribly.

"Easy," Letitia said. "Don't tire yourself. I need to talk to you. Please . . ."

Grandmama coughed, unable to go on. Letitia mopped her brow and soothed the old lady to the best of her abilities. Finally, the coughing eased and Grandmama subsided into an uneasy stupor.

Why should she think or hope that Grandmama would change at the end? Letitia asked herself. Honoria Sinclair always hated and despised her granddaughter, and now she'd finally explained why.

Grandmama roused. "Letitia, come closer and—" Coughing again choked off the dying woman's speech.

"Can't you find it in your heart to forgive me?" Letitia pleaded.

"No! You're not a Sinclair—Oh God!" The old woman's awful breathing cut off her words.

"I'll get Opal. You mustn't talk like this."

"You'll read it in my will soon enough, but . . ." Grandmama managed to control her cough for a moment. "Every Sinclair . . . who counted for anything. Dead . . . in this awful war. I'll not have . . . the undeserving ones . . . in my house. I've left . . . everything . . . I own . . . to Saint Andrew's Church." She paused, gasping for air, and then continued. "In God's sight . . . I know I'm doing . . . the right thing. I regret nothing . . . I've done . . . in this lifetime."

The wrinkled, age-spotted fingers released their grip and fell back on the covers. "Get away from me. I won't have you at my deathbed. Don't lean over me like that. I don't want you. I never have."

Letitia backed away, her hand at her throat, fighting not to show her pain and despair. Grandmama claimed to be a God-fearing woman, but Letitia couldn't help questioning what sort of God. . . .

The old woman struggled to sit, clawed at her throat, and fell back against the pillows, the ragged sound of her breathing filling the room.

Letitia couldn't stand it any longer. She ran to the door and screamed, "Opal!" but by the time the heavyset black woman joined her, Grandmama's fight for breath had her arched against the pillows. The old woman's eyes widened, a surprised expression settled on her features, and she gasped weakly. Letitia grasped Opal's hand for comfort, and thick silence filled the room. It seemed to Letitia as if her grandmother shrank as the life force left her body.

"O my Lord! Miz Sinclair is gone!" Opal wailed, dropping heavily to her knees beside the bed. "What will happen to us now? Sweet Jesus, save us poor sinners."

Letitia knelt beside Opal and clasped the black woman's hands, her own fear driving her to seek comfort.

Her voice as remote as her emotions, Letitia said, "Grandmama told me Clay Jewell is my father."

"Oh my Lord." Opal's fingers tightened around Letitia's own. "Why in the name of God did she have to do that to my poor baby?"

"It's true, isn't it?" Letitia asked.

Opal nodded. "But it wasn't Melanie's fault. Clay Jewell, he's got mighty taking ways around womenfolk. My poor Melanie, she never had a chance when he looked at her. She was fascinated by him, just like the way a moth dances around a candle flame. There's no going back—not for the moth, not for Melanie."

Opal dropped Letitia's hands and Letitia saw tears gather in the housekeeper's eyes.

"It's not your fault, honey," Opal said. "Don't take on so. You may know the truth now, but that knowing doesn't make you any different. You're still the same person."

"No," Letitia said. "I'm different now. Everything is different now. Grandmama told me she'd left Bellewood to the church."

"She left this place to the church?" Opal's voice rose, and for the first time in Letitia's memory the housekeeper broke down and sobbed. "To the church? Oh Lord, Miss Letitia. They'll make us all leave. I don't know no other home. None of us do. And now we have to go?"

To Letitia, it seemed as if the center of her world was spinning away like a child's brightly colored top. Clay Jewell was her father, Grandmama was dead, and Bellewood was lost. Letitia stared at the pattern in the red Turkish carpet, and an odd detachment settled over her, cushioning her from any more blows. And with the detachment came a strength she'd never known before.

"Listen to me," she said. "When I talk to Father Jerome I'll try to convince him the church should keep Bellewood. Then you and the others could stay on and run the place."

Opal tried to smile, but her trembling lips wouldn't obey. "I know you'll try. You got a good heart, child."

In her sparsely furnished room, Letitia poured water into the washbasin and cleaned her hands, washing away the touch of her grandmother's fingers. She had tried so hard to win Grandmama's love and still failed. Failed miserably, failed absolutely. Why couldn't—?

No. She wouldn't think about what might have been. Her fingers tightened on the basin. She was a fool to think Grandmama would ever love her granddaughter. She was a bastard, a blight on the Sinclair name. Shelly hadn't cared about that, but he was dead, too. . . . Oh, why did he have to die? He was the only one who'd ever loved her, who'd ever . . . No, she wouldn't think about Shelly either.

Letitia lifted the basin, tipping its contents into the slop jar. She tried to control her whirling thoughts and the shaking of her hands. The china bowl dropped from her suddenly numb fingers. She cringed at the echoing crash, dreading the scene that would follow when Grandmama discovered the destruction.

Then she laughed hysterically. "You'll never punish me for this, Grandmama," she whispered.

As Letitia bent to pick up the pieces of china, she realized that her world, as hated and as restricted as it was, had shattered irreparably, just like the basin. Frightened by the overwhelming enormity of her aloneness, she asked the echoing silence, "What will happen to me now?"

The sewing lay bunched in Letitia's lap while she wound a length of thread around her index finger until the eye of the needle was snubbed painfully tight against her knuckle. Then she unwound the thread, but releasing her finger didn't free her from the troubles surrounding her.

Opal knocked and then came into Letitia's room. Her eyes were red-rimmed from crying. "Father Jerome from Saint Andrew's Church is here."

Letitia folded her sewing neatly and stood. It was time to confront her problems. "Is he in the morning room?"

"No." Opal crossed her massive arms over her chest. "He's in Miz Sinclair's office, going through her papers. It's not right! She's still laid out in the parlor, not even in her grave, and that—that man's taking over just like he owned the place."

Letitia sighed. "He does—or he may as well. Grandmama did leave Bellewood to the church."

"It's not right," Opal repeated.

"What is?"

Letitia left her room and walked down the stairs, her fingers trailing along the polished banister. She didn't love Bellewood as Grandmama had, but she didn't disdain what it had represented until now—security. She'd made her bid for freedom by marrying Shelly, and look how disastrously that had ended.

Father Jerome glanced up from the papers he'd spread over Honoria Sinclair's desk and said, "Come in, my dear. We have a great deal to discuss."

Letitia sat in the chair he placed for her and looked at the clergyman. Her lips tightened as she gazed at the open ledgers. Opal was correct—it wasn't right—but when had that mattered to Grandmama?

"I grieve with you at your time of loss." Father Jerome's words of condolence did not lighten the tense atmosphere. He fingered the edge of the ledger, his saintly halo of white hair at odds with the glint in his brown eyes. "But we must never forget our duty to the living."

"No, of course not." Letitia bowed her head, inwardly shaking, knowing that her future, and the future of the people of Bellewood, depended on this avaricious man.

First Father Jerome discussed the running of Bellewood, asking her questions about the crops and the stables. She answered him calmly, forcing herself to sit erect in her chair, her hands folded in her lap as became a lady, maintaining an outward composure she didn't feel.

"The church is very pleased with Mrs. Sinclair's—dear Honoria's bequest," he said, as a conclusion to his questions.

Dear Honoria? No one, not even Father Jerome, had been on a first-name basis with Grandmama. Letitia resisted an urge to wipe her damp palms down the length of her skirt. "What will happen to Bellewood and the people who live here?" she asked.

Father Jerome leaned back in his chair, placed his fingertips together to form a steeple, and rested his wrists on his paunchy stomach. "No decision has been made yet, naturally. But I expect the church will follow my recommendation to bring in a manager. We'll continue to run Bellewood—at least for the present. We certainly couldn't realize its true value if we were to try to sell during these unsettled times."

She nodded, knowing she mustn't show her relief. Opal, Basil, and all the others who lived at Bellewood would be safe, at least for a while. She decided to try her luck. Grandmama had told Letitia she must leave the plantation, but the old lady was dead and perhaps only she had heard that last harsh decree.

"Father Jerome," she said. "I'm sure you know Grandmama used me as her eyes and legs this last year. I know a great deal about the plantation and the running of the stables. I'm sure I could assist your manager."

The clergyman looked impassively at her and she steeled herself to return his gaze.

"That's not possible," he said flatly. "In dear Honoria's bequest to the church she made certain conditions. One of those conditions concerns you, Letitia. You may not remain at Bellewood."

She shifted uncomfortably in her chair. It was no different from what she'd expected. "I see."

"I am sorry, my dear." His words said one thing, but his expression clearly contradicted his speech. "Your cousin Cecily will help, I'm sure—she is, after all, your mother-in-law."

Letitia nodded, her throat dry at the idea of pleading with Cecily for assistance. Cecily had never forgiven her son's rash marriage to his cousin, but . . . Perhaps, for appearance' sake if nothing else, she'd help his widow.

Father Jerome leaned forward, tidied the papers into a pile, thrust them inside the ledger, and stood. "We must be practical, but I can assure you the church won't be unreasonable. Certainly we don't expect you to leave Bellewood before the end of the month. However, I'm sure you're anxious to settle into your new life as quickly as possible." He picked up the ledger and tucked it under his arm. "I'll see you tomorrow. It is such a privilege to officiate at dear Honoria's funeral."

Letitia stood as Father Jerome left and then dropped back into her chair. Her throat tightened and she fought back her tears. She was expected to leave by the end of the month? That gave her exactly ten days to figure out what to do. She had no training for anything, except being the mistress of a plantation, and the war had ended any chance of her ever realizing that ambition. If Cecily wouldn't take her in, what would she do?

* * *

The mourners gathered in the drawing room at Bellewood, glad to be out of the cold, blustery weather. They drank Honoria Sinclair's sherry, discussing her passing and the unsettled politics of the day. From Letitia's vantage point by the French windows leading to the garden, she watched a black manservant wheel the invalid chair holding Richard Sinclair to a position by the fire.

Her throat tightened as she gazed at her cousin. Richard had lost both his legs and the liveliness of his personality at the Battle of the Wilderness. Shelly's formerly vigorous father had drifted off into a half-life of his own where nothing and no one could reach him.

That could be Shelly, Letitia thought, fighting grief. She tried to console herself with the thought that Shelly would prefer death to being a cripple, but consolation was not to be found. She wanted her husband back, even crippled. Oh, how she wanted him.

Nevertheless, duty had to be faced. She crossed the room and took the invalid's hand. "Hello, Richard. Thank you for coming today."

He didn't respond.

Cecily Sinclair sailed into the room, pausing inside the door as if to take stock of the people gathered there. Letitia looked at her and remembered how pretty Cecily had been before the war began at Fort Sumter, bringing about the loss of her only child and her husband's ill health. Circumstances had etched lines in a face that could no longer be called lovely.

Cecily joined her husband and Letitia, greeting her daughter-in-law with an airy kiss somewhere in the vicinity of Letitia's left ear.

Without preamble Cecily said, "I don't understand why Aunt Honoria didn't leave Bellewood to us. Father Jerome spoke to me outside. He told me your grandmama has left Bellewood to the church and that you must leave. What do you intend to do?"

It had to be faced. Letitia swallowed hard. "I would like to talk with you about that. Perhaps tomorrow—"

"I can't help," Cecily said flatly. Her hands moved in a fluttering motion. "I'm sorry to tell you I have to . . . we're . . . we've decided to sell Mount Royal. I haven't your grandmama's resources. There's nothing left—we can't stay in Kentucky."

Letitia stiffened, and Cecily glanced at her husband.

"My sister has offered us a place with her at her home in Baltimore. My position is almost as bad as yours."

"I understand," Letitia whispered. She looked at Richard, but he gazed unseeingly at the opposite wall.

Cecily nervously touched the mourning brooch of Shelly's hair that she wore at her throat. Letitia knew her thoughts were unworthy and selfish, but she just didn't care. She couldn't stop envying the small piece of jewelry. She had nothing of Shelly's, not even his tintype.

Cecily's words broke into Letitia's thoughts. "It's not as if any of us have a choice any longer. Things may be better in Baltimore. Perhaps my sister will know of a woman who needs a companion. You're used to attending old ladies."

Letitia couldn't bring herself to reply. Spend the rest of her life chained to one querulous old lady after the next? She tightened her lips. She'd find something else to do—something!

But what? Marriage was out of the question. She didn't know of a man who would consider marrying her—especially in her penniless state. Teaching? Her own schooling had been sporadic. She could read and write and figure sums, but not much more. She'd read the contents of the Bellewood library but that didn't constitute an education.

Unfortunately, Cecily was right, Letitia realized. The only thing she knew was how to be a companion. Yet Cecily's promise of help was vague and Letitia realized she couldn't count on her.

She excused herself and left Cecily and Richard. She'd find a way. She had to.

Anson Cunningham, one of Shelly's friends, approached Letitia and offered his condolences. She tried to reply suitably, but Anson stopped her with a smile. The movement of his lips twisted the saber scar that ran from his temple to his chin. She willed herself to maintain eye contact with him and not to let her pity show. Once, he'd been a good-looking man, and he was still a proud one.

"I won't play the hypocrite," he said. "I never cared for your grandmama and she certainly never deigned to look my way. Thing is, I'm afraid her death has created a terrible tangle for you. I heard Father Jerome saying she'd left Bellewood to the church."

"Yes," Letitia said. "But I'll be fine."

"In case you're not—"

"I will be."

"In case you're not," Anson repeated, "Margaret and I want you to come to us. Shelly was a good friend."

"Yes. Thank you." Letitia bit her lip, wondering how to refuse gracefully. Margaret was expecting their third child, and certainly the Cunninghams couldn't afford another mouth to feed.

Anson pulled a letter from his pocket. "The post-

master asked me to give this to you. Seems as if old
Father Jerome has already instructed him to deliver all
Bellewood mail to the church, but he didn't want to do
that, since this was addressed to you personally."

Letitia took the letter. It had come all the way from
California. She thanked Anson and added, "It's from
Papa."

"Hunt Ramsey"

Letitia nodded. "He writes whenever he can."

"I didn't realize you were still in touch with the
man. Didn't he leave Bellewood after your mama
died?"

"Yes, and that was ten years ago. But Papa was
always kind to me while he lived at Bellewood."

She half smiled, remembering how kind Hunt Ramsey had been to an unwanted child, especially after her
mother had died and Grandmama proved with her every word and action that she didn't care for her daughter's child.

Now the day Cousin Felicity had been so cruel took
on a special significance. Felicity Sinclair had had everything; loving parents, doting grandparents, adoring
older brothers, and curly hair. Somehow, she'd even
managed to turn the scattering of freckles on her up-
turned nose into an asset. Plus she'd always been the
leader when games were played.

Letitia remembered how Felicity had declared herself Queen Felicity the Fair of Fayette County and then
dubbed Shelly, Sir Shelly the Magnificent, and Anson,
Count Cunningham the Courageous, until all the children had titles, except Letitia.

Felicity snickered and said to Letitia, "I know something about you no one else knows. When I give you

your title, everyone will know. I'll call you Belle-wood's—"

"No, you won't!" Shelly, who was always so mild, grabbed Felicity's arm and twisted it so hard she cried out in pain. "I don't believe you know anything. You enjoy tormenting Letitia, and I won't have it."

Felicity jerked free and slapped Shelly as hard as she could, the sound of the blow echoing in the silence as the stunned children watched. "You can't stop me, Shelly Sinclair! I do so know the truth and I'll tell," she cried.

Grandmama joined the children ringed around the two combatants. Her voice a whiplash, she demanded, "Tell what, Felicity?"

Felicity faced Grandmama for a long moment. But the young girl was no match for the older woman's steely determination. Her head low, her voice just above a whisper, she said, "Nothing, ma'am."

"That's right." Grandmama drove her lesson home. "You know nothing and you'll never, ever repeat scandalous gossip about the Sinclairs."

"No ma'am."

"No ma'am, what?" Grandmama demanded.

Felicity's fists knotted until her skin showed white over the knuckles. "No ma'am. I won't gossip about your side of the family, or . . ." Felicity lifted her chin ". . . your daughter." Her voice underlined the last word spitefully.

"Get out of here," Grandmama said. "All of you. Get out of here this instant."

Frightened, all the children scattered, and Letitia ran as fast as she could, back to the house, straight to her papa. She found him in his office, gasped out her story, and asked, "What is it that Freckled Felicity knows about me? Grandmama said she was lying, but she knows something, doesn't she?"

Letitia gazed at Papa, watching those strange eyes of his as he tried to find the words to answer her.

"Your cousin is just jealous of you," he said finally. He pulled her up so she could sit on his knee. "It's like those fairy stories Mama used to tell you. You're the true princess—not Felicity—she's like an ugly stepsister. She has to make up stories to prove her importance. Someday, the whole world will acknowledge Letitia Ramsey's intelligence, grace and beauty. And when they do, I'll be the one saying I told you so. *I've* always known how special my treasure is. Don't be frightened, child, I'll always protect you. You know that, don't you?"

"Yes, Papa," young Letitia had whispered gratefully.

At last the mourners were gone, except for Father Jerome.

"Well." He rubbed his hands together in a proprietary fashion. "I think it went well. Dear Honoria would have been pleased at the showing, especially in these troubled times." He poured himself a fresh glass of sherry. "I saw you talking with Cecily. I assume that disposes of your worries about leaving Bellewood."

Letitia bit back what she wanted to say. "It's all taken care of," she said. She'd never let this dry, unfeeling man know how desperate her case was. "As we agreed, I'll leave Bellewood at the end of the month."

"Good. Good." Father Jerome finished his sherry. "You needn't bother to see me out. I know the way."

She watched him leave, the enormity of what was

happening to her finally taking full possession of her thoughts. She dropped into a chair and the hard edge of Hunt Ramsey's letter poked through her pocket into her thigh. Seizing on any distraction, she removed the envelope, opened it, and read the flowing copperplate script.

She scanned his report of his health and the events taking place at his ranch in California. Then she read:

> I know how hard times must be for you with-out the protection and care of your husband. I have learned of your grandmama's failing health. Knowing Honoria Sinclair as I do, I fear she will not provide for her only granddaughter as she should. Only the good Lord knows how future events will transpire. However, I fear I can be of little help to you, living as I do on the edge of the wilderness. My involvement with the Sinclair family has been over for many years, yet I wish to offer you my assistance, should you ever need it. Only you will know how, or if, I may ever help you, but please don't hesitate to ask. If it's within my power, I'll do it.
>
> Your loving papa,
> Hunt Ramsey

Letitia's hands shook as she fought to hold the letter still enough to read the last paragraph of her papa's letter again. Like a message from God, here was the answer to her problems. Except Papa was thousands of miles away and it would take time, precious time she didn't have to spare, for him to respond to her plea for assistance.

Anson had offered to help, but she shrank at the

idea of landing herself on the Cunninghams—his farm barely supported his growing family. As she fingered Hunt Ramsey's letter she was swept by a longing to see him again. He'd solved her childhood troubles with kindness and intuitive sensitivity. Now she wanted him to step in and resolve her current miserable situation. If only she could find a way to join Papa in California.

Then an idea, startling in its simplicity, grew in her mind.

Letitia knew she wasn't the only bastard Clay Jewell had fathered. She also knew, as everyone in Fayette County knew, that Clay Jewell took care of his own, even if they didn't bear his name.

Perhaps it would work. It had to.

Letitia pulled her bay mare to a stop in front of the colonnaded entrance to Clay Jewell's house. He'd supported the Union and, during the past four years, had clearly prospered. A stable boy ran up to hold the mare's reins, as the majordomo appeared at the head of the steps, ready to usher her inside.

"I'd like to see Mr. Jewell," Letitia told him.

"Yes'um." He showed her to a settle in the entrance hall. "I'll tell Mr. Clay you are here."

Letitia gazed curiously around the entrance hall. A curving staircase rose gracefully from the center of the room and spiraled up two full stories. The walls were decorated with hand-painted wallpaper. The pattern was dominated by large, dark green leaves that made her feel as if she were deep in a forest. She reminded herself to rehearse her story once again.

"This way, ma'am."

The majordomo's deep voice startled her. She rose

with what she hoped was an air of great calm. He nodded and motioned her to precede him down the hall. The servant probably knew everything, she thought. Who she was, what she was, and even what she wanted.

Letitia tried to imagine that she was Grandmama. *She* never cared what anyone thought.

The man opened the door to Clay Jewell's office, and she walked inside. She'd never seen her natural father up close—and now she could understand why Grandmama had made sure of that. Rude as it was, Letitia couldn't stop staring at him. Yes, she had his blue eyes all right.

Jewell returned Letitia's stare. "Since you're here, I can only assume the old harridan, Honoria Sinclair, finally told you the truth."

Letitia wasn't sure how to reply to his simple statement of the facts. Dry-mouthed, she simply said, "Yes."

"There's more of me in you than there is of Melanie," he observed. "Pity. She was a pretty woman. Now, it's been said I'm a handsome man, but my kind of looks don't do so well on a woman's face."

He smiled with great charm and guided Letitia to a chair. As his lips parted, she saw one thing she hadn't inherited. Jewell had crooked teeth. She ran the tip of her tongue along the even ends of her upper teeth, strangely relieved to remember that she did have a Sinclair trait after all.

"Well." He smiled again, and in spite of the circumstances Letitia felt herself relaxing. She didn't feel any kinship with the man, even though he was her natural father. What she did feel was a lightening of her tension, a lessening of her worries. No wonder he's been so successful with women, she thought. He could charm the birds right out of the trees.

She warned herself to be careful. The man was an accomplished manipulator. He was used to bending women to his will.

"I can't say I'm truly sorry to hear of your grand-mama's passing." Jewell sat down in the chair opposite Letitia. "Old Mrs. Sinclair sure hated me." He smiled, this time ruefully. "With reason, I might add. I fear she turned her abhorrence of me to you."

Letitia didn't know how to reply to this plain speaking.

"Your mother and I . . . if things had been different . . . but they weren't. I doubt you came here today to hear about that."

It seemed as if the smile and charm had never been, and the bleak expression on his face frightened her. She shifted uncomfortably. "No, I didn't."

"I thought not."

Jewell rose and poured a glass of whiskey for himself. He waved his hand toward the decanter, and Letitia shook her head no.

He returned to his seat. "Let me make this easy for you. It's all over the county that Honoria left Bellewood to the church, and knowing the old bi—witch as I do—did, I'm willing to bet she didn't make any provision for you."

Letitia nodded again, feeling a wash of color climb up her neck. Would she ever stop feeling humiliated? Did everyone in Fayette County know she was penniless and a bastard?

"All the Sinclair men are dead, except for Richard, who may as well be dead. And as for Cecily . . ."

Jewell's lips thinned. "You're truly in an impossible position, aren't you, my girl?"

"Not exactly." She wished she hadn't refused that whiskey. She could use its false courage now. "My papa—that is, Hunt Ramsey—has offered me a home with him in California." She hoped Jewell wouldn't guess that she was embroidering the truth. "The thing is, I haven't the resources to go to California, and I can't stay here until Papa makes the arrangements."

Jewell sipped his whiskey, waiting.

"I . . . I . . . Letitia gripped her hands together, willing herself to go on, to stop stammering.

"I . . . I'd . . . would you advance me the money for the journey?"

He said nothing and Letitia rushed to fill the silence with words. "It'll be paid back, I promise you. I'm only asking for a loan."

"I see," he said at last. "You may look like a Jewell but you're a Sinclair at heart. Proud as they come, aren't you?"

Letitia gazed at the wall opposite her, refusing to respond to his taunt.

"Easy." He'd read her mind, or perhaps her rigid posture. "I meant that as a compliment. If Melanie'd been more like you, she'd have left this ingrown, evil society when I asked."

"You asked Mama to run away with you?" Letitia asked, clearly incredulous. "You? Already a married man?"

Jewell swallowed what was left of his whiskey in a quick gulp and returned to the decanter for more. "You have no good opinion of me. Why should you? But yes, and this is God's truth, I wanted Melanie to go west with me. No one would have known we weren't legally man and wife. But the old bi—your grandmama discovered our plans."

Jewell raked his hand through his silver gray hair and walked over to his desk. "That's ancient history and all the talking in the world won't change it." He opened a drawer and removed a cherrywood money box. "The least I can do is give you the wherewithal to get out of this hellhole."

To Letitia's amazement, her pocket was soon weighted down with the generous amount Jewell felt would be sufficient to fund her journey.

She stammered out her thanks, scarcely able to believe her plan had worked. She was going to California—to Papa—to someone who cared for her.

Jewell gazed at her steadily. "I haven't even the right to ask you to write—but . . ." He cleared his throat. "Jewell and Sinclair. It's a good mix, daughter."

She felt overwhelmed by the contradictory emotions warring inside her. This man, this sad, charming stranger, was her father. He meant nothing to her—yet what she wanted to do, more than anything else in the world, was to put her head on his shoulder and sob out all her anger, frustration, and fear. But she could never do that.

"I'll write," she promised, her voice little more than a whisper. Her vow seemed so inadequate, but she could only repeat, "I'll write."

"Do that." Solemn now, he guided her through the entrance hall.

Hearing a noise above her, she paused and looked up the staircase. Jewell's wife stood, frozen, at the first curve, staring down. Her face was composed, but her eyes glittered with hatred.

"Even Honoria Sinclair couldn't instill a sense of dignity in you," Flora Jewell accused, her shrill voice carrying to every corner of the room. "You're no different from all his other bastards—they all come whining and crying behind my back."

Appalled, Letitia glanced at Jewell. Tight-lipped, he stared at a point on the wall opposite them, refusing to be a part of his wife's scene.

"You're a slut, just like your mother," she went on.

Letitia twisted her hands together and bent her head. Flora Jewell's words couldn't cut any deeper than Grandmama's had. *All I have to do is endure it,* Letitia thought. *Sooner or later it will be over and I can go.*

Then she realized that Flora wasn't Grandmama. Fear turned into indignation, and the healthy emotion liberated her. She glared up at Flora. "It's true I'm illegitimate. Nothing can change that. You're as twisted up in your hatred as Grandmama was. You'll die like she did, alone and unloved. I felt nothing but pity for her—the same pity I feel for you."

"How dare you speak to me in that tone of voice!" Flora cried. "I won't be pitied by someone like you."

Letitia pulled her gloves on and turned, her actions dismissing Flora.

For a long moment no one moved. Then Jewell's hand was gentle as he led Letitia to the door.

She didn't know what to say to break the uncomfortable silence as she waited for her horse to be brought around. She watched a muscle twitch in Jewell's jaw. Even his famous charm couldn't smooth over what had happened inside.

She didn't want it smoothed over. She wanted to laugh and dance, celebrating her freedom. For the first

time in her life she'd stood up to someone, and it felt
wonderful. Life, in fact, was wonderful. She was on
the threshold of a great adventure.

Suddenly, she realized if she were to truly free herself from her old life, she had to shed the name Sinclair, the one Shelly had given her. Grandmama had
placed that name above all kindness and compassion,
and look where it had gotten her. She'd be Letitia
Ramsey from now on, she vowed. It was her passport
to a place where she'd always be cherished, always be
the loved daughter. She'd never be an outsider again.

The stable boy led her mare to the mounting block.
Jewell motioned the boy to move the horse a few steps
further, then helped her to mount. He looked up at
Letitia as she threaded the reins through her fingers.
"Don't forget you promised to write," he said.

"I won't. And thank you. You've given me a future."

Jewell smiled, his charm back in full force. "I
thought I did that twenty-three years ago."

"So you did. But now, it's up to me."

"You'll do just fine," he said. "It's a curious combi-
nation—Jewell and Sinclair. Whatever it is, it makes
you quite a woman. I'm proud of you—daughter."

Letitia leaned forward, and her horse trotted away
from the plantation house. Deliberately, she loosened
the rein controlling the curb and urged the mare to a
wild gallop. The wind whipped her face and her
mount's flying mane stung her cheeks as she let the
racing horse carry her toward her future.

"I'm free," Letitia shouted. "Do you hear me? I'm
free at last."

2

San Francisco, California, 1867

Adam McCormick threaded his way through the crowded streets, his shoulders hunched against the persistent chill of the damp fog. He entered his hotel, his thoughts centering on the ranch he'd purchased and its advantages. It was less than twenty miles from the huge spread Hunt Ramsey controlled.

Hunt Ramsey, Adam thought grimly, the man who had destroyed his grandparents and his father. The man who—

"Adam? Adam McCormick!"

He turned, searching the lobby for the person who'd called his name and saw his half brother. Adam decided that in the month he'd been away, Swen had grown at least another inch.

"Swen." Adam swiftly covered the space between them. He wanted to embrace his younger brother but knew Swen's fragile dignity would never survive, so he settled for pumping Swen's hand up and down. "It's good to see you. Are you hungry?"

A few minutes later, seated in the hotel restaurant and waiting for their food, Adam eyed his brother. Even though they'd been in San Francisco for two months now, the boy still looked out of place. "How are you? Did you get along all right while I was gone?"

Swen fidgeted with the array of forks laid out on the snowy tablecloth. "Oh, I don't know," he said moodily. He gestured at his well-tailored clothes. "I'm not sure I'm cut out for the life of a leisured gentleman."

Adam opened his mouth to speak, but his brother went on, not noticing. "It's not that your friends haven't been kind while you were gone—they have. It's just plain wrong for you to support me. I need something to do. You were a captain during the war. I thought I might join the army."

Unpleasant memories crowded into Adam's mind, and he laughed mirthlessly. "I can't say I'd recommend the military as a line of work. I didn't enjoy it much—it's mostly dirty and boring."

"But the battles—? Weren't they exciting?"

Adam remembered the reckless exhilaration of a cavalry charge, the fear somehow clearing his mind and turning him into a killer. The joy when he realized he was alive and the enemy dead—and then later, the guilt and anger over that simple joy.

"I wouldn't recommend soldiering as a profession. There's no glory in it. Even so, I'd never try to stop you from doing something you want to do. Do you really want to be a soldier?" Adam asked.

Swen sighed. "Well, I have to do something, and I'll be damned if I'll go back to being a farmer!"

"It's a good thing I came back when I did. I've got an alternative plan I'd like to discuss with you. I've bought a ranch."

"A ranch? Really?"

"It's in the mountains north of San Diego," Adam said. "I bought it from a widow. She and her husband were just getting the place going when he died. It's going to take a lot of work to put it on its feet and I'd hoped you'd work it with me."

"Sure I will," Swen's voice rose with enthusiasm. "Being a rancher is a lot better than being a farmer."

Adam smiled. "Maybe. It's only a small place, and what cattle are left are wild."

Swen's eyes narrowed. "If it's in that bad a shape, why did you buy it?"

Adam paused, trying to collect his thoughts. "Did Ma ever say anything to you about my pa? My real pa, I mean."

Swen blinked in surprise. "Your pa? Why . . . why, she never said a word of him to me that I can recollect. My pa now, he had plenty to say. Said you were Ma's—" Swen swallowed hard, but he couldn't force the word out.

"Bastard." Adam finished Swen's sentence softly, for Robert had used that epithet to refer to his stepson often enough. "But it wasn't true. Ma was married to my father."

Swen's head swung up at the tone of Adam's words.

"I don't know for certain, but my father has to be dead," Adam said. "Ma had to have been a widow, or she never would have married your father."

"That's true."

Adam reached back into the dim recesses of his childhood memories. "All I can remember of that time is a fire that burnt our house. Then it was just me and Ma until she married Robert. Strange, the only thing I can recall about my father was he had one blue eye and one brown eye."

"I've never seen a man like that."

"I've never seen another. Anyway, I'm certain he's dead."

Adam paused and drew her letter from his inside coat pocket. He'd read it and reread it until he knew the words by heart, but he continued to carry it with him as a talisman that this time he wouldn't fail her. He handed it to Swen. "It's time you read this."

Their meal came just as Swen finished reading. He handed the letter back to Adam.

"I don't know what to think," Swen said. "All that stuff about you being God's instrument of revenge against Hunt Ramsey. As I see it, the only way any of it can make sense is the fact that Preacher Morrison had a real hold over Ma. He's a real hellfire-and-brimstone type. I'm sure he didn't help her any. Especially near the end she . . . she didn't seem right, like she wasn't Ma anymore. Because of him, when she died, I . . . I decided to stop going to church."

Adam paused, his knife and fork poised over his steak. To his way of thinking a man's religion should be between himself and his God. But he couldn't blame Ma for turning for comfort wherever she could find it. There was one hard fact in that letter, though.

"Ma said that Hunt Ramsey destroyed my grandparents and my pa." Adam's lips tightened into a thin line. "I'll bring Ramsey to justice, not because of God, but because she wanted me to do it for her. I let her down too many times. I don't intend to fail her again."

"Ma understood why you had to leave. When you came back from California a rich man she was glad—"

"But she wouldn't take a dime of my money," Adam interjected.

"She couldn't! Because of Pa and, and . . . I think Ma was glad you'd gone your own way. She prayed for you and rejoiced in your success . . . at least she did until the last."

"I'm just disappointed she wouldn't let me help her," Adam said. "But it doesn't matter about me. What matters is that I owe Ma. It may be almost thirty years too late, but Ramsey is going to pay."

Swen glanced down at his plate and then looked at his brother. "I've never heard of Hunt Ramsey. Ma sure never said anything about him to me. What do you know about him?"

"I traveled to San Diego to find out what I could about him, but he's holed up at that ranch of his, guarded as if it was the mint here in San Francisco rather than just a ranch. The foreman wasn't about to let me see the boss unless I told him what I wanted."

Adam smiled. "I suppose you could say we reached a bit of an impasse. You know how Ma used to say there's more than one way to solve a problem if you only look for it."

Swen nodded.

"Well, I'm looking for another way."

"What has Ramsey done to make him so careful of strangers that he'd hole up like that?" Swen asked.

"He's pretty well known in that part of California, and the word is he makes enemies wherever he goes. He's powerful, but he isn't so strong he can't be stopped. He's trying too hard to protect himself, and I say a frightened man is a vulnerable man."

"Then all we have to do is find his weak spot," Swen said.

Adam nodded. "True. People hate him, but they fear him as well, because of the power he wields. Talk is he's got political aspirations, not just for the state, but in Washington, too. They tell me he's a dangerous man."

"That doesn't matter to me!"

"Nor to me. I've met up with some folks I used to know in the goldfields—the Bickles. They've got an old score to settle with Ramsey and I think they can help us. I haven't figured it all out yet, but I'll find a way to stop Ramsey. If I can keep him from getting what he wants, bring him to justice, I figure I'll have kept faith with Ma. Are you with me on this?"

A wide grin lit Swen's face. "You bet."

The stagecoach left Yuma just after dawn. Now the sun was high in the morning sky, and Letitia swayed as the coach lurched in and out of a larger-than-normal hole. Since she'd left Kentucky, she'd learned, through necessity, to master the relaxed state of total numbness required to endure the journey. She was so tired and so dirty she knew she'd willingly sell her soul to the devil for a hot bath and a clean bed.

Not that he could provide such luxuries, though this was definitely the devil's county. On the long, weary way to Yuma they'd passed tall red pinnacles of rock twisted into fantastic spires and shapes that reminded her of the stories she'd read about Aladdin's cave. Anything could exist inside those odd-shaped monuments. But she bet the devil would be hard pressed to find a bed or a bath in this strange new world that seemed as foreign as the places she'd read about in her favorite novels—Russia or maybe India.

A torrent of abuse, aimed at the horses by the driver, who drove like Jehu, roused Letitia from her reverie. He used words she'd never heard of and could only imagine the meaning of—it could have been Russian or Hindustani he was shouting at his team—but she knew they were words Grandmama wouldn't approve of.

Even so, Letitia stored the phrases in her memory. She delighted in knowing Grandmama wouldn't have approved of them but Letitia doubted she would ever find the courage to say them out loud.

This journey didn't require courage, only desperation. She looked down at her slender hands, her right index finger rubbing the place where Shelly's ring had rested, ever so briefly. Grandmama had insisted that Letitia's wedding band go to fund the Confederate cause, and try as she might, Letitia had been unable to defy the old woman. It felt so strange, frightening in fact, to finally be free of Grandmama.

Letitia thought gratefully of Clay Jewell and how strange their parting had been. She'd write to him no matter what, even after she returned his money.

His money—her ticket to freedom—was tucked inside a special pocket sewn into her corset, which was pinching her most uncomfortably. She knew she should have put her corset cover back on, but the knitted garment was dirty and smelly and she was so tired she just didn't care.

Damn it! Letitia thought, using her newfound freedom with profanity. *Why did Shelly have to die? He did love me! He did! None of this would have happened if he hadn't marched off to war.*

The catharsis of facing up to Jewell's wife had faded, and Letitia couldn't recapture the rush of joy she'd experienced when she'd claimed her freedom. She was once again beset by her fears and uncertainties. What would Papa say when she suddenly appeared without any warning?

Henry Fletcher, the preacher sitting in the corner of the stagecoach, shifted his weight trying to cross one leg over the other. His action forced his fat wife, Constance, to lean away from him, and her heavy arm pressed into Letitia's side. Letitia scrunched further into her corner and promised herself the next time they stopped she'd ask Bella, the woman sitting opposite, if she'd like to trade seats.

Of course, Constance would have a fit, since the heavily made-up woman sitting with her back to the horses was clearly a prostitute. Grandmama had always pointed out women like that to Letitia, telling her that was what she'd be doing for a living if not for the bounty of her grandmother's kindness.

The man sitting in the other corner didn't strike Letitia as someone she wanted to sit next to, either. He'd boarded the stagecoach in Yuma and introduced himself as a guard from the territorial prison. He smelled of that grim place and worse, he suffered from flatulence. Considering the amenities and the food she'd been offered, the guard's private habits didn't surprise her, but it certainly didn't make him someone she'd want to share closer quarters with.

She shifted her weight again, trying to ease her pinching corset and the ache in her back when several loud bangs rang out.

"What was that?" Constance demanded.

"Gunshots, lady." The prison guard replied. "Probably bandits."

The driver whipped up his horses and shouted profane defiance as the stagecoach lurched forward at headlong pace.

Letitia's chest tightened with fear and she hung onto the strap beside the leather curtain for dear life, her feet braced on the floor.

"Lord," Henry Fletcher intoned. "Deliver us poor sinners . . ."

Constance's shrieks drowned out her husband's words.

"For God's sake be quiet!" Bella exclaimed. "We can't do a damned thing except hang on."

"And pray," said the minister.

"Fat lot of good that'll do," the prostitute retorted.

The preacher's reply was lost in the ear-blasting percussion of several gunshots being fired outside the coach. A strangled cry, a sharp thump, and a scuffling, dragging sound on the roof drew the passengers' attention. Letitia bit back a shriek of her own as she saw the stagecoach guard falling past the window opposite her, screaming in agony.

"Oh, God!" the prostitute cried.

Henry Fletcher clung tightly to a strap, but he still managed to take the prostitute to task as he bounced all over his seat. "That's right, woman. Take the Lord's name in vain. You'll burn in hell, you hussy!"

Too scared to think coherently, Letitia tried to control her fear. There was another scream, a curse, and a repeat of the ominous bump and thump. The driver fell off on her side and she could almost touch his leather vest as his body dropped by her window.

"Oh no!" Constance wailed. "We'll all surely be killed. No one's driving!"

None of the passengers contradicted her. There were more shots, and the stagecoach swung wildly from side to side. Everything happened too quickly for thought, and Letitia concentrated only on survival as she skidded into Constance's soft side, rebounded into the solid corner, and slid across the seat again.

The scream of a horse carried over the pandemonium inside the stagecoach as it pitched to the right. Letitia glimpsed the prison guard's carpetbag flying toward her and, as the musty satchel hit her square in the chest, another sharper, harder blow knocked first the breath and then the sense from her body.

Letitia heard someone moaning, the monotonous sound filling the air and pressing down on her ears. She struggled to open her eyes and realized it was she who was making the sound. A sharp pain bolted through her head. She shut her eyes against the white light lancing across her vision.

The next time she opened her eyes, she managed to control the pain and focus on the carpetbag lying on her chest. She grunted, shoved at the satchel, and tried to sit up. It appeared that the stagecoach had rolled on its side and, as Letitia pushed her hair away from her face and righted her bonnet, she saw the prostitute twisted in the opposite corner.

Bella's head leaned at an unnatural angle, and Letitia feared the woman was dead. She clambered over the debris in the stagecoach and reached for a pale wrist. "Bella?" she whispered. She licked her lips and tried again, her voice louder. "Bella?" Letitia pressed her fingers hard against the inside of the woman's wrist, searching for a pulse.

She was dead. Letitia wondered why she was still alive. Wildly, she glanced around the interior of the coach, oddly disoriented by the seats stretching upward on either side of her. Where was everyone?

Desperate to be free of the confined space, she looked through the open door above her head. The need to breathe fresh air somehow propelled her through the opening. Halfway in and halfway out, she sagged over the side of the stagecoach, fighting the dull throb in her temples and the cruel pinch of her corset. She shut her eyes against the bright sunlight and felt as if she were floating away.

Rough hands grabbed her and hauled her the rest of the way out. She floated back into her body as she stumbled and fell on the hard earth, hot grains of sand scouring her palms when she landed on her hands and knees. She craned her neck, blinked, and blinked again, trying to focus on the three men ringed around her.

At first, to Letitia's confused gaze, they seemed to be replicas of one another in dirty denim pants and shirts and sweat-stained hats pulled low over their eyes. The way they stood—one stooped, two straighter —betrayed their ages, one old, two younger.

One of the younger ones stepped forward and, with his toe, prodded Letitia's side. She fell to the ground, again shutting her eyes against the pain throbbing in her head. She wished the floating feeling would come back but it didn't.

"Look at what we got here," the man said. "Pa, Billy, we got lucky. She ain't dead after all."

The older man stepped forward and hauled Letitia

to her feet. She looked into his hard, vacant blue eyes. A thrill of fear coursed through her bloodstream. She tried to twist away, and her gaze fell on the crumpled, bloodied bodies of Henry Fletcher and the prison guard. Bile rose in her throat. She swallowed desperately, trying to keep her stomach in place.

"This one is a bunch better, Pa." The first man shouldered aside his father and squeezed Letitia's breast, hard. Grandmama had drummed into everyone what they must do if the Yankees came to rape the women and children at Bellewood. Without thinking, Letitia instinctively bent her leg and tried to knee her tormentor in his groin.

"Son of a bitch!" The man avoided Letitia and slapped her.

She didn't see the blow coming but she sure felt it. Stars exploded in her head. She fell to her knees, but she didn't faint, as much as she wished she could. No one, not even Grandmama, had ever hit her before, and she sobbed in astonishment and disbelief.

"Leave it, Walt," Pa ordered. "There'll be plenty of time for that tonight."

"But, Pa—"

"C'mon, Missy." Pa hauled her to her feet. "Time to ride."

"Wait! Where are you taking me?"

"Mexico," the one called Walt said.

"Why?" Letitia looked at the man's feral face and realized the stupidity of her questions. It seemed as if Grandmama had been correct about Letitia's ultimate fate. To these men, a woman was good only for one thing, and all women were Bellas.

"Oh." She realized what they intended to do to her. "No! You can't!"

"Don't you worry none about Mexico, Missy." Pa's voice was kindly but the leer on his face was anything but. "It's a fair way to the border and Walt and Billy and me have been mighty lonesome lately."

"Wait!" Letitia frantically searched for a way to save herself. "My . . . my papa is a wealthy man. If . . . if you take me to him, I'll say you saved me from bandits and Papa will pay you, handsomely, for saving me. I . . . I know you'll be richer if you take me to Papa instead of Mexico."

"Richer?" The older man looked Letitia up and down. "If you're rich, my name ain't Jonas Bickle. Missy, with that accent of yours, I knows you was on the wrong side and I knows us Yankees ain't left nothing for you rebs. And even if I didn't know that, all I'd have to do is take a look at you. That dress of yours is old and all wore out. You ain't got no rich papa. No way, no how."

"You're wrong!" Letitia succeeded in pulling away from Jonas, only to have Walt grab her close. "Listen to me!" She shouted, struggling in his arms. "My papa will pay whatever you ask! I promise it!"

"Some promise," Walt sneered. "Pa has the right of it. You're the begging type. By the time we get to Mexico you're gonna be begging us to keep you."

He thrust Letitia away and she staggered, falling again, this time on her backside. She struggled into a sitting position, drew her knees up, and buried her head on her forearms. This couldn't be happening to her.

It had to be a bad dream. If she shut her eyes very tightly, ignored her aching body, and quelled the sick turning of her stomach, the Bickles would go away and she'd wake up, safe and secure in Kentucky.

She opened her eyes and peered at the triangle of sand she could see through the frame of her left arm. It didn't look like Kentucky dirt. She shut her eyes and tried again.

A touch on her shoulder made her lift her head.

"Ma'am?" Billy asked. "We're leaving now. Pa's cut the horses free and you'll be able to ride one, won't you?"

With Billy's hand under her elbow, she managed to stand. A sudden scream made her whip around. Walt had Constance's two pudgy wrists tightly clasped in his left hand while he brandished a wicked-looking bowie knife in his right.

"Save me, dear Lord," Constance shrieked.

"Be quiet!" Walt bellowed. He thrust his knife into the fabric of Constance's skirt, approximately at knee level, and dragged the blade downward, slashing Constance's skirt and many petticoats in two.

She continued to pray for deliverance while Walt twirled her around and applied his knife to the back of her skirt as well.

"Billy!" Walt yelled. "Over here. Help me get this tub of lard on one of the horses."

The youngest Bickle joined his brother, and with much swearing on their part and praying on Constance's, they managed to boost her onto the broad back of one of the stagecoach horses.

Walt turned, the knife once again in his hands, and approached Letitia. She drew herself up, forcing her mind to the state of blankness she always hid behind when Grandmama raged at her.

She felt the tug of the knife at the brown fabric of her skirt and felt stitches popping at her waist as Walt slashed her skirt in two. A breeze tugged at the fabric and she modestly tried to pull the ragged edges together.

Walt repeated his attack on the back of her skirt.

"My papa truly is a wealthy man." Letitia put all the calm conviction she could muster into her words. "You're making a terrible mistake. He'll come looking for me when I don't arrive in San Diego as I'm supposed to. Taking me to him is easy money."

Walt fondled her backside. "Taking you is going to be easy, all right." She jerked away and he pulled her back.

"Quit messing around," Jonas ordered. "We got a long way to go to find water. You get Missy on the back of one of them horses pronto."

She knew what was coming and she also realized it would be impossible to resist. They wouldn't listen to her, they were stronger, but that didn't matter. She had to figure out something. She had no idea what, but *something* would come to her. It just had to.

Billy led up a roman-nosed chestnut. Letitia didn't hinder, but she didn't help either as Walt shoved her onto the draft horse's broad back. In an untidy whirl of dragging petticoats and ragged skirt she managed to get her right leg in place. The horse's sweaty sides felt rough and unpleasant next to her stocking-covered legs, and the width of his shoulders stretched her thighs unpleasantly.

Walt ran his hand from her ankle up to her knee, his unkempt, grimy fingers stroking up and down. Letitia looked away, bracing her hands on her mount's withers, willing herself to ignore him.

"Hey!" Jonas bellowed. "Let's get a move on."

Walt tilted his head and his blue eyes seemed to

burn in his tanned, oddly youthful face. "Later," he promised as he sauntered away.

He mounted and grabbed the reins of Letitia's horse. Billy did the same with Constance's mount. Jonas picked up the lead rope to his pack mule. He shouted, "Let's get outta here!" and the little cavalcade started out across the desert.

The abandoned stagecoach's wheels pointed toward one of the distant mauve mountains. The bodies of dead people and horses were a mute testament to the violence of the morning. Already, large, dark buzzards circled the sky. The sickly sweet smell of blood, fouling the pristine desert air, clogged Letitia's senses.

They rode without stopping through the heat of the midday sun. When Letitia let herself think, she remembered longingly the sharp winter cold she'd left behind in Kentucky. In this land of Satan, even in springtime, the sun shone fiercely, evaporating all moisture, until she imagined the inside of her mouth was as dry as the sand the horses trotted across.

She hated this place. If she thought prayer could help she would have willingly imitated Constance, but harsh reality kept creeping into Letitia's thoughts, and she knew only *she* could help herself now.

Constance prayed softly, monotonously, but finally the awful, oppressive quiet of the desert seemed to overwhelm her. As the sun started its journey down the western side of the sky Constance's silence changed to heavy, rasping wheezes as she fought to breathe.

Part of Letitia feared for the older woman. Constance's breathing sounded like Grandmama's just before she died. The other part of Letitia's mind fought to block out all sound and sensation as she tried to cling to the idea that none of this was actually happening to her—it was all a terrible dream, and if she didn't give in to it, it would simply go away.

Their shadows were long when Jonas finally led them into a wash that opened into a canyon. The horses stepped out eagerly, smelling water in a tiny pool at the head of the canyon. Dazed with exhaustion, Letitia wound her hands in her horse's mane and wondered how Constance managed to hang on, sounding the way she did.

The horses halted, and the older woman fell across her mount's neck and then slid to the ground, landing heavily, an ungainly lump of flesh and bones.

Letitia slid from her horse and went to help. She knew the Bickles didn't care. Somehow, she found the strength to turn the preacher's wife onto her back.

"Help . . . me . . . sit. . . ." Constance wheezed.

Letitia drew her companion in misfortune forward. "Is this easier?"

Constance seized Letitia's hand in a bruising grip and tried to nod, the air rasping in and out of her throat as her lungs labored. Her fear-stricken eyes gazed at Letitia from a face the color of putty.

"O Lord, save thy servant who putteth her trust in thee," Letitia whispered. The preacher's wife coughed and gasped, and Letitia felt as if the bones in her hands were turning to water as the older woman held on, fighting the betrayal of her body. The air whistled in and out of her lungs one last time and she toppled over to lie on her side, her blank eyes staring at the faded pastel blue of the sky.

"And grant her an entrance into the land of light and joy." Letitia closed Constance's eyes, looking away, fighting tears, focusing on the spindly legs of the Bickles as they crowded around.

"Hell and damnation!" Jonas swore. "She wouldn't have brought much, but any kind of woman is worth something." He pointed toward a jumble of boulders. "Billy, Walt, put her behind there."

"Aren't you going to bury her?" Letitia asked.

Jonas shrugged. "What for?"

Letitia gaped at him. "Because it's the right thing to do."

"Right!" Jonas spat. "Hell. Don't you understand? A body don't last long in these parts—you cain't bury 'em deep enough to keep the coyotes away."

The horrible image Jonas's words painted forced Letitia to argue further. "I don't believe you. You—we *can* bury Constance deep enough. It's the only Christian, the only human thing to do."

"Well then, Missy." Jonas pulled a shovel from the mule's pack. "You want her buried, you do it."

"I will. Just see if I don't!"

Letitia struggled to force the shovel into the earth. The sand was only about six inches deep, and below that the dirt was hard as a rock.

"Damn you, Jonas Bickle, for being right," Letitia cried. "I don't care, I'll do whatever it takes, but I *will not* leave Constance for those animals."

Eventually, Letitia managed to scoop out a shallow trench. She tugged Constance's body into the grave, ripped a piece from her tattered petticoat to cover the woman's face, and resolutely replaced the dirt. Plenty of rocks littered the ground so she piled as many as she could move to mark Constance's final resting place.

When Letitia was done she searched her mind for an appropriate prayer, but nothing came to mind. She folded her hands together and simply said, "Dear Lord, please accept our sister, Constance. Keep her . . . keep her," Letitia swallowed hard. "Keep her free from harm and guard her—"

Jonas joined her. "Ain't you done yet?"

Letitia turned and looked at him. "Go away."

"Unh-uh," he said. "I've got better things for you to do, like cooking our supper. I'll build the fire because I reckon you don't know how to, Missy. You cain't say I'm not a kind man. But you watch me close, hear, because tomorrow building the fire is gonna be your job."

Letitia struggled to cook beans and foul-smelling bacon over the tiny campfire. No matter which way she turned, the smoke followed her, curling into her smarting eyes.

She couldn't forget the expression of fear on Constance's face. No one deserved such a death. She wouldn't let those animals see her cry. Letitia dashed her hands at the tears on her cheeks. It was the smoke making her cry. It was.

Finally, she presented full plates to the three men. They chewed stoically through the greasy, unappetizing meal, but after taking her first bite, Letitia knew whatever she ate would be rejected by her queasy stomach.

She set aside her food and leaned against a boulder, trying to wrap her destroyed skirt modestly around her ankles. She endeavored to blank out what she feared the future would hold, but she couldn't control her thoughts any longer. Panic welled up before she could fight it down.

She wouldn't submit tamely to what the Bickle family had planned for her, she just wouldn't. But what could she do? She didn't think about the desert she'd traveled across for days or the fact that she couldn't survive on her own in the wilderness. All she could think of was escape.

Do it now or you never will, she told herself. She stood, deliberately hanging her head, keeping her hands hidden in the tatters of her skirts.

"Where you goin'?" Jonas demanded.

She bit her lip. "I . . . I . . ." She gestured awkwardly at a pile of boulders. "Just behind those rocks, for a moment—please?"

"The lady needs privacy," Billy said.

She wished she could blush on order like a proper Southern maiden. Instead Letitia settled for a murmured "thank you" before she fled.

The night seemed as black as the inside of a cave she and Shelly had explored when they were children. In the pale starlight it was almost impossible to make out the few stunted trees and the ever-present boulders littering the canyon floor. Thinking the darkness would aid her, she prayed the moon would rise late, or, even better yet, not at all.

In Cooper's Leatherstocking tales the characters were always undone by a twig snapping beneath their feet. She didn't think there were many twigs lying around but she tried to place her feet squarely and softly, just like Natty Bumppo. She felt her way through the stygian gloom, all the time fighting down an almost overpowering urge to race blindly into the night.

In the darkness behind her she heard Jonas shout and knew the Bickles had discovered she was missing. With a little sob she forgot everything and ran. In spite of her wild flight she sensed, more than heard, the jingle of metal and the creak of leather.

She wasn't alone any longer, and she turned away

from the sound, tripping over an unseen rock, sprawl-
ing on the ground. Panic drove her back to her feet,
but before she could turn away the horse and rider
were upon her.

The horse neighed and tossed its head, its white-
rimmed eyes gleaming in the darkness. The rider
swore, commanding his mount to stillness even as he
reached down and yanked Letitia up onto the horse
with him.

She knew he couldn't be one of the Bickles. If she
could somehow unseat him she'd have a horse and a
good chance of outdistancing her captors.

"Be still, woman!" the rider ordered, his arms
wrapping around her as he tried to subdue her with his
greater strength.

"No!" She struggled wildly. If only she could get
free. "No! I won't!"

"Damn it!" He swore again. His horse danced nervously, threatening to unseat them both. "Stand still,
Buck."

He twisted her around, one hand imprisoning both
of hers, dragging her left leg against the pommel of his
saddle, as he fought to keep her in place.

The three Bickles materialized, their sudden appearance and their shouts frightening the horse again and
making it rear. Letitia felt herself sliding across the
rider's knees and falling. . . . The saddle creaked
alarmingly. Simultaneously, he managed to control his
horse and pull Letitia back across his lap.

"Who's that?" Jonas demanded. "I'll have you
know that woman's ours."

"Jonas?" the rider questioned.

"Adam? That you?"

The rider grunted his assent.

"Well, come along to the fire. Didn't expect to see you till next week. You can bring Missy, too."

"No!" Letitia hollered. She tried to see her captor's face, but aside from a flash of even white teeth she couldn't make out his features under his hat brim. "I'm not theirs." She spoke as fast as she could, desperately trying to convince him. "They've kidnapped me! I tried to talk to them but they won't listen. My papa lives in California. He's a wealthy man. If you deliver me to him safely, he'll make it worth your while. I guarantee it."

Privately she prayed Papa would make her promise good. Of course he would. Any compassionate human being would rescue her from the Bickles. She tried again to make out the man's face, but in the darkness she couldn't see if he had sympathy for her or not.

Adam's horse caught up with the Bickles, and Jonas said, "She's already tried that story about her pa on me. But I reckon it's a waste of time. She ain't got no wealthy pa and even if she did we may as well sell her in Mexico and be shut of it."

Letitia moaned when she realized this Adam was probably one of them. His arms tightened around her and he leaned forward, encouraging his horse to step into a narrow break between two massive boulders. "Please," she whispered, unable to give up. Maybe she could influence him against Jonas. "Please get me out of this."

"Keep your mouth shut and maybe I will."

She wondered if she could believe this stranger. She didn't have much choice—she'd have to hope, to pray for the best.

The horse walked ahead eagerly, encouraged by the smell of water and the presence of others of its own kind. Adam guided his mount past the fire to an informal picket line, swung down, and helped Letitia to the ground. She hesitated, not sure what to do next, watching as he freed the cinch strap and dragged the saddle from his horse's back.

The moon had at last risen above the horizon, the glow from its fat, lopsided orange face combining with the firelight to reveal the man's face. She stared at him, wondering if she could trust him. His chin was strong and square, his cheeks lean, his nose long and straight. A face of planes and angles, finished off with blond stubble. With his hat pulled low over his brow she still couldn't see his eyes.

Walt grabbed Letitia's arm, yanking her roughly against his chest. "It don't pay to try and run away from me," he warned, his voice harsh. "Now I'm gonna have to teach you a lesson."

3

"Howdy," *Adam said* as he joined the younger man, forcing himself to ignore the indignities Walt was inflicting on his captive. Adam had a flask in his saddlebag, but he debated if he should pull it out. The Bickles were plenty mean sober. He decided rum wouldn't help. "Come to the fire," he said. "We've got some catching up to do. Haven't seen you in a while."

Walt adjusted his belt. "In a bit. I've got some more important catching up to do first."

Adam looked at the woman shrinking away from Walt. Even under the dirt and tearstains he could tell she wasn't especially pretty. Not that it mattered. He'd heard Walt had some loathsome tendencies where women were concerned, and, in spite of her dirty and disheveled appearance, her soft Southern drawl betrayed her gently bred background. A virgin, he guessed. No woman's first experience should be with a snake like Walt. For that matter, no woman should have to experience him, ever.

Adam tried to come up with a distraction but Jonas saved him the effort.

"Walt!" Jonas shouted. "Use your brains for once. Women are a dime a dozen, and that skinny miss ain't much of an armful. You come to the fire, be sociable, and listen to what Adam has to tell us."

"Damnation, Pa!" Walt yelled back. "She's run off already once. If I don't show her what's what right now, we'll have nothing but trouble."

Adam watched Jonas look shrewdly from Walt to the woman and then back at his son. "Missy *is* trouble, boy. It's writ across that plain face of hers, clear as day. She ain't much to look at, but she's smart. There ain't nothing worser in this world than a smart woman. Now you come along to the fire. Missy can wait, Adam cain't."

Grumbling and swearing, Walt shoved Letitia aside and strode away. Adam watched her sway, her right hand pressing against her temple. Her hand dropped to her side and he could see a bruise on her gently rounded cheek. Perhaps it'd be best if she just fainted. Showing her compassion wouldn't help him achieve what he'd decided to do.

"Here's a little something to warm your innards." Jonas handed a jug to Adam. "Iffen you want something to eat, I'll have Missy here fix it. I give you fair warning, she ain't much of a cook."

Adam resisted the urge to wipe his own none-too-clean hand across the top of the jug, tilted the container to his lips, and swallowed cautiously. No one knew how Jonas did it, but he always had a jug of the best white lightning west of the Mississippi. The liquor slid easily over Adam's tongue and down his throat. By the time it hit his stomach, his body had figured out what was happening and a fiery glow spread out across his chest and arms, bringing warmth even to his fingertips.

"This'll do just fine." Adam took a second sip.

The jug passed around among the four men and, although Adam didn't betray his emotions by a single flicker of muscle or eyelid, he couldn't deny his prickling awareness of the woman Jonas called Missy slumped against a rock, her knees drawn up tight against her chest. Escorting her to her papa would take time he didn't have. Still, it couldn't be helped.

Jonas belched and took another pull at the jug. Adam stiffened, his distaste for the Bickles almost overwhelming him. When he'd bumped into Jonas and heard his hard-luck story about Ramsey, Adam had decided he could use the Bickles. Now he wasn't so sure.

It takes a scoundrel to catch a scoundrel, he tried to convince himself. Except that line of reasoning wasn't as solid as it'd seemed a few weeks ago. Setting the Bickles on Ramsey was bound to include something illegal, but he'd reasoned that fair means wouldn't bring Ramsey down.

"You boys find anything useful?" Adam asked.

"Depends on what you call useful." Jonas lowered his voice. "You were right, he's spreading into the territory. Got himself a ranch beyond Tucson and he's got a couple of banks as well. I heard tell he fancies himself as one of them railway barons."

"That'll be decided in Washington," Adam said.

"Yeah, but the deciding will be decided by money."

Jonas grinned and reached for the jug. "You did yourself fine back in Placerville, but I hear tell our friend has done even better than that. He's a rich man, Adam, and you're twisting a rattler by the tail. Iffen he gets word of what you're planning he'll squash you like a little ole bug."

Adam didn't reply. Instead he looked levelly at Jonas.

"Yeah." The old man spat and continued. "I reckon as how you've got the right of it. He's the one oughta be squashed and I'm betting you're the man to do it. If that son of a bitch hadn't jumped our claim back in fifty-seven, I reckon I'd be the big bad baron and you'd be a-trying to squash me."

Adam didn't deny it.

Jonas leaned forward. "What d'ya plan to do next?"

"Find out more about those banks. He needs money to finance his plans, and that may be the way to stop him," Adam said.

"Hah!" Jonas cackled and waved the jug. "Your ma didn't raise no dummy."

Adam glanced quickly at the Bickles' captive. Her tense posture suggested that she was listening to every word they said, even though she had the good sense to keep her mouth shut like he'd ordered. When he judged the Bickles were at the precarious stage between mellowness and mean drunkenness, he tilted his head toward the woman and asked, "What are you going to do with her?"

Walt snorted but Jonas answered. "Taking her to Mexico. We started off with three, but it's been an unlucky day. Lost two of 'em already."

"You know that ranch of mine in the mountains northeast of San Diego?"

Jonas nodded.

"I reckon I could use her." The woman jumped to her feet and Adam glared at her. "It'll save you the trouble of taking her south. Besides, I need you boys to get working on the next project right away. What d'you figure she's worth?"

"Wait a damn minute!" Walt sat bolt upright. "Sure, we're gonna sell her, but that's days off."

"Get your head outta your pants, boy," Jonas ordered. He stared at Letitia, hard. "Sit down. What we're doing don't concern you."

"Doesn't concern me!" Letitia cried. "I'm no slave to be bought and sold."

"Old Abe may have freed the slaves, but he didn't free you, Missy." Jonas cackled at his wit. "If you don't sit down and shut up, I'll let Walt take care of you." His son started forward, but Jonas warned him back. "You sit, too. Adam's right. It's gonna take time we ain't got to get her to Mexico. Time we could put to better use right here in the good old U.S. of A." He reached for the jug, his expression crafty. "Adam, I'll tell you what, I'll sell her to you for five hundred dollars."

He took the jug from Jonas. "I said I wanted her for the ranch. A man in my position doesn't need a courtesan."

"A court-a-what?"

"Besides," Adam continued. "From the looks of her she's just a scared virgin. She doesn't know the first thing about looking after a man. You already told me she can't cook."

"True, she cain't cook," Jonas agreed. "But Walt here'll teach her all about men."

"No offense intended to Walt," Adam said to Jonas, "but that's bound to lower her value."

Jonas nodded. "Make me an offer."

Adam paused, considering. "Fifty." He saw her flinch in astonishment. He'd explain later, maybe.

Jonas whooped with laughter. "Think you're a crafty horse trader, don't you?"

Adam lifted the jug in a silent salute. "You admitted she isn't much of an armful."

"Damn!" Jonas reached for the jug and backhanded his mouth. "Seeing as how we knew each other back in the goldfields and we're business partners now, how . . . how about two-fifty?"

"How about it?" Adam shook his head. "Look Jonas, I'm a reasonable man, but I'm not all that rich. I'll go a hundred."

"You call that reasonable!"

Jonas reached for the jug. Adam knew he had to close the deal now or Jonas would dig in, simply for the joy of thwarting him.

"Don't listen to him, Pa," Walt urged. "You don't know what you're doing!"

"Don't I?" Jonas turned on his son. "I damn well know what I'm doing. Don't you got enough sense not to interrupt your Pa when he's doing a spot of horse trading, boy?"

Walt swore viciously and reached for the jug.

"My last offer." Adam stood.

He watched her hands twisting in the tatters of her skirt. He knew he'd lied. He'd do whatever it took to rescue her from the Bickles. He had to fight his revulsion as he gazed at Jonas. Why had he involved himself

with this group of murdering thieves? He loathed asso-
ciating with them, had to keep reassuring himself that
the ends justified the means. At least some good had
come of it already, he'd rescue the woman Jonas called
Missy.

"I'll give you two hundred and you throw in a
horse."

Jonas blustered.

"In gold," Adam added softly.

"Damn, but you're a hard man." Jonas nodded and
offered Adam the jug. "We'll drink on it."

Adam took one last swallow, feeling slightly lightheaded. Jonas' home brew packed one hell of a wallop.

"Moon's up," Adam announced. "She isn't used to
the desert like we are. I reckon we'll ride."

Jonas belched. "Wish you luck—you're gonna need
it. Missy here ain't much of an armful and besides
that, she's an *awful* cook."

"Come on." Adam hauled an unresisting Letitia to
her feet. "We're leaving." He could feel her hand shaking in his.

She looked from him to the three Bickles, still sitting
by the campfire, passing the jug back and forth.

"Remember, you did ask me to get you out of this,"
he said softly as he moved away.

She followed him. "Yes, but . . . two hundred dollars gold. I don't know whether to be insulted or gratified."

"Wait until you see the horse. Besides, it doesn't
matter."

"Yes, it does, my papa—"

"We'll never reach your papa if we don't get a move
on." When he took her arm, she flinched at his touch
and he swore under his breath. "Walt there gets plenty

ornery when he's drunk and it looks as if he's planning to get drunk tonight."

Letitia turned away. She decided she had nothing to lose, and followed him to the picket line. Adam led one of the stagecoach horses to her side and helped her up onto its back. She groaned as her already sore thighs were forced to accommodate her uncomfortable mount once again.

Her torn skirt and petticoats bunched under her knees. She sensed him staring at her exposed legs. She felt herself flushing and struggled to rearrange her garments. He pulled his hat lower on his forehead and mounted his gelding, leading the way past the Bickles and out of the canyon.

She followed him around a curve in the trail and looked back. The Bickles' fire had been blanked out by distance and the intervening boulders. It had been a bad dream, she told herself fiercely.

She looked at Adam's broad back and square shoulders and wondered what she'd done. He couldn't be like the Bickles in any way, shape, or form. He might look as rough as they did, but he had an educated man's way with words. Not that education counted for trustworthiness, but it couldn't hurt. Besides, he had a kind voice. If she could only see his eyes.

He headed due west across the desert, arrogantly not looking, not checking to see if she followed. She drummed her heels hard into the coach horse's broad sides, trying to keep up, wondering if she'd fallen from the frying pan into the fire.

Her horse ducked its head, trying to free the reins, and she sagged forward over his neck, the whalebone from her corset digging into the tender flesh below her breasts.

Lightheaded from the pain and hunger, she forced herself to maintain her seat and control her horse. Fatigue seemed to rise up from the desert floor, a tangible force battering her insensible.

She didn't care. She was so tired and sore, she just didn't care anymore.

After a while, the sky lightened to gray and behind them the horizon took on rays of deep pink, red, and gold as the sun rose. She hardly noticed. She saw a line of trees in the distance, but they meant nothing. Instinct forced her to stay on her horse's back, but she had no memory, no recollection of Adam taking the reins from her. Finally, the horses stepped forward eagerly, sensing the water running in a stream threading its way through the cottonwoods, but she didn't notice that either.

When her horse thrust his head into the water, she fell forward across its neck and realized they'd come to a stop. Dully, she looked around and wondered how she'd unwind her hands from her mount's mane. The task seemed too difficult.

Adam swung from his horse and walked to Letitia's side, gently untangling her hands. He pulled her free and she sagged against him, her head burrowing into the curve of his shoulder. Her eyelashes fluttered and she lost consciousness.

"Damn!" he muttered, compassion and pity for her sweeping through him as he ducked under a low branch and settled her in the shade of one of the trees. "What in the hell are you doing out here?"

She might be a lightweight, he thought, and perhaps not the prettiest thing around, but what there was of her felt soft and gently rounded—except for that stupid corset wrapped around her middle like a piece of old-fashioned armor. She looked so defense-less as he watched her sleep. The sight of her profile was as pure as that of a cameo, and her skin was incredibly smooth. He shook his head to rid himself of his strange fancy. Blinking, half-dazed with tiredness, he left her to go tend the horses and make their camp.

It was well past midday when Letitia woke. She was lying on a horse blanket, and she wrinkled her nose at the smell of it as she rolled onto her back. She seemed to be resting in some sort of a roughly built lean-to, the branches rising to a point less than two feet above her head. She turned, shading her eyes against the bright sunlight filtering through the twisted tree limbs.

Adam lay on a blanket, stretched across the opening of the crude shelter, his face shaded by his hat, his soft snores a comforting drone. Wondering what he looked like in daylight, but still too tired to bother sitting up, she drifted off to sleep, waking again when the glow of sunset filled the humble lean-to.

The smell of frying bacon tickled her nose, and her stomach grumbled raucously in response. Every muscle protesting, she crawled on her hands and knees until she was clear of the branches piled above her and struggled to her feet, one hand cupping the tender muscles at the base of her spine.

He heard the soft rustling of her skirt as she stood. He balanced the fry pan on one of the rocks ringing the small campfire, turning to watch her. She stepped closer, her hands twisting in the tatters of her skirt, and he was reminded of a half-wild cat he'd discovered living in the tumbledown shed that doubled as a barn on his ranch.

The cat clearly knew about humans, and clearly knew they weren't to be trusted. Damn the Bickles for revealing life's harsh side to this unprotected girl. She reminded him of a magnolia. Obviously, she was unsuited for this barren land. He looked away for a moment, clearing his mind of his fanciful imaginings. He'd take her to San Diego. What happened to her then wasn't his problem.

He looked back at her and a question popped into his mind. "What's your name?"

"Letitia . . ."

"Didn't think it was Missy."

"No."

He watched her eyes widen with fear and silently cursed himself for reminding her of the Bickles. "Forget it," he said. "Just forget it. I'll take you to San Diego and all this will be over."

"I wish it were."

He rose from his squatting position by the fire and smiled. "Well, then. Wishes do come true."

When she finally saw his eyes she suppressed a gasp. They were as blue as cornflowers, the color as clear as the morning sky on a sunny day. She hadn't expected anything as compelling as those eyes, as fascinating as that smile, his even white teeth contrasting with his deeply tanned face.

Tiny lines radiated from each side of his eyes, but in spite of his expression, she didn't think they were smile lines. Something about him convinced her he hadn't had much to smile about for a long time.

His words broke into her thoughts. "Feel like eating?"

"Mmmm, yes." Letitia gestured at herself, hating to

imagine how dirty and disheveled she appeared. "I—is there anywhere I can clean up, just a little?"

Adam pointed with his chin toward the stream. "It's pretty dirty, but do the best you can. I wouldn't recommend bathing in it, it's scarcely fit to drink."

He reached for his saddlebags, rummaged around, and handed her a blue bandanna and a bar of soap. "Be sure to go downstream. I don't figure soapsuds will improve the flavor."

She did her best, but the muddy, sandy water didn't leave her feeling much cleaner as the silt clogged her pores, drying to a fine grit. She shook her head at the state of her dress and petticoats. They were ruined, not even fit for rags, but they were all she had. If only she could be free of her uncomfortable corset. What would Papa think when he saw her?

She shuddered and combed her fingers through her hair, wishing that she could wash it or at least brush it. Most of her hairpins were gone, so she ripped a piece free from one of her petticoats, braided her hair into a single rope and tied it back. She decided it was best she couldn't see her reflection in the stream.

At the campfire Adam had divided the food between the fry pan and a single plate. He handed the plate to Letitia and turned his attention to his meal. She inhaled the tantalizing aroma and greedily shoved the rice seasoned with pepper into her mouth. He was a much better cook than she was. She blushed at her lack of manners and lowered herself to the ground, wincing as the whalebone from her corset bit into her side again.

Adam's eyes narrowed. "Where are you hurt?"

"I'm not." Letitia forked up a mouthful of bacon and chewed vigorously, savoring the taste.

"Like hell," Adam said. His unshaven cheeks took on a faint tinge of pink. "Pardon me. Seems as if I've been away from polite company a bit too long."

Letitia shrugged. She'd heard much worse the last few days. "Thank you, but it doesn't matter."

"Yes, it does. Well. Jonas said he'd taken you off the stagecoach. If anyone could louse up a simple stage robbery, they're the ones to do it. Did you hurt your ribs in the struggle?"

"No, I don't think so. I'm fine, aside from some sore muscles."

She vowed she would take off the miserable corset no matter what and find another way to hide her money. She gazed through the trees to the expanse of sunset-lit desert beyond the stream. It wasn't as if she needed a corset. A lady simply always wore one. Even so, it didn't seem as if ladylike attributes were worth much out here.

Her meal finished, Letitia stood and nodded at the pot of water heating on the coals. "I'll wash these." She picked up her plate and Adam lifted the fry pan. When she bent to take it from his hand, the whalebone stays dug in again and she bit her lip against the pain.

A sudden ache throbbed against her temples and her stomach lurched. She closed her lips tightly against the nausea, her vision blurred by frantically dancing dark spots. From far away she thought she heard Adam call her name, but she couldn't hear him clearly. The spots took over, coalescing into one great, overwhelming blackness.

"Hell!" Adam shouted, catching Letitia as she fainted, crumpling in his arms.

His right hand encountered a damp, sticky patch on her left side, just below her breast. Blood! God in heaven—what a little liar, he thought. She'd broken a rib and the nearest doctor was days away.

He gently laid her beside the fire and sprinted for his saddlebags and the blanket she'd left in the lean-to. When he returned to her side, she was still deep in her swoon, and he prayed she wouldn't come around until he'd discovered the extent of her injuries. What he had to do would hurt her, and the thought of causing her pain tightened his jaw and created a faint echo of that agony in the pit of his stomach.

He knelt beside her, ripped open the buttons of her bodice, then leaned her against his chest to pull her arms free from the sleeves. There, above her corset, was a vivid ring of rust overlaid by a bright patch of fresh scarlet, staining the purity of her long-sleeved white camisole. He laid her on the blanket and applied his knife to the strings of her corset. Again he raised her, peeling away the rigid stays like the skin of an orange.

He tugged the camisole free from the waistband of her voluminous petticoats and tried to pull the garment over her head but it stuck to the wound in her side.

Damn! He'd have to soak it free. He reached for the bandanna she'd used earlier, dunked it in the pot of water steaming beside the fire, folded the cloth into a pad, and gingerly applied the hot compress to her side.

Letitia moaned. The rubbing from her corset had become a red-hot poker digging into her side. She tried to twist free from the relentless heat, but she couldn't get away.

"Easy," Adam said, brushing her hair away from her forehead with his free hand. "Just take it easy."

The sound of his voice brought her to full consciousness. "What—?"

But she could go no further. She wrenched herself free of his hands, rolled to her uninjured side and, unable to stop herself, violently emptied her stomach.

Her body shuddered, the spasms coming fast, one after the other. Still, she was dimly aware of Adam's comforting hands as he held her forehead and helped her endure the vile sickness.

Finally, it was over. She felt as limp as a dishrag.

"Through?" he asked.

"Yes," Letitia whispered, the humiliation of what she'd just done sweeping through her. *Oh Lord,* she thought, *what can happen to me next?*

She kept her eyes averted as he helped her to lie back on the blanket. Strangely, she felt much better. He levered her against his chest, his arm coming around her good side to offer her a mug of water.

"Here, rinse out your mouth."

She complied, and that was when she discovered that her upper body was covered only by her camisole.

"Oh, no!" she moaned. Frantically, she tried to pull away from him, but his arms, as strong as iron bands, held her close.

"Don't struggle, you little fool. That rib is bad enough as it is." He lowered her to the blanket and knelt beside her, holding her still when she tried to move away from him, his blue eyes filled with concern. "I'll try not to hurt you any more than I can help, but you've got to let me doctor you."

"No!" She endeavored to struggle to a sitting position, but he held her down. "You don't understand!"

"Damn it!" This time he didn't apologize for swearing in front of her. "Do you want to kill yourself?"

"Of course not. But I'll have you know I'm a re-spectable woman."

"That's not the point. It's perfectly clear to me you're a total innocent." He paused and ground his teeth together. "Listen to me. I'm no rapist. You're hurt and you *will* let me take care of you. I'm not a doctor either, but that rib—"

"It's not my ribs," she interrupted. "I'd know if I were really hurt." She bit her lip. "One of the whale-bones poked through my corset and it's been rubbing me—"

"—raw from the looks of it." He reached for the steaming pot of water. "Don't argue. If you haven't broken a rib then that's good news. But I have to be sure, and that means the rest of your clothing is com-ing off whether you like it or not."

"You can't!" Letitia exclaimed. "I won't let you."

"You don't have a choice," he said. "So spare me your maidenly protests."

Unable to think of a way to stop him, she twisted her head away, her hands clenching into fists. How could she endure this—this invasion on top of every-thing else? If only he'd listen to her—but it was clear he wouldn't. She shut her eyes, wishing she could pre-tend this final indignity wasn't happening to her.

"Scratch a woman and find a martyr," Adam mut-tered. Still, when he applied the hot compress to her side, he did it as gently as he could. She yelped and drew back, but he was ready for her. He held her close, his right arm circling her shoulders, wedging her be-tween his knees.

He could feel the soft underside of her left breast and the instinctive hardening of her nipples brought a response from deep in his loins.

The girl was a virgin, he reminded himself, gently bred, and frightened. But that didn't stop the slight tremor in his hands or the aching desire to lower his lips to hers. But he controlled himself. He was no rapist.

"I think that should do it," he said, his voice harsh and raspy. He lowered the pad, revealing her firm, taut flesh.

"Raise your arms."

Without looking at him, Letitia obeyed.

"I'll try to take this off without destroying it."

"Thank you."

Still, the sodden fabric stuck to the wound in her side as he tried to tug her clothing over her head. She moaned, swaying at the pain.

"Sorry!" He pulled the camisole back down, reached for his knife and with one smooth tug slit the garment from neck to hem.

The two halves fell away, exposing Letitia's soft flesh, glowing in the firelight. While small, her breasts were tempting mounds, pleasingly shaped, firm and topped by dark pink nipples, now tightly puckered against the cold and pain.

She could feel her nipples tingle and the betrayal of her body completed her mortification. She sensed Adam's gaze and turned to look at him. Those blue eyes, now darkened almost to the color of indigo, regarded her steadily, his expression unfathomable. He said nothing, but his gaze dropped and she knew he was looking at her naked flesh. Her lashes swooped down, veiling her eyes, but she couldn't control the blush rising up from her neck, crimsoning her cheeks.

His finger traced the curve of her jawline. "Don't be frightened," he said gently.

"I'm not," she whispered.

His voice carried a thread of amusement. "Little liar."

"Yes."

No one had ever seen her like this, no one but Shelly, and she tried to banish the memories of the week they'd spent together before he marched off to war. Tried and failed.

How could she think of Shelly at a time like this? Was Grandmama correct? Was her granddaughter a wanton, tainted with her mother's and Clay Jewell's bad blood? How could she react like this to a strange man if she wasn't? She bit her lip, fighting the tears that were dangerously close to the surface.

He gently peeled the camisole away. "It's not that bad," he said.

His exploration of her injury was mercifully brief, his touch as delicate as any woman's. Letitia shut her eyes and endured, her lips closing tightly to hold back the whimper building in her throat. At last he was through.

"Thank God you were right. I don't think anything is broken."

He reached for a small pot of salve guaranteed to cure either man or beast and spread it on the wound. When his hand accidentally brushed across her tightly erect nipple, they both tensed, neither daring to look at the other. The silence vibrated between them, the space between their rigid bodies heavy with longing.

Not looking at her, Adam reached for the tapes to her petticoats and untied them. "I'll help you out of these. I want to find the cleanest fabric to use as a bandage."

Wordlessly, she obeyed. The petticoats pooled

around her feet, and clad only in her boots, stockings, and drawers, she gave in and crossed her arms across her chest, hugging herself tightly.

His knife slashed through the cambric material, the sound of ripping cloth harsh in the still night.

"Lift your arms," he said quietly, not meeting her eyes, as he helped her to sit.

He wrapped the bandage around her middle and over her shoulder to keep it in place, tore the end, and tied the cloth off neatly, using a square knot. "That should do for now, but we'll keep your petticoats handy because you'll need rebandaging."

He pulled a chambray shirt and faded trousers from his saddle bag and handed them to Letitia. "Put these on. Your dress is ruined."

Her arms rippled with gooseflesh and she reached eagerly for the garments. If only she could hide her thoughts as easily as she could hide her body. His shirt covered her thighs and the sleeves drooped past her hands. She rolled up the cuffs, stepped into the trousers and did up the buttons. The pants immediately sagged past her hips and she grabbed at the waistband, pulling them back into place.

Adam grinned, applied his knife to his lariat and handed her a short length of rope. "Here." When she finally had his trousers firmly in place, he added, "Have to say they look a whole lot better on you than they ever did on me."

Letitia sniffed, and rolled up the bottoms of the pants, too. She took a few experimental steps. The scuffed, scratched patent leather toes on her boots looked ridiculous as they stuck out from the impromptu cuffs. The fabric felt bunchy and odd around her waist and legs and she missed the concealment of her skirts.

Adam cleared away his medical impedimenta, and while his back was turned, she swiftly transferred her money from her corset to a pocket in her borrowed trousers.

He turned and looked at her. "Now you're rested and treated, I want to clear up a few things. All I know is I'm taking you to your pa and he lives near San Diego. What's his name?"

She settled back on the blanket, drawing a meaningless pattern in the dirt with a handy twig, grateful for his return to what passed for normalcy in this strange, savage place. "Papa lives near San Diego and his name is Hunt Ramsey."

Adam's blue eyes blazed. *"Hunt Ramsey?"*

"Yes. That's right." Frightened by his grim expression, she wondered why he'd reacted so, why his shoulders were suddenly so rigid. Did he know Papa?

Adam shook his head and swore. "That's not possible."

"Of course it's possible. My name is Letitia *Ramsey.*" She decided to abridge her story, considerably. "When Mama died, Papa left me with my grandmama and came out West. He remarried and now he's living on a ranch. When Grandmama died he wrote, asking me to come and live with him." She bit her lip, knowing she was embroidering her tale, just the tiniest bit. But Papa would help—she knew he would!

Adam swore again. He didn't believe in God, or at least not much. Yet in Ma's letter she'd set him on Hunt Ramsey's trail. But Letitia? It seemed like too much of a coincidence, but what if it wasn't? What if this chance meeting had been meant to happen?

He'd bought a ranch in the mountains above San Diego to be within striking distance of Ramsey, he'd fostered an acquaintance with the Bickles simply because Jonas wanted to bring Ramsey down as much as Adam did, and he'd taken, as his own, his mother's wish for vengeance to bring his grandparents' and his father's destroyer to justice.

Still, none of this had gotten him close to Ramsey. In a weird, twisted way Adam realized it made sense that Letitia had come into his life. He instinctively knew she would be the key to reaching Ramsey and bringing him down.

"What's wrong?" she asked. "It's something about Papa, isn't it? Is he all right?"

Adam looked away, his gaze focusing on the starlit sky. "I wouldn't know."

"Then what is it?"

"Nothing," Adam said, shifting uncomfortably.

She didn't believe him. The silence stretched between them, full of unspoken questions and disturbing, confusing undercurrents. "Do you know my papa? Do you know Hunt Ramsey?"

"No."

Even though Adam still wouldn't look at her, she sensed he was telling the truth this time. "But you know about him, don't you?"

"Leave it alone." Adam sprang to his feet. "Don't you know you don't ask direct questions of a man out here? If he wants to volunteer information, that's fine. Otherwise, it's none of your business."

"But it is my business." Letitia stood up too. "You're taking me to Papa."

Adam raked his hand through his blond hair. "Look, I asked you to leave it alone." He sighed. "I'll take you to Ramsey. I said I would and I will. How I do it is another matter entirely."

"But—"

"No buts."

The hard gleam in Adam's eyes forced Letitia to swallow the words she wanted to say. It seemed as if nothing had changed, not really. First Grandmama, then the Bickles, and now Adam. What made her the sort of person who was always ordered around? What was wrong with her?

He pointed toward the rustic lean-to. "You'd better get some rest. We've got a long way to go tomorrow."

"I'm not tired."

"You should be."

Adam remembered his mother's letter and the arousing sight of Letitia's breasts, her firm, supple flesh glowing in the firelight. God, or whoever it was that ordained the running of a man's life sure had a twisted sense of humor.

4

Adam watched the stars slowly fade away into the pale gray of the predawn sky. In the waiting hush, he could hear the sound of Letitia's heavy breathing as she slept. Rest was the best thing for her but as soon as the sun was properly up, he'd have to wake her. They had to be on their way.

When breakfast was over, Adam picked up her plain brown bonnet. "Here," he said. "Put this on."

She reached for the sadly stained piece of headgear. It hadn't been much of a hat to begin with, as plain and as worn as her traveling dress. She tried to brush the worst of the dirt from the brim and held it in front of her. She'd look even more ridiculous than she did now if she combined her bonnet with Adam's shirt and trousers and her boots.

She looked up at the perfect blue sky framed by meager branches of the cottonwoods. Bright sunlight sharpened and defined the landscape. She knew if she didn't shade her face her nose'd burn to a crisp by midday. Sighing, she jammed the bonnet on her head. Who cared anyway?

Adam stood by his horse, waiting. She sensed he didn't want to talk to her. She wondered what her papa had done to make him so black in Adam's eyes. Hunt Ramsey had always been a bit of an adventurer, making his way through the world relying on his wits and intelligence, but he wasn't evil—she was sure of that.

She frowned. In many ways he was just a shadowy memory—his letters to her were more real than the man. Residents of Fayette County had disliked papa, but that was because he wasn't one of the closely in-bred group. She wished she knew what Papa had to do with Adam. She put that disloyal thought out of her mind as quickly as it'd surfaced. Papa hadn't done anything. He wasn't that type of man. Adam had to be the one at fault, somehow.

Letitia shrugged away her thoughts, walked to her horse, looked up at his broad back, and sighed.

"Ready?" Adam didn't wait for Letitia's answer, he just boosted her onto her horse.

He settled down into his saddle and said, "It'll be two days before we see fresh water again. I've got only one canteen full for the four of us." Adam's gaze took in the horses. "We're on rationing."

She nodded, her throat tightening in response to his words. What did she know about this man, really? Could she even rely on him to find water again? She had to trust him, she realized, because she knew she couldn't even find her way back to this muddy stream.

She gazed at Adam as he thrust his right leg forward, leaned over, and checked the girth. His saddle creaked as he straightened up. She knew there was a sense of command about him that made her want to follow him implicitly. *Stop that!* she thought. *He's your guide—nothing more.*

He urged his horse forward. She drummed her heels against her mount's side and fell into line behind Adam. The horses splashed through the silty river. She urged her gelding to catch up. He lowered his head, refusing to go any faster. Clearly, he was a natural follower.

She borrowed some of the language the driver had used the day before yesterday, whispering words softly toward the long hair that rimmed her horse's ears. Maybe he'd respond to that.

"What?" Adam turned in his saddle to look at Letitia. What's going on back there?"

She felt her face burn and knew her cheeks must be scarlet. "Nothing."

He had to have ears like a switch-wielding schoolmaster if he'd heard what she'd said. She blushed all the harder, praying he hadn't.

Adam focused his attention on the trail before him, wondering if she'd said what he thought she'd said. No, she couldn't have. Where would a woman like Miss Letitia *Ramsey* have learned words like that?

The desert was getting to him, he decided. If he didn't watch out he'd be one as peculiar as the old prospectors who haunted the mountains around here.

*　　*　　*

When Adam judged it to be midday, he stopped his horse, waiting for Letitia to catch up. "We'll rest here."

She slid down her mount's side and staggered a few steps. She felt tired and stiff, but the blinding exhaustion she'd experienced yesterday hadn't engulfed her yet. Her wound was still sore but much better than before. How wonderful it was to be free of her corset. She moved, relishing the emancipation from her skirts.

"Why do women always wear dresses?" she asked.

Adam frowned. "I have no idea. Women wear skirts and men wear trousers and that's the way it is."

"I bet if more women had a chance to wear trousers they'd give up skirts for good."

Adam grinned, shook his head, and turned back to his horse.

Neither mode of dressing really helped much in the desert, she decided. Back in Kentucky it was still winter, but here it was hot and dry. She thought longingly of the fountain in the courtyard at Bellewood where cool, fresh, delicious water was piped in from the stream that ran behind the slave quarters. When she was little, when she could escape from Grandmama's eagle eyes, Letitia had played in that stream, the water splashing up around her ankles—

"Don't." Adam's voice interrupted Letitia's thoughts.

"Don't what?"

"Don't think whatever it is you're thinking."

"How do you know what I'm thinking?" she demanded.

He reached for his canteen, yanked the bandanna from his neck, soaked it, and held it to the coach horse's nostrils. "It's as plain as that stand of cholla you're thinking about water. You keep that up and you'll be ten times more miserable."

She turned her back on him and stomped away. So she'd been thinking about Bellewood—so what?

A light touch on her shoulder made her whirl around. He offered her the canteen. "Three swallows. You can have more when the sun goes down. Anything you drink now you'll just sweat off."

She took her three swallows. The musty water tasted awful, but at least it eased the dryness of her throat. "How can anyone survive out here?" Her gaze took in the grayish green cacti and the faded pastel purple and coral and beige of the low, bare mountains in the distance. "There's no water, no shade, no nothing."

"It's not that bad when you know how. Couple hundred years ago a Spaniard by the name of de Anza marched his men through here. Can't say it's been a steady stream ever since, but if you're sensible you can survive the journey. The Mormon Battalion came through this desert before the war." Adam narrowed his eyes against the noontime glare. "I'll admit it isn't a picnic. I'd never do this in the summertime."

Last night he'd lectured her on the impropriety of asking a man his business, yet once again she found herself wondering what he was doing out in the desert if he owned a ranch near San Diego. What had brought him to this desolate place?

Adam watched her expression. He could sense her mind turning as busily as a spinning wheel, yet when she spoke, her question surprised him.

"I can't figure it out. You're not at all like them. What were you doing with the Bickles?"

"Didn't I tell you not to ask a man about—"

"Yes." She handed the canteen back to him. "You did. But I'm curious, and how will I ever know anything if I don't ask?"

Adam jammed the cork back in the canteen's neck and scowled. He didn't have to explain his affairs to her. "Like I said, it's none of your business." He turned and marched back to the horses.

"Hell!" she muttered under her breath. She knew why men swore. It made them feel better, and wasn't it just like a man to deny a woman even that little bit of pleasure?

Adam continued to lead the way west until it was almost too dark to see. He guided the horses along a tiny wash between two small, flattish hills. A single, stunted cottonwood grew in the pocket where the hills joined together.

"This is it," he said. "We'll camp here. Sorry, but I can't build you a lean-to. Whatever wood I can find will have to go for the fire."

Letitia wrapped her arms around her chest, trying to conserve precious body heat. When the sun went down, the air got cold, and it became winter in the desert, too.

Later, wrapped in Adam's jacket and his single blanket, she looked across the glowing embers of the fire, making out his lean form stretched on the sandy earth, his legs inadequately covered by his saddle blanket. She pulled her own covering higher and tucked her hands under her armpits. Before, she'd slept the sleep of total exhaustion. Tonight, even though her bones ached with tiredness she couldn't fall asleep.

"What's wrong?" Adam's voice filled the space between them.

"I can't sleep."

"Are you trying?"

"Have you ever *tried* to go to sleep?"

"Is your, uh, side bothering you?"

"Not really." She paused and then said, all in a rush, "I'm so cold!"

He sighed deeply, unable to ignore the plaintive note in her voice. He was cold, too, but he'd learned long ago to ignore bodily discomforts.

In the light from the campfire he could see her shoulders quiver. He raised up on one elbow to look at her and he saw the blanket covering her body ripple as another shiver convulsed her body. Next thing, her teeth would start to chatter and he'd be up all night listening to her. That definitely wouldn't be good.

As long as he kept the fire going they might not freeze to death, but he knew they were both in for an unpleasant time. The clearness of the night sky meant it would be plenty frigid in the hours before sunrise. Still, he'd been cold before and he'd more than likely be cold again.

He knew what he had to do and steeled himself to use an old Plains Indian trick. Personally, he always hated to do it—it always reminded him of the fire that night long ago, a memory that could still bring a shudder of horror when it intruded into his consciousness. But it couldn't be helped. Tonight it was freezing.

"Hell!" he grumbled.

He moved the pile of wood some five feet from the fire and then carefully used one of the burning brands to kindle a fresh blaze. He pulled a small spade free from his saddle and used it to transfer the rest of the fire to its new location.

With his foot, he spread out the warm dirt that had

rested under the fire, shook his blanket out on top, and said to Letitia, "Move over here where it's warm."

"I can't," she said, clearly shocked by his suggestion that she share his blanket.

"Suit yourself. Freeze to death then."

He forced himself to lie down where the fire had burnt a few minutes ago. In the stillness he could hear the chattering of her teeth.

"Look," he said, "you may not realize it, but people actually do freeze to death in the desert. If you wish to survive this night you'd better move."

"Are you serious?" she quavered.

"Dead serious." His voice ironically underlined the word dead.

"Oh . . . okay."

In a quick rush she scrambled over to join him, her blanket tightly clutched around her shoulders. He inched closer so she could share his body warmth.

She moved closer, keeping her hands tucked firmly along her sides, her body rigid. He could tell she was too cold to worry about proprieties in spite of the fact that some old biddy somewhere would raise a ruckus if she could see what they were doing.

Letitia seemed to be greedy to share his warmth, and he felt strangely protective as her body snuggled up to his.

"Thank you," she whispered, her voice barely audible.

She shivered again, and he could feel her muscles tense as she tried to control her involuntary reaction to the cold.

"Just go to sleep," he said softly, doing his best to make his voice low and hypnotic.

He slid his arms around her, just below the soft

curve of her breasts. He felt her relax. And then she was asleep, her heavy breathing verging on gentle snores.

Tantalized by her soft curves, he realized that now *he* couldn't sleep.

Eventually, he relaxed and drifted off until his mind was invaded by the images of the dream. It was always the same—a fire engulfing and destroying everything and everyone. Terror pervaded his senses, smoke choking him and red heat rising up from everywhere to destroy him.

"No!" he shouted, sitting bolt upright, still seeing the reflection of the flames burning in his dream and not the stillness of the desert night.

"What's happening?" Letitia was clearly confused by the disturbance. She shoved her hair away from her face. "What is wrong?"

"Nothing," he said abruptly. "Go back to sleep."

"But?"

"Be quiet!" he said. "Don't say anything. Just go to sleep."

He forced himself to add fresh wood to the fire and then lay back down, memories of the dream crowding into his mind. Always it came back when he least expected it, a tormentor he'd struggled with all his life. He knew it was linked to the night of the fire he'd experienced when he was a small boy, before his father had left. To an extent, he'd learned to fight it. In the dream, he always knew something awful, more awful than just the destroying flames, was going to take place, but somehow, he'd managed to train himself to wake up before it actually took place.

If only he could stop the dream from recurring.

He half-turned on his side, listening to Letitia's

even, exhausted breathing. He knew he couldn't trust himself to sleep again tonight.

Daybreak found Adam boiling a small amount of their precious water to make coffee. He knew he shouldn't take the risk, with their supply so low, but he needed the comfort of the warm beverage.

Letitia sat up and looked at him. What had happened in the night to make him shout so? She didn't understand, but she sensed it was something she shouldn't ask him about.

She wandered away from the campsite and gazed at the stunted cacti standing on the hillside. They grew perhaps every five feet, not more than two feet tall. She bent down and counted eight twisted arms on the plant in front of her, each protrusion less than an inch in circumference if one discounted the long, wicked thorns sticking out like needles in a pincushion. Nestled among the spines, what could be only flower buds were about to bloom. It made sense—cacti were plants after all—but blossoms? The concept was as incongruous as the idea that Grandmama had ever felt a gentle emotion.

Letitia stood, adjusting the rope belt around her waist. Her attention was caught by an odd, persistent buzzing noise. She turned, startled to find a snake, not three feet from her, raising its head from the wicked coil of its body, its tongue flickering as it hissed.

Her hand flew to her throat. She tried to scream, but she couldn't force sound past her stiff lips. The snake's tail pointed straight up as it repeated its alarming rattle.

Finally, she managed to wail, "Adam!"

The explosion of a shot shattered the early-morning quiet. Time seemed to stretch out into eternity as she watched the snake's body uncoil and soar into the air. She felt flying grains of sand sting her face and hands as the bullet plowed into the earth. The raw smell of gunpowder was everywhere. When the dust cleared, she saw Adam standing twenty yards away, his smoking pistol dangling from his hands.

She stumbled toward him, trying not to sob as he came to meet her. Her arms clutched him. She rested her head against his shoulder and heard his rapid heartbeat.

He lifted her chin. "Did it bite you?"

"N-no," Letitia stammered. "I turned around and there it was, making that awful sound."

"Thank God."

It seemed the most natural thing in the world when he lowered his lips to hers. She shut her eyes, blocking out the sunlight, pressing her body against his. His mustache prickled, but his lips were firm, reassuring. Without thinking, she opened her mouth and his tongue slid between her teeth as if it belonged there. He pulled her even closer, molding her body against his. Her arms wound around his neck as she returned his embrace. Time seemed suspended, sensation reduced to the pleasure of his lips, the enticement of his tongue.

Adam hesitated, his chest heaving as he fought to breathe. She stared up at him, trying to understand the emotion in his eyes.

Before she could say anything his head lowered again. If the first kiss had been arousing, the second was purely devastating. Desire flamed within her. With a little moan, she tore her lips from his and buried her head in the hollow of his shoulder. She couldn't hear his heart for the pounding of her own blood as it raced through her veins and beat in her head. She knew what was happening to her—knew what she wanted—but she didn't know what to do about it.

That is, her body knew what it wanted, but she wasn't so sure. Just because she'd never met anyone as compelling as Adam and just because she knew the infinite delights of surrendering to a man, that didn't mean she should let those two soul-shattering kisses lead to the logical conclusion.

It wasn't a logical conclusion anyway. A good woman didn't surrender herself, except to her husband, no matter how much she might wish to do so. She tried to convince herself she was a good woman.

Adam gazed at Letitia's bent head, her tousled brown hair gleaming almost auburn in the sunlight. Gently bred girls didn't kiss like that—or perhaps they did. He'd met enough of the Northern version of Letitia at balls during the war years and he remembered more than a few stolen kisses fondly.

So she wasn't totally unawakened. That thought made his lips tighten, and he pushed unwanted jealousy away, reminding himself who her father was. She was to be the instrument of his revenge, not his love.

He stepped away, forcing himself to ignore her gentle sway as she put out one hand to steady herself.

"One good thing about all this." He forced a grin. "You found us breakfast."

"What?" Letitia turned on him, furious with herself over the betrayal of her body, and even more furious with him because he clearly intended to ignore what had just happened between them.

"You can't mean you intend to eat, to eat . . ." Her stomach churned at the thought. "I won't!"

"Suit yourself." Adam strode away, his knife in his hand. "I've heard people say rattlesnake tastes like chicken. Don't know where they figured that out—it tastes like snake, to me."

"Ohhhh!" Letitia whirled away and stomped to the fire. She snatched up the cup, dashed the dregs to the ground, and poured the small amount of remaining coffee into the cup. She sat down, stretching her legs straight, and sipped cautiously at the hot liquid. It wasn't easy to drink the coffee Adam made—the grounds kept floating to the top. She hated this, she thought.

He returned. The skinned snake that dangled from his hand looked like a pale, rubbery length of rope. "If I had the time," he said, "I'd turn the skin into a belt to replace that piece of rope you're wearing. But I don't, so here's your trophy." He dropped the rattles into Letitia's lap.

She shrieked and batted distastefully at the dark buttons until they fell into the dust. "Ugh!" she cried, shuddering.

Adam ignored her. He sliced the snake into pieces, skewered lumps of meat onto a stick, and roasted them over the small morning fire. When he judged the meat to be done, he put a piece on his plate and handed the food to Letitia.

"Eat it," he said, not unkindly. "If you're going to make it on this journey, you're going to have to do your damnedest just to survive."

The smell of the cooked snake tantalized Letitia's nose, not unpleasantly. She watched his strong teeth tearing into his portion and her stomach rumbled. He looked up and smiled, the flash of his teeth white against the stubbly golden beard covering the lower half of his face. "Go on, try it," he said. "Please?"

Undone by his request, she gingerly lifted the meat to her mouth and nibbled at it. He was right. It didn't taste like chicken—it was too rubbery. She swallowed and bit off another tiny mouthful. Snake didn't taste all that great—more salt would help—but it was possibly better than her recent diet of rice and beans.

"What do you think?" Adam asked.

"I think it tastes like snake." She took another tiny bite, chewed vigorously and swallowed. "So?" She smiled brilliantly.

He blinked, astounded by her attractiveness when she smiled. The expression transformed her grubby, almost plain face.

"You should smile more often," he said.

She picked up the last piece of meat. "Why?"

He stood, wiped his fingers on the seat of his pants, clapped on his hat, and marched off to tend the horses. "Damned if I know."

He stood with his compass flat on his palm, mentally charting the course they must take. Letitia joined him, peering at the instrument in his hand.

She fingered the glass face of the compass. "I've always wondered how this works. I know it points to the north, but then what?"

Adam turned and the vibrating needle moved with him. "Just like you said, a compass always points the way to true north. We want to go due west today. See that gap in the mountains over there? It's about ten degrees short of true west. We'll head for the gap and then when we get closer we'll have to veer to the right, to the north, so we're heading due west again."

She gazed at the instrument. "I thought it was complicated. But it's easy, isn't it?"

He snapped the case shut and placed the compass in his vest pocket. "Let's ride. I have a surprise for you."

Afternoon shadows were long on the ground when Letitia heard the oddest rushing sound. Her horse tossed his head, drawing the reins forward to hang against his neck, and trotted forward eagerly.

"Whoa!" Letitia tried to stop him, bracing herself against his rough, unpleasant gait. Her mount had the bit firmly between his teeth as he rushed across the desert floor.

Amazed, Letitia saw a small stream of crystalline purity gurgling in a small ditch cut into the earth. Fresh water in the middle of this wasteland didn't make any sense. Her horse slid to a stop, stuck his nose into the stream, and sucked greedily at the water. It had to be a hallucination, she thought, one she was sharing with this miserable excuse for a lady's hack.

Adam's better-trained gelding stopped beside her. Adam loosened the reins so his horse could drink, too.

"Shall we join them?" He swung from his saddle and knelt by the stream, cupping the fresh water in his hands.

The stream was real!

She scrambled from her horse's back, falling to her knees, reaching eagerly for the blessed, pure liquid. Delightedly, she drank her fill, splashing the water on her face and forearms.

"It's amazing," she murmured. She gazed at the ever-present cactus and the barren mountains stretching across the horizon. "This is more than amazing—it's a miracle."

"That's enough, Buck." Adam pulled his gelding from the stream and reached for Letitia's mount. "Greedy hog," he said to the coach horse. "Drink too much of that on an empty stomach and you'll be one sorry nag."

She stood, drying her hands on the legs of her trousers. "I don't think that horse understands anything anyone says to him. Actually, I don't understand, either." She gestured at the stream. "It's a miracle this is here. I don't see how it can be possible, unless it's a collective hallucination."

"The stream is real enough." Adam smiled. "The water comes from a spring at the head of that canyon." He pointed beyond the fold of a hill. "But I agree, it _is_ a miracle, and a very pleasant one."

Adam lifted Letitia back onto her horse and led the way into the canyon. The stream tumbled over huge boulders, and cottonwood trees grew thickly by the water's edge. The tree's foliage showed bright and healthy green compared to the cactus crowded farther away on the still-barren hillsides. Game had beaten down a rough trail, and Adam followed the path as he led the way deeper into the canyon. Letitia's horse snatched a mouthful of leaves from one of the trees and chewed.

A final turn, and the trail led into a clearing. At the head of the canyon, about twenty feet up the bare red rocky wall, water from the spring gushed out in a steady fall, filling a pool. The water was so clear Letitia could see boulders lying at the bottom and could make out fish lazily moving with the current. She had no way to judge the depth of the pool, but it stretched out perhaps ten feet wide and twenty feet long.

She looked at the trees grouped along the edges of the water. At least they seemed like trees, but like none she'd ever seen before. They looked almost like feather dusters stuck into the ground, the trunks oddly ridged in a diamond pattern and the foliage composed of tattered fronds. Then she remembered the Lenten season and knew what the trees were. They were palms. It made sense—Galilee was a desert, too.

Grass grew at one side of the pool, where Adam pulled his horse to a halt. The gelding tore eagerly at the fresh green growth and Letitia's mount did the same. She slid down and struggled to get her horse's head up so she could free him from his bridle. "Adam's right," she said. "You're too greedy for your own good. Come to think of it—that's your name, too. Greedy."

"Suits him," Adam said.

Greedy ignored them, swinging his head away to gather another mouthful of grass.

"What do you think?" Adam asked with the air of a conjurer pulling a rabbit from a hat. "Impressive, isn't it?"

"Words fail me," she said. "I called the stream a miracle and this is . . ." She gestured at the palm trees. "It's amazing, that's what it is."

He pulled his soap and the remnants of Letitia's petticoats from his saddlebags. "Remember the pool we passed just below this one?" he asked.

She nodded.

"Ladies have the first chance at the bathtub."

She grabbed the soap and the petticoats, not even

stopping to thank him, and rushed back downstream. A bath in this wonderful water! What heaven!

Stripped, except for the now sweaty and stained bandage just below her breasts, she lowered one foot into the stream. Glory! This water was cold!

The result could be more than worth freezing half to death, she told herself as she stepped farther into the pool. She felt her nipples puckering against the chill as she waded, the water lapping above her knees as she reached midstream.

She dunked down into the water, a small shriek escaping her lips as the icy liquid cascaded on her chest. She moistened the soap and started to lather, wincing as the suds soaked into the sore flesh below her breast. The bandage floated free, and she bent back, tilting her head in the water until her hair streamed out behind her.

She sat up, the wet strands of hair falling about her face as she applied the soap to her scalp. It felt so good to know she would finally be free of all her dirt and sweat. Never again would she take such a simple thing as a bath for granted. She leaned forward, holding her eyes tightly shut against the soapsuds, letting the gentle current wash her hair clean.

Shivering, for the sun was starting to set and the warmth was leaving the air, Letitia reached for the soap and began her bathing ritual all over again. Just once wasn't enough. She intended to be so clean that every inch of her squeaked.

Adam finished gutting the last of the fish he'd speared by the simple expedient of lashing his knife to a branch from one of the cottonwood trees. Rattlesnake this morning, fish this evening. He grinned to himself. A feast fit for a king, even though he reckoned not one king had ever made it to this part of the world.

When the fish was ready, Adam rose to his feet. What was taking her so damn long? He wanted a bath before the sun went down, too. No one had ever accused him of living a fastidious life, but he definitely wanted to wash himself. He smelled as rank as any desert rat.

He made his way around the boulders to the bathing pool. Letitia stood, thigh-deep in the water, her hair streaming down her shoulders, the setting sun gilding her pale flesh. He was reminded of a painting he'd seen during the years he'd lived in Europe. It'd been done by some fancy Italian and showed the goddess Venus rising from the waves, standing on a sea shell, of all things.

Except that Venus had her hair and hands wrapped modestly around her opulent body. This goddess stood with her head back, her shoulders squared, her naked, firm breasts emphasized. That Venus had been plump, pleasing to some, but this one didn't have an ounce of wasted flesh on her tight, flat stomach or on her long, shapely legs.

Adam gazed longingly at her. He swallowed hard, feeling the hot rush of his blood as he imagined what it would be like to take that wet, supple flesh to his, feel those strong legs wrap around him—

He shook his head angrily, trying to banish his thoughts. He retreated noiselessly to the other side of the boulder. He forced moisture back into his dry mouth and then whistled and called, "Letitia?"

He heard splashing.

She called out, "Go away. I'll be through in a minute."

"Are you all right?" The memory of her gleaming breasts teased him. "Do you need any help with your bandage?" *Fool.* She hadn't been wearing anything, and he'd never even noticed her wound.

"No." Her voice sounded tense. "I'm dressing now. Go away."

He stood his ground and when she reappeared, he asked. "Save any soap for me?"

"Here." She thrust the bar and the sodden petticoats at him, not meeting his eyes.

Guiltily, he wondered if she'd realized he'd been lurking behind the rock, staring as hungrily as a small boy in front of a candy display. He shook his head and stomped down the trail. What did it matter?

He left his clothes on the bank and strode into the stream, the cold water splashing up his legs. This icy stream should cool him down. He plunged in, burying his head in the water, and came up, gasping for air, already shivering. He'd best make haste.

Letitia wandered back to where Adam had set up their camp and looked approvingly at the fish he'd laid out on a frond appropriated from one of the palm trees. She supposed she should start frying them, except he hadn't lit the fire and the tinderbox was in his pocket.

His comb and clean socks rested on top of his saddlebags. She reached for the comb and tugged it through her snarled hair. That done, she shook the damp tresses behind her shoulders and wandered around the small campsite.

Adam's been gone for quite a while, she thought. She remembered how good it felt to get clean, really clean, and she expected he was indulging himself the same way she had.

The thought of him, naked, in the middle of the pool made her mouth go dry. She'd felt the strength of his arms each time he lifted her onto her horse. She couldn't help but wonder what he looked like without his clothes.

She picked up a blanket and draped it around her shoulders. She knew she shouldn't, but her footsteps drew her irresistibly to the boulder shielding the pool. She peeked over the top and saw Adam, bent over, his head buried in the stream as he washed his hair. He shook his head like a dog, his blond mane flying as droplets of water sprayed everywhere. He swore, cupping his hand to bring water to his face so he could wash away the soap in his eyes.

He stood and Letitia sucked in her breath. He wasn't much taller than Shelly, but where Shelly had been slight, almost soft, Adam was lean, all of him pure, sculptured muscle. Shelly had had very little body hair, but Adam's chest was furred with the same blond hair that covered his head. The hair trailed in a thin line over his navel and down to . . .

Letitia bit her lip. She shouldn't be here, she shouldn't be looking at him, but oh, he was beautiful. Beautiful like a statue of a Greek athlete, wide shoulders, narrow hips, perfectly formed, perfectly muscled.

Letitia turned, knowing she must go back to their campsite when her foot dislodged a small stone. She froze, the sound of the rolling rock in the sunset hush as loud as cannon fire.

* * *

In reaction to the sudden noise, Adam crouched down in the stream, his movement as lithe and supple as a mountain lion's. His gaze darted to his clothing and the pistol he'd left on the river bank. Damn! Just because he hadn't expected anyone else at this oasis was no reason—

He saw a quick, jerky movement just beyond the boulder he'd hidden behind earlier. Someone had stolen into the canyon and was now between him and Letitia. If he didn't act they could both die.

He gauged the distance to his gun and lunged for it, the icy water fanning up and around his shoulders. The rocks at the edge of the stream bruised his knees. On his feet again, he pulled on his pants and his fingers closed around the butt of his pistol.

The small, steep defile echoed with the sounds of someone recklessly forcing their way through the underbrush. He disregarded the sharp rocks underfoot as he raced down the game trail, intent on reaching the pool and Letitia. Once he had her safe he could confront the unknown.

From the noise, he could tell he was gaining on the intruder. For a moment, he saw his quarry's shoulders. He raised his pistol, taking aim. The trespasser stumbled and fell, with a soft cry of pain.

Adam burst into the small clearing by the pool and saw the intruder struggling to stand up. Transfixed, he skidded to a halt and stood, staring at her.

Letitia, it'd been Letitia all the time. He thought of how he'd almost shot her and shuddered. Then anger swamped him and a totally different emotion raced through him, shaking him much worse than his earlier fear.

"You little fool!" he shouted.

She stared back at him wordlessly, her eyes as wide and as frightened as a cornered doe's. "Don't," she begged. "Please don't."

He thumbed the safety catch back into place and laid his pistol aside. He'd shake her, shake her until she was silly, until she knew never, ever to do such a thing to a man. Intent on teaching her a lesson, he grabbed for her. She fled from him, racing across the clearing. She stumbled over the open bedroll and fell onto the blankets, twisting away, trying to regain her feet. He seized her, his hands closing around her shoulders. He felt the soft flesh covering her bones and the terrified shudders shaking her. Her legs tangled with his, her supple body trapped beneath him, her breasts flattened against his chest.

She gazed up at him, her tongue nervously moistening her lips. In a flash, all the emotion raging inside him turned to burning need. His hands cupped the back of her head, his fingers tangling in the soft cascade of her unbound hair. "Ah, hell!" he swore.

And then he kissed her.

5

Letitia felt Adam's lips grind against hers. Her thoughts were confused and incoherent. She opened her mouth to protest.

His tongue swept inside to stroke the moist interior of her mouth and he pulled her even closer. Trapped, she struggled to free herself. Yet she couldn't deny the mastery of his overpowering embrace. Her arms seemed to have a life of their own as they slid across the oddly corrugated ridges on his shoulders and linked around his neck. His back and his legs were icy cold, but as he pulled her closer, feverish heat seemed to bloom wherever their bodies touched.

He was as hard as the rocks surrounding them, as hard and as unyielding. She had to feel him closer. She needed to feel the strength of his body, needed the sweet oblivion of passion.

Her shudders of terror changed into tremors of excitement as his tongue continued caressing the inside of her mouth. His demanding embrace wiped away the last of her fear and an echo of his desire took possession of her senses.

Finally, his lips left hers. She tried to speak but he forestalled her.

"This has been building up since I first kissed you," he said, his voice husky. "It's inevitable."

"No," she moaned, knowing she should protest. "No."

His eyes blazed at her, demanding the truth. She stared at him for a long moment before she surrendered to him with a whispered, "Yes."

She linked her arms around his neck and pulled him closer until her lips met his. She could no longer deny the passion that ignited in a consuming flame as his mouth touched hers.

His eyes darkened, almost to indigo, and he kissed her again. Like dry wood kindled by a spark, she responded freely, her fear miraculously transformed into a desperate yearning for satisfaction.

His fingers impatiently worked apart the buttons of the shirt she wore, revealing her taut breasts as they were freed from the restraining cloth. His hand closed around her flesh, his thumb teasing the nipple. His lips closed around her excited skin. She fell back, gasping, lost to sensation while he tasted one nipple, his fingers tantalizing the other.

A stream of fire swept through her, finally centering low, in the pit of her abdomen. It was unbearable. She twisted, moaning. She had to be free. His mouth moved to her other breast and the unendurable changed to a glorious ecstasy.

Finally, he raised his head and stared deeply into her eyes. She gazed back at him. He reached down to free her feet from her boots. His fingers traveled up her legs, tracing a path of sensation up her calves, stroking them under the loose fabric of her trousers. He reached higher. Then, frustrated by the restriction of the cloth, he withdrew his hand and impatiently undid her rope belt.

She drew a faint, shuddering sigh as he tugged the trousers free. Again, his hands slid the length of her legs, his hard fingertips leaving her soft thighs trembling from the desire that consumed her thoughts, her mind, her body. With quick impatient movements he stripped away his pants.

Passion overwhelmed her. In a daze of aching need, swept beyond any thought or imagining of what might be right and what might be wrong, she lay on the blanket, knowing what was coming next and welcoming it.

He gently spread her legs and shifted his body into position over her. Letitia reached for him and guided him inside her.

Somewhere, a portion of his brain protested. No. It wasn't right. She was a virgin. She shouldn't know anything about this.

He couldn't resist. He plunged deeply into her. Dimly, he heard her cry at his intrusion. Once he'd felt the moist enticement of her he could no longer be distracted, could no longer deny his rocketing senses. He could concentrate only on the driving movement that would bring him release.

He heard her cry out and arch her back as her hips rose up to meet him. His head jerked back and he felt complete and total fulfillment as his seed spilled forth.

* * *

Letitia had no idea how much time had passed before she became aware of her surroundings again. Adam's head rested on her breast and a particularly pointy rock jabbed through the blanket at the middle of her back. She wiggled, trying to find an easier position.

He lifted his head, but he didn't look at her. He stood and turned away. She hugged her arms to herself, feeling suddenly bereft without his comforting presence pressed tightly to her body. He stepped into his pants and nudged her borrowed clothing with his toe.

"Put those on," he said. "It's getting chilly. I'll start the fire."

Fighting sudden tears, she complied with Adam's order. She wondered what had happened to make him treat her so coldly. Where was the wonderful warmth and companionship she and Shelly had always shared when they were through? Where was the total relaxation of complete satisfaction? What had happened? Or did these special things happen only between people who loved each other? Worse, did they only occur to people within the sacred bonds of marriage?

Guilt coursed through her. *That's what you get,* she told herself sternly, *making love with a man when you shouldn't.* She had confused love with lust. Now she was a ruined woman, just like Mama. No wonder Grandmama had lectured so on the evils of the flesh. Suddenly, Letitia felt like weeping.

Adam added fresh wood to the fire and balanced the pan full of fish over the flames. Silence stretched out between them, as heavy and as tangible as a thick, frozen fog.

Letitia watched a muscle at the side of his jaw pulse. She sniffed and swallowed hard. She would *not* cry, damn it!

He looked up, trying to contain his anger. She'd started it, damn it, running from him the way she had. It wouldn't work, her moping around as if he'd just deflowered her. He knew better than that. She was no virgin, and she couldn't convince him otherwise.

He turned the fish and rocked back on his heels, trying to decide what to do next. Why in the hell should he feel guilty? She'd wanted it, too. What was wrong? Why did he feel as if he'd just defaced a beautiful painting or shouted obscenities in church?

He placed two of the fish on his single plate and handed the meal to Letitia. "Watch out for the bones."

She kept her head down and nodded.

He ground his teeth together and his temper snapped. "What's wrong with you, woman? You can forget the injured virgin role with me. It won't work."

"What?" Letitia gasped. "What do you mean? Of course I'm not a virgin. I never pretended—"

"Didn't you?" Adam yelled. He heard the echo of his shout lingering in the rocky defile and tried to moderate his tones. "Your pretended innocence, your misplaced modesty, your—"

"My misplaced modesty? My . . ."

She was so mad she couldn't articulate. He reckoned those tears in her eyes were tears of rage.

"You're the one who started this," she finally shouted.

"Oh, yeah?"

"I'll have you know I'm a perfectly respectable

widow, or I was. . . ." Her voice broke and dropped
to a whisper. "Until I met you."

"Widow?"

"Yes, a widow!" Letitia snapped. "I don't care if
you believe me or not. Shelly fell at Gettysburg and I
wouldn't even *be* in this mess if he hadn't gotten himself killed by you, you . . . you *damn* Yankee!"

Adam flinched, remembering the gray faces of the
dead. "I wasn't at Gettysburg."

"It doesn't matter." Letitia rubbed her finger where
her wedding band had so briefly rested. "It doesn't
matter," she repeated fiercely. "If I hadn't given my
ring to help finance the Confederate cause and you'd
have had outward proof of my marriage, you still
wouldn't have treated me any differently, would you?
Grandmama said all men were beasts. If Shelly had
lived, he probably would have grown into a beast,
too."

"No. Wait." Adam crossed the space between them
and took Letitia's hands into his own. She looked up
at him and he could see the tears welling in her eyes as
she bit her lower lip and tried to control her emotions.

"Tell me about it. I want to know."

She tried to pull her hands free but he wouldn't let
her go.

"Tell me." It was a request, not an order.

"There's nothing to tell," she said dully. "I married
Shelly and a week later he marched off to war. Then
Grandmama died and my papa wrote. You know the
rest."

"Now I do," Adam said softly.

She tried again to pull her hands free.

"Ah, Letitia." He gathered her close, trying to find

the words that would melt her rigidity. "I didn't understand. I thought you were willing. . . ."

"Perhaps . . . I was," she admitted honestly, her
voice muffled against his shoulder. "Grandmama was
right. I am as abandoned as Mama."

Adam swore softly and wished he could bring himself to be as honest with her as she was being with him.
But she was Hunt Ramsey's daughter, and Adam realized he'd just complicated the situation beyond belief,
for he'd never experienced a woman as giving, so capable of pure enjoyment in her lovemaking as Letitia.

"I didn't understand," he repeated. He lifted her
chin so he could look into her confused eyes. "But I do
now." He knew that in spite of her brief marriage, she
was still truly an innocent in many ways.

"What happened was good." He smiled broadly.
"Let's be honest. It was great, and something like that
doesn't happen very often. You've made me a very
happy man." He sobered and decided to be as open
with her as he could, under the circumstances. "It's
never happened to me that way before. I think that's
why I lost my temper, again, when we were through. I
know I shouldn't have let it happen, but there was no
way in the world I could stop."

"No," she said. "I suppose not. But I should have,
and that's what frightens me. What if I lose control
like that with other men?"

Jealousy knifed through him at the thought of Letitia with another man. Her late husband—well, he was
dead, so Adam had to convince himself the guy didn't
matter now. But someone else!

Again, Adam decided on honesty. "I can't answer
that question for you. It could be there are other men
out there who'll attract you, but it doesn't necessarily

follow that you'll make love with them. Have you ever been tempted before?"

Letitia thought about her life with Grandmama and laughed, a short, bitter sound. "Hardly."

"Then don't worry about it. Maybe I'm the only man who'll ever affect you that way." He paused and grinned. "Modest, aren't I? What I mean is you don't strike me as the sort of woman who'd enjoy that sort of life. You're the sort of woman who makes a man think about settling down."

He reached for his now-cold fish. To Letitia, it looked as if he intended to say something else. He hesitated for a long time. Breathlessly she waited for him to continue, unsure what she wanted him to say. She only knew she wanted him to say more. The silence dragged on and still he didn't speak.

Disappointed, Letitia glanced down at her clasped hands. Certainly, he hadn't said romantic words of reassurance. Yet, he had said, more or less, that she was the sort of woman he'd like to spend the rest of his life with. That was definitely a start.

And just because she'd made love with him didn't necessarily mean she'd fall into every pair of male arms she happened to encounter. She'd come across plenty of men since she'd left Kentucky and she'd never felt that insistent tug of attraction she felt for Adam. She'd loved Shelly, still loved his memory, but she couldn't ever remember being so swept away by their lovemaking.

Of course, there was the possibility she might get pregnant, but—well, she'd cross that bridge if she came to it. After all, it hadn't happened with Shelly.

She picked up her plate, separated the succulent flesh of the fish from the bones, and tried to eat.

Still . . . No matter how she put it, she'd just committed a cardinal sin—according to Grandmama.

What made Grandmama always right, other than the fact that she thought so? Letitia smiled to herself. Adam was right—it had been good.

She stood, walked to the side of the pool, knelt, and washed her hands. Adam joined her and handed her the cup. Murmuring her thanks, she dragged the tin mug through the pool and lifted it to her lips. The water was pure and icy enough to make her teeth ache.

He'd shrugged into his shirt and now he draped his jacket around her shoulders. "Come back to the fire," he said softly, his words holding a promise.

She looked up and read the desire in his eyes once again. She placed her hand in his. What was done was done and there was no going back to undo it. As he drew her down to lie next to him on the blanket, she knew she didn't want to undo a single second. No matter what Grandmama and convention might say, with Adam it was simply, undeniably right.

He rained tiny kisses down Letitia's throat, as he helped her free herself from her clothing. "Don't be sad," he coaxed.

"No," she whispered, gasping sharply as his hand found her breast. His blond head bent and he tasted first one rose-tipped nipple and then the other. His hands tangled in her hair, piling it above her head.

A tiny river of fire shot through her and she moaned, her head tilting back as she let him work his magic spell once again. He shucked off his own clothing and tugged her trousers free.

His lips touched her ankle, his breath warm on her naked skin. Expert fingers traced a path up her calves, massaging them until he reached the juncture of her legs. His palms and fingers spanned the backs of her thighs, and he touched his mouth to the hollow behind her knees in tantalizing, quick kisses that exploded into shivers of desire.

"Every part of you is perfect," he said huskily. "But especially your long, lovely legs." His fingers followed a line down the silken side of her thighs. "It seems as if all I've thought of is wrapping them around me."

His tantalizing touch so close to the heart of her filled her with longing. She shivered in a daze of wanting, anticipation, and love.

"Are you cold?" he whispered.

Before she could reply, he answered himself. "I'll fix that."

His left hand inched up to her breasts and circled her nipples one at a time. His other hand slipped between her legs. Instinctively, she moved her knees further apart, giving his right hand free access to the silky curls.

Her hands clasped his arm and wrist for support and her head fell back. Her eyes drifted shut, her lips gently parted as she absorbed the delightful things he was doing to her.

Within seconds hard shivers racked through her. Her hands clenched around his arm. He held her tightly, his thumb exciting the storm raging inside her.

She finally stilled, gasping for air, and clung to him while he lowered her to the blanket. He stood above her for a second before he joined her again. He pulled her close and she felt her breasts flatten against his chest. He kissed her, deeply, and she tasted the enticing interior of his mouth. Need for him ran like an uncontrolled fire though her.

He knelt before her and wrapped her long legs

around his waist. With his hands, stroking her burning flesh, and then with his tongue, he raised her to a new level of excitement.

Slowly, with exquisite patience, he entered her and began to move inside her. Her head twisted from one side to the other as she absorbed the power of his thrusts. Her legs tightened around him. She cried out in delight as shudders of fulfillment raced through her. As if from far away, she heard him cry out too as release swept through them both and delivered them to a place of exquisite gratification.

When Letitia had at last fallen asleep, Adam rolled onto his back, linking his hands behind his head, thinking. What he'd told her was true. She was the sort of woman a man could share his life with. What he hadn't told her was that it would be impossible with him.

The words from Ma's letter went inexorably through his mind. There wasn't any way around it— he'd just made love, had the best experience of his life, with the enemy. Except that Letitia didn't know yet that she was his enemy.

Guilt threatened to swamp him. Why had he lost control so completely? What a hell of a mess. She was so obviously an innocent, no matter what her experiences might have been. She expected and deserved only the best from a man—marriage, in fact.

And Ma . . . She was counting on him to save her immortal soul.

His good intentions had been overtaken by his overwhelming longing to make Letitia his own. And not just once, either. Cursing his weakness, he turned and gazed at her profile, glaring in the flickering firelight.

What could he do? He owed honor and duty to two women now. Which one had the greater claim on him? How could he decide?

He couldn't, not now. Perhaps later. He'd decide later, when he had to. There had to be a way to satisfy Ma. Her battle was with Ramsey, not with Letitia.

He rolled back and cradled her sleeping body gently within his arms. He vowed to find a way to honor Ma and keep Letitia as his own.

6

Early-morning sunlight shone over Adam's head, the rays transforming his blond hair to burnished gold. Letitia, watching from her nest of blankets, felt her breath catch in her throat. While he wouldn't appreciate being told so, he was beautiful, in perfect harmony with the beauty of the desert oasis.

Her thoughts returned to her folly of the night before. But it couldn't be folly. Folly wouldn't feel so right.

There was no way in the world she could have stopped Adam, because, to be honest, she'd wanted last night to happen. Passion had overwhelmed her sense of right and wrong. Maybe her Grandmama was right. Maybe the way she'd responded to Adam proved her depraved nature.

But it didn't matter, really. He'd said she'd never

have to worry about being attracted to other men because he'd be there. Didn't that imply permanency? And he'd said she was the woman he could spend the rest of his life with.

Could. She twisted around in the blankets, her legs tangling in the itchy, woolen folds. He'd said a lot last night, but he hadn't said he loved her and he hadn't asked her to marry him. He would, she promised herself. She knew he'd ask her to marry him. It was the only right thing to do. She knew he was an honorable man.

"Good morning." Adam's greeting broke into her thoughts as he handed her a cup, steam rising from the fresh coffee. "I reckon we'll spend the day here. The horses can use the rest." He smiled and she felt herself blush when he added, "So can we. It was quite a busy night. It could be a busy morning, too. . . ." His lips claimed hers and his hand insinuated its way into the covering of blankets to tease one of her nipples.

She gasped and shifted uncomfortably. As gentle as his touch was, parts of her were tender from their night of unrestrained passion.

"I'm sorry." His hand moved lower to gently cup her breast. "I know you're not accustomed to love-making. You're so tempting that I forget I have to go slowly."

Embarrassed, she searched her mind for a way to change the subject. He was right. She was sore. Worse, the memory of her uninhibited behavior of the night before seemed totally inappropriate for the prosaic atmosphere of daylight.

He removed his hand and rocked back on his heels. She smiled at him, her heart filled with love and trust. She wanted to know everything she could about him.

"You told the Bickles you have a ranch near San Diego. Have you always lived there?" she asked.

He grinned. "You'll never learn not to ask direct questions, will you?"

"No." She smiled back, secure in his companionship. "My answer is still the same. How will I ever learn anything if I don't ask?"

Adam took the cup back from her and sipped. "I haven't owned the ranch for very long. I bought it last fall." With the honesty that Letitia always seemed to drag from him, he added, "After the war, I felt as if I wanted to build something."

But even her silent demand for truthfulness couldn't draw out his real reason for selecting just that ranch—its nearness to Hunt Ramsey.

Adam reckoned that when he'd satisfied his mother's last request, he'd sell his ranch because it wouldn't be useful any longer. But he'd buy another one, a better one. Maybe he'd settle north of Santa Barbara. It was pretty country up there. In a rare moment of insight he accepted the fact that he wanted to settle down, raise some cattle and some children—

His jaw tightened as he realized where his thoughts were leading him. Children meant a wife first, and after he'd finished with Hunt Ramsey, Letitia would be through with Adam McCormick for life. She trusted him now—but later? What a damnable situation to be in, he thought.

"You fought for the North." Letitia's flat voice made the question into a statement.

Adam nodded, for once welcoming her questions to distract his thoughts. "I was with the Army of the Cumberland—I fought in the western campaigns." He grimaced. "Does it bother you that you've been consorting with the enemy, my girl?"

Letitia shrugged. "Shelly claimed we were fighting for our way of life. I wasn't so sure of that. There were plenty of slaves at Bellewood. The whole institution of slavery always seemed wrong to me, but I never dared say so. Why should I live in the plantation house, with a room to myself, clean clothes, and an education, while the Negroes were crammed into small cabins and forced to work every day of their lives? It seems impossible, but when I was little, I actually envied their children. It seemed to me that they all belonged to loving, happy families."

Adam looked at her incredulously.

"Grandmama believed in keeping families together if she could," Letitia explained. "She said it made them happier. Ultimately, it all seemed pretty relative to me. Happier than what? They were still Sinclair possessions."

Adam nodded. "I didn't fight to end slavery, although that's a good enough reason in itself. I believe it will take a powerful federal government to keep our nation strong. Like Lincoln said, I fought to preserve the Union."

"You said you'd just bought that ranch of yours. Didn't you have a home to fight for like Shelly did?"

Adam sighed and reached for the coffeepot. She'd certainly hit the nail on the head. "I don't think I've ever had a place I could call home. My pa left Ma and me when I was just a little tyke. I don't even remember him. . . ." He fell quiet, trying once again to recall something, anything, about his father, but all he could bring to mind was the man's strange eyes—one blue, one brown.

"It takes more than just a place to live to make a home," Letitia said. "Bellewood was never a home, especially after Mama died. Then Papa left and I felt so abandoned. I lived with Grandmama, but she didn't want me. That's hard for a ten-year-old child to understand."

Adam sipped at his coffee. "Why didn't she want you?"

Letitia fidgeted with the edge of the blanket. As close as she felt to Adam she couldn't bring herself to tell him about her illegitimacy. It was just too shameful.

"Grandmama didn't want me for a lot of reasons," Letitia explained. "Maybe if I'd been a boy things might have been different." She knew she was lying. Grandmama wouldn't have cared—she never could have forgiven the insult to the Sinclair name.

"You're an only child?" Adam asked.

"Yes. And you?"

"I've got a younger brother, Swen."

He sighed again, somehow unable to stop the cathartic experience of telling his life story to Letitia. He'd never unburdened himself with anyone before, but with her he couldn't stop talking about his past. "Ma remarried when I was five, almost six. My stepfather had a farm—it wasn't much—just outside Elmira, New York. Robert, the man she married, I didn't like him, but at six there isn't much you can do about that. Ma said he was our only chance for security.

"When I was sixteen Robert decided we'd go to the Oregon Territory. I hated him, but it was a way out of Elmira." Adam scowled. "I didn't want to leave Ma. And, to be honest, I didn't want to miss out on the adventure of going west."

"So what happened?"

"Well, we made it, and Robert settled us on a farm on the Willamette River, south of Oregon City. That's where my brother was born. I hate farming—and that didn't help the situation any. Robert worked all of us like dogs. He believed in using his belt to keep me in line, and, well, things just got worse and worse until staying didn't make sense any more. So I ran away to the goldfields in California."

Letitia realized what had caused the odd corrugations on Adam's back. They were scars—scars from beatings received from his stepfather. She knew the marks were one more thing she couldn't ask him about. Instead, she said, "You were a forty-niner?"

"Not quite. I ended up in Placerville. The first wild rush was over, but it was still pretty wide open. Thing is, I couldn't see the sense of grubbing in the dirt alongside thousands of other miners. So I decided to go off on my own, looking for my own strike."

"Go on," Letitia said. "This is better than any book I've ever read. Did you find your gold?"

"What I found was a valley—no, it was El Dorado. Lord, it was beautiful. The prettiest stream ran right through the center." He reached for a pebble lying in the dust and fingered its smooth shape. "I didn't bother panning for dust, I just scooped up the nuggets lying there in the water. It was freezing cold and I was laughing and dancing around like a regular jackass."

"So you did find your gold."

"I found more than that," he replied. "I got smart and went looking for where the gold in the river came from. I found the mother lode. And that beautiful valley is now buried under the slag heaps from my mine—the Ingrid."

He bared his teeth in an expression that wasn't a smile. "I'd done what I'd set out to do. I was a wealthy man. But when I went to get Ma, she wouldn't leave Robert. Said she'd married him under God's holy law and she couldn't break her vows no matter what I wanted." He shrugged. "In the end I had to leave—she wouldn't even touch the money I wanted to give her— said it wasn't right. I didn't know what to do, didn't know where to go."

"Oh, Adam. Perhaps your mother didn't mean it. Perhaps your stepfather made her say those things."

"Perhaps."

Letitia knew she didn't have the power to ease Adam's deep disillusionment. How terrible it must have been for him, young and idealistic, to reach his goal and have his achievement thrown back in his face.

"What did you do next?"

"Next?" Adam laughed mirthlessly. "I only knew two things. How to be a farmer and how to be a gold miner. I didn't fancy the first and I'd heard a lot of the boys were leaving for Australia to look for gold there. So I went back to San Francisco and bought a passage on a clipper ship called the *Ferdinand*. Cost me one hundred and fifty dollars to share the first cabin with five other people."

"How long did it take?"

"Sixty-seven days."

"And then what happened?"

"Well, the hills around Melbourne look a lot like they do in California, except the trees are all different. I still didn't believe in working a claim, so my mate and I—that's what you call your partner there—we went looking for a strike. What a crazy country." Adam shook his head. "There wasn't any water to speak of, so there wasn't any way to pan for color. There's millions of dollars just lying around and there always will be, because there's no way to take it out of the dust."

"Just lying there so you can pick it up?"

"You've got to find it first. It's all a coarse wash— little chunks of gold in the gravel. Some of them aren't so little. Tom and I were doing pretty good, but you're always hoping you'll find a really big nugget. Nugget!" Adam laughed again, this time with genuine humor. "What we literally stumbled over wasn't a nugget, it was a regular boulder."

"You found gold a second time?" Letitia asked incredulously.

"Yeah. It still amazes me when I think about it. Most of the miners managed to at least make a living. Me, I hit it big twice."

He tossed his pebble at the pool. The stone hit the water with a soft plop, ripples spreading out in perfect circles across the still surface of the water.

"Our 'nugget' weighed over two thousand ounces, and it was almost pure gold. We took it to Mount Harryratt where the troopers will buy your gold. Water there had to come from at least twenty miles away and it sold from anywhere from fifty to seventy-five cents a gallon. It was like that everywhere. The price for anything was simply outrageous, just like it'd been in California. I told Tom we might be wealthy men, but we'd only stay that way if we left Australia."

She asked, "So you came back to America?"

"No." Adam reached for another pebble. "Tom had left England for what he called 'Australia and adventure.' After we found our gold he reckoned he'd had enough of both and decided he wanted to go home. So,

Tom—Thomas Mitchell Arbuthnot, Baronet, to give him his full title—convinced me to go back to England with him. I didn't want to go back to America and I sure didn't want to stay in Australia. If you're important like Tom, everything is just fine. But if you're just a digger, or worse, a Yankee . . ."

"But you were a Yankee in England, too. How could it be different?"

"It's different when your mate is a baronet," Adam said bluntly. "Since I was with Tom, everyone tolerated me, even though there were a lot who thought I was some sort of oddity. And he helped me smooth off some of my rough edges." Adam sipped at his coffee and made a face at the tepid contents of the cup. "After a while, I almost felt as if I fit in. I must say we had a good time introducing me to the glories of the Old World. I was in Berlin when I heard the war news. It gave me a reason to come back."

"Your mother?" Letitia asked softly.

"She died." he said flatly. He recalled the words from Ingrid's letter. *Right the wrong you did to me by avenging our family.* He'd never been able to help his mother during his lifetime. He had to fulfill her last request and honor her faith in him. But Letitia? What about Letitia?

"What a life you've lived," she said enviously. "I wish I were able to travel like you, make my own life, do things. I wish I were a man."

"I don't." Adam stood and tossed the dregs of his coffee on the ground.

She looked up into his eyes and blushed. It wasn't proper to want him the way she did.

*   *   *

Letitia rolled over onto the warm spot Adam had left behind in their nest of blankets. In the predawn hush, the birds resting in the palm trees were twittering and chirping, making enough racket to raise the dead.

She knew Adam intended to leave their oasis today, but she snuggled deeper into the blankets and tried to ignore the noise. She didn't want to leave this pristine place. It was a gift, a place out of time . . . almost like a fairy-tale land where only good happened.

He knelt beside Letitia and brushed her tousled hair from her face. She reached out for him and their lips met in a gentle good-morning kiss; then the embrace deepened, arousing her to an aching need in spite of how much love they'd shared in the last twenty-four hours.

He tore his lips from hers. "Enough. We've got things to do today."

He'd fought a stern battle with his conscience during the night as Letitia slept beside him. No matter what he felt for her, and he feared he already felt far too much, he had to stand firm in his resolution to follow through and wreak his mother's vengeance on Hunt Ramsey. Adam forced himself to harden his heart. He had to. Perhaps, someday, Letitia could forgive him. But Ma could never absolve him if he failed her.

Letitia had to be the key to his goal. Adam acknowledged to himself that he didn't quite know how he'd achieve it. Even though he lacked his mother's stern trust in God, he knew Letitia had been sent to him. He also knew he couldn't simply let the opportunities she represented slip through his fingers.

He had to figure out a way to satisfy Ma and somehow keep Letitia with him. She'd hate him when she found out what he planned to do. Clearly, she loved her papa. And just as clearly, Adam knew he would destroy the man.

How could he resolve the situation? He gazed down at Letitia and tried to relegate his frustration to the back of his mind. He'd deal with trouble the way he always had, one piece at a time.

"What sort of things do we have to do today?" she asked provocatively as she wrapped her arms around the back of his neck.

"Not this sort of thing." Adam unwound her hands and pulled her to her feet. "We've got mountains to climb today."

The oasis seemed a dream as they made their way back to the barren desert floor. Tall mountains reared up in front of them, and Letitia could see trees growing higher up where the edges of the earth seemed to fold together. Adam led the way into a canyon that twisted and turned, carrying them ever upward, deeper and deeper into the wilderness.

Soon she noticed they'd climbed high enough to leave the ever-present cactus behind. Stands of scrubby bushes covered the hillside, and she wished she could name the dusty gray-green plants. The trail opened into a meadow. She knew the trees dotting the surrounding hills must be oaks because of the letters Papa had written. But the trees didn't look like oaks at all. Nothing in California made sense, Letitia thought. She gazed at the steep, rocky hillside in front of them. When they reached the end of the meadow, she realized that their climb would begin in earnest.

She could tell that the trail cleaved to the hillside.

Greedy scrambled up the path until she could see a ravine opening up to the right. The trail narrowed until she followed Adam down a faint path that led between a high mountain wall and a sheer cliff falling away into the defile below.

Don't look down, Letitia warned herself. She knew she wasn't brave when it came to heights. But she couldn't resist an urge to know the worst and took a quick glance over her right shoulder. It must have been at least a hundred feet to the bottom of the ravine. "Oh, no," she moaned.

It reminded her of a nightmare, except that in a dream, the horrible sensation of falling always ended in sweaty, shaking awareness. This was reality. If she fell she wouldn't wake up in bed.

Greedy stumbled, his head bobbing up and down as he tried to regain the rhythm of his slow walk. She wrapped her right hand tightly in his mane, clinging to the reins with her left, frightened by the sudden change in her mount's gait.

"Adam!"

He pulled Buck to a halt and twisted in his saddle to look back at her. "What? This is no place to rest."

The coach horse stopped, too. "I know that," she shouted. She relaxed her grip on the reins just the slightest bit, since her mount stood so patiently. "I think there's something wrong with Greedy. He stumbled and then his walk changed. I think he's cast a shoe."

"The right fore?"

"Yes. How did you know?"

"It figures. When I cleaned his feet this morning I noticed his shoes were worn, especially the offside front one." He swore. "Trust Jonas to sell me a horse who needs a trip to the blacksmith."

"Now what?"

"We'll have to go on." Adam turned to look ahead. "The trail opens up when we get to the head of this ravine. I'll see what I can do for Greedy then. In the meantime, let's ride."

Adam leaned forward, his reins slackening. Buck obediently obeyed the signal and walked on. Greedy fell into step, and Letitia could definitely sense the difference in her horse's gait. On this rocky surface she knew he'd soon be favoring that front leg, but she couldn't do anything for him. There wasn't even room to dismount and lead him.

The trail wound on, the sickening presence of the ravine to her right a constant reminder of danger. The reins slipped between her sweaty fingers. She tightened her grip, praying.

"Don't give up," she told her horse. "Please, just get us out of here."

Greedy flicked his ears back at the sound of her voice and stumbled. She swayed with the movement, her knees gripping his sides, her free hand burrowing deeper into the coarse hair of his mane. His walk changed again, his right shoulder falling away with each step as he limped forward.

Letitia groaned. Greedy's head went down, the reins slack against his neck. The trail turned and Adam twisted in his saddle, his mouth grim. "Hang on. We're almost there."

Ahead, she could see the ravine narrowing as its steep sides joined together, perhaps five hundred feet farther along the trail. It was still a long way down to the bottom of the canyon, perhaps fifty feet, but the sheer precipice had changed into an extremely steep, chaparral-covered hillside. In just a few minutes this nightmare ride would be over.

A hawk, soaring on the thermals formed by the mountains, folded its wings and dived, swooping down on its prey. A panicked rabbit erupted from a fissure in the earth, dashed under Greedy's nose, and disappeared into the ravine.

The horse shied violently, his head tossing in fear, his unshod hoof unable to support him as he lunged sideways. He tried to regain his feet, but the edge of the trail crumbled under his weight and he fell over the side, taking Letitia with him.

It all happened too fast for coherent thought, but the sensation of falling did not feel at all dreamlike. She lost her seat on Greedy's back and slid away from him. It hurt as dirt and rocks hailed down and the chaparral cut into her hands and face as she tumbled ever downward. The sound of Greedy's wild scream and the rumble of falling rocks filled her ears.

Frantically, she clawed at the bushes as she crashed down the ravine, trying to stop her fall. Her hands connected with a strong branch and her wrists almost snapped from their sockets as she desperately hung onto the limb.

Greedy hurtled on down the almost perpendicular hillside, the sound of his tragic fall and the resultant rumble of an avalanche of rocks echoing again and again. Dust rose up, and Letitia choked on the grit as her questing toes tried to find solid footing on the ravine wall. Her feet found a ridge of rock, and she found she could rest the soles of her boots on its narrow support while her heels dangled out into space.

"Adam," she moaned. "Help me. Oh, *please* help me."

"Letitia!" he shouted. "Letitia! For God's sake, answer me. Where are you?"

"Here," she croaked. She swallowed, trying to clear the dust and overwhelming fear from her throat. "Here. Over here."

A rope with a large loop in the end snaked down to dangle, tantalizing, by her shoulders.

"Get that around you," Adam ordered, his rough voice reflecting his fear. "And I'll pull you up."

"I can't," she cried. "I can't. If I let go of this brush and grab for that rope, I'll fall again. I can't do it."

"You can do it," he encouraged. "Keep hanging on with your right hand, it's the stronger one. Grab the rope with your left and get that loop over your head and shoulders. Go on. Do it now."

His level tone of command penetrated her paralyzing fear. She knew if she made one slip she'd pay for it with her life, but she also knew only she could save herself now. She loosened her grip, her cramped, sweaty palm sliding along the prickly rope as she grabbed at it. Pebbles trickled, in a steady stream, from beneath her feet. Carefully, cautiously, she slid the rope into position.

"Okay. Now hang on to the rope with your left hand and get that loop under your right arm."

Letting go of the bush was probably the hardest thing she'd ever done. But, sobbing under her breath, she did it. At last she held on to the rough hemp surface with both hands, the rope cutting into her shoulder blades.

"Ready?"

She nodded, speech impossible. The rope tightened

painfully across her back, and her knees banged against the ravine wall as Adam hauled her back to safety.

He helped her crawl over the edge and then drew her up to stand on the narrow trail. She saw Greedy's body draped over a huge boulder, his neck bent back and his legs twisted askew. It could have been her. Letitia sagged, but Adam's strong arms were there to catch her. She gulped, replayed in her memory the awful moment when she and Greedy had plunged over the edge.

She burst into tears.

"Easy. Just take it easy. You're safe now." He lifted her into his arms and strode carefully along the uneven surface of the trail.

She buried her head in his shoulder, unable to stop the shudders of reaction shaking her body. "I . . . I knew . . . you'd . . . you'd come."

"Hush," he said tenderly. "It's all over."

"I . . . I knew you . . . you wouldn't let me fall. I knew—" She choked on a sob. "I knew you'd be there."

He wrapped his arms around her and hugged her shuddering form as tightly as he could. He felt weak-kneed himself at the narrowness of Letitia's escape from tragedy.

He closed his eyes, but the image of Letitia and her horse crashing down the ravine seemed to be permanently imprinted on his brain. He gazed at the top of her head and gently pulled a twig free from her dusty hair. He'd never felt this overwhelming need for anyone before. It frightened him.

"Thank God you're safe," he breathed. "When you fell I realized what I feel for you, what you—"

The meaning of the words flowing from his mouth penetrated his brain and he bit back what he intended to say. He couldn't admit, even to himself, what she meant to him. If he did, then he couldn't go through with what he had planned. Ma was depending on him. He had to honor her last request. He had to!

Letitia gazed up at him. "Adam?"

She licked her lips, the quick movement of her tongue, the sheen of moisture enticing him. He groaned and pulled her even closer. It was madness. Undeniably, he'd pay for this, but he simply had to taste the sweetness of her mouth, if for no other reason than to prove she was still alive and not lost to him, yet.

It was well past midday when, riding double on Adam's horse, they finally made it to the top of the mountain. He reined his mount to a standstill. He freed his right leg from its stirrup and twisted in the saddle so he could hook his knee over the pommel. "Look." He pointed to the east.

Letitia swiveled around, her gaze following his finger. She gasped as she caught her breath. The earth dropped away as sharply as any cliff. She looked out across the desert floor, thousands of feet below them. The sandy beiges, mauves, pinks, and grays stretched out to the horizon, a barren, unfriendly, awe-inspiring sight.

"We crossed that?" she asked incredulously. "It's not possible."

"We sure did." Adam whooped triumphantly. Buck pricked his ears and stepped forward. "It doesn't matter that I know where to find water—it always amazes me when I make it safely back. It's one hell of a journey, even in the springtime."

"Yes, it is certainly that." In the midst of her fatigue and soreness, she couldn't help sharing Adam's satisfaction. If anyone had told her she could survive a journey across that desolate waste, she simply wouldn't have believed them. In fact, back in green, gentle Kentucky, she never would have been able to comprehend the awful totality of such an empty land.

Adam dropped his leg back into the stirrup and pulled his horse's head around. "It isn't far to my cabin." His lips twisted into a lopsided smile. "In fact, we're on my land now."

This time they traveled to the south. As the sun started to set, Letitia shivered.

Adam pulled Buck to a halt and looked over his shoulder at her. "You're cold. I'll untie my jacket from the cantle for you."

He reached around her and then handed her the oiled cotton garment, and she slid her arms into the overlong sleeves, appreciating its warmth. She realized just how far they'd climbed by looking at the tender green shoots of grass just starting to appear under the sere yellow mat of last year's growth. This mountain fastness had barely been touched by spring.

She leaned forward, her breasts flattening against his back, appreciating his warmth and his nearness. She felt almost feudal, riding pillion behind her brave knight.

The oak trees thinned to reveal a long, sweeping meadow. A pile of five boulders, each as large as a small wagon, guarded the entrance. A small shack and a somewhat larger barn crowned a flat hill at the upper end of the grassland. She gazed at a small herd of cattle grouped around the stream that flowed through the middle of the meadow.

The animals were a scruffy-looking group, clearly unkempt and untrained. One of the cows sighted the horse and its two riders. Within seconds, the whole herd raced away, their tails up, their ungainly gait making Letitia smile.

Adam watched his cattle run away and sighed. "They're as wild as March hares. No one's lived on this place for some time—it's going to take a lot of work to get it into shape."

Letitia nodded, even though he couldn't see her.

"After the cows drop their calves I'll hire some men for a roundup. We'll get this place on its feet, eventually."

"You live out here all alone?"

"Yeah."

The tone of his voice clearly indicated this was not a time for her to ask questions. She wondered what could have happened to all the gold he'd found. Clearly, Adam wasn't a rich man any longer. Not that it mattered to her. She'd been attracted to him before he told her he'd been wealthy.

The small cabin, a shack actually, sat only a few yards ahead now. She shivered at its primitive appearance. Even the people Grandmama contemptuously branded "poor white trash" lived better than that.

Still, it didn't matter. Adam had said she was a woman he could live with the rest of his life. She knew she had to make that statement a reality.

She slid to the ground. He dismounted and she followed him as he led Buck into the barn. She watched as Adam rubbed his horse down and grained him.

Adam squared his shoulders. "May as well go inside. I'm sorry—it's not much. Certainly not what Miss Ramsey of Bellewood is used to, but . . ."

She sensed his unease over the poor appearance of his ranch and tried to reassure him. "Miss Ramsey of Bellewood never existed, not really."

Adam scowled and took her arm. "Like I said, let's go inside. We've got something to discuss."

She felt relief spreading in her chest, lifting the heavy weight that had been resting there ever since they'd sighted the cabin. He intended to speak to her. Shelly had been nervous, just like this, before he proposed. She knew what her answer to Adam would be as she admitted to herself how easily she could come to love this man.

What wasn't there to love about him? He was a tender, accomplished lover, a resourceful pioneer, an interesting conversationalist, a man capable of rescuing a woman from a certain death.

He pulled at the rawhide strand that controlled the primitive bar on the door and ushered Letitia into the dim interior of the cabin. She wrinkled her nose at the musty smell. The crude furniture and the dirt floor conspired to make his cabin much worse than any of the slave quarters at Bellewood. Something would have to be done.

Adam tossed his hat on the table. He raked one hand through his hair before he crossed the small room to the stone fireplace. He kindled the wood lying there with his customary carefulness. When the flames were burning to his satisfaction, he rocked back on his heels, his tanned complexion glowing in the firelight.

"You'd better sit down," he said, pointing to the single bunk. "You're not going to like what I've got to tell you."

Stunned, more by his harsh expression than his words, she dropped down onto the wooden shelf. "What do you mean?"

"I mean I'm not taking you to Hunt Ramsey tomorrow."

It would be all right. She exhaled an almost silent sigh of relief and said, "I see."

Adam swore, his violent words barely audible. "You don't see at all. You promised me if I'd rescue you from the Bickles, your father, *Hunt Ramsey*, would make it worth my while. I intend to make it worth my while, but I'm not interested in any reward."

She nodded, trying to understand his words. Knowing him, it made sense that he didn't want a reward. "Yes?"

He pulled the only chair from the small table, twisted it around and straddled it so his elbows could rest on the chair back. "Before I bought this ranch I tried to see Hunt Ramsey. He refused. Your papa has holed up on that ranch of his and he doesn't see anyone he doesn't know. When he goes anywhere, he goes with armed guards. Hunt Ramsey has made some very serious enemies and there's more than one person who'd like to kill him."

Letitia's eyes widened. She had no idea Papa had become involved in such dangerous doings. His letters always spoke of his placid life as a rancher. What had he done since he'd left Bellewood?

"Are you one of the ones who want to kill Hunt Ramsey?" Letitia asked softly.

Adam's lips tightened. "Maybe. Probably," he added honestly. "I do know I'll do whatever it takes to bring him to justice. That's why I bought this ranch, why I got involved with the Bickles, who had their claim jumped by Ramsey years ago—"

Letitia stiffened. "I don't believe you," she said. "Papa would never—"

"Believe what you want," Adam interrupted her. "I'll do whatever it takes to achieve my ends. I need a means to make Ramsey come to me. I reckon he'll come running when he learns I'm holding his daughter hostage."

7

"*Hostage?*" *Letitia's voice* rose. "You're not serious? Are you?"

"Dead serious." His low voice was flat and exhausted. "In case I didn't make myself clear, you are my ticket to Ramsey."

"You mean you . . . ?" Letitia sputtered, totally at a loss.

"I mean to do what I have to do," he said.

Finally, she understood. "You didn't mean to . . . ? Oh, no!"

A scream built inside her chest, but the pain blocked her throat so tightly no sound could escape. *Oh, God!* she cried silently.

He had never meant to marry her, she realized. She'd let him use her. Grandmama was right. All men were beasts! The realization of just how thoroughly he'd manipulated her transformed her anguish into rage. He'd not only used her to satisfy his lust, he intended to use her to hurt Papa. Later, she'd find some way to deal with her devastation. But now . . . Not while that . . . that *beast* thought he could hold her hostage as a way to threaten Papa!

She leaped to her feet. "You can't be serious. What you're accusing Papa of doing, of being, it just isn't true."

"Ah, but it is. In one of Hunt Ramsey's many underhanded dealings, he managed to marry the daughter of one of the old Spanish dons and take over the property. Except his wife died in childbirth along with their baby. I understand the only thing Ramsey wants more than power is an heir. I reckon that's why he sent for you." Adam smiled wolfishly. "A female heir is better than nothing at all. He'll end up with just that—nothing at all—unless he cooperates with me."

"That's ridiculous. I don't believe you."

"That Ramsey wants you as his heir?"

"That . . ." Pain threatened to overcome her. She fought it back and brushed her hair away from her face. This couldn't be happening to her. It just couldn't! "That you're ransoming me. I told you Papa would pay you a reward. Why do you want to harm him?"

"That's my business. No amount of pleading for your father will change my mind." Adam folded his arms across his chest. "I took you from the Bickles because I knew you'd be useful to me. That's what you're going to be, useful."

"No." Letitia refused to accept his words. "No. You can't—this is all wrong!"

He glared at her. "What do you mean? You're Ramsey's daughter, aren't you?"

She certainly couldn't tell him of her illegitimacy now. "Papa isn't the man you're describing. He's always helped me. He's kind, he's good. You admitted you've never met him. You don't know the truth. Papa isn't evil, he isn't bad."

Adam looked at her, his gaze level, his expression giving nothing away. "You know Ramsey so much better than I do? You saw him last when you were how old?"

"Thirteen." Letitia sank back onto the bunk. "But . . . It doesn't matter. You're wrong. I know you are."

Even as she defended Ramsey, a corner of her mind doubted. Adam was right, it had been ten years since she'd seen Papa. She never really knew him, for how can a child truly know all the nuances of a man's nature? But of course a child could tell. The way Papa'd treated a lonely little girl proved his nature.

Adam simply couldn't be right. Papa had written his letter before Grandmama's death. He hadn't asked Letitia to come to California and become his heir. He'd just held out a vague promise of help should she ever need it. She squashed her niggling doubts. Papa was her savior, and Adam . . .

Anguish threatened to swamp her. She fought back the horrible sense of betrayal building inside her like black storm clouds racing to block out the sun. She'd deal with the disastrous reality of her situation later. Not now. Not while Adam stood there watching her, his face as still as if it'd been graven in stone, his eyes flat and almost gray.

"I don't believe any of the horrible things you're

saying. Papa isn't like that, not at all. He's an honorable man. Which is more than I can say of you, Adam . . . Adam . . . !" Dear God in heaven, she'd made love with this man, decided she'd marry him, and she didn't even know his last name!

Adam stood, shoving his chair away. "As far as I'm concerned, this discussion is over. You know the reason you're staying here and that's enough."

"No it's not!" Her fingers twisted together, as she fought back tears of despair. "You're no better than Grandmama or the . . . or the . . . those Bickles!" Her chin wobbled dangerously as she realized just how completely she'd let Adam use her.

Something inside her seemed to snap. She faced him, welcoming the anger burning through her veins, since it washed away all her pain. "I won't be this stupid ever again. All my life people have used me and now I understand why. They use me because I let them do it. That's all in the past. No one is ever going to use me again. Especially not you, Adam! What's more," she added, "I don't give a damn what your last name is! You're not going to use me to hurt my papa, do you hear? I won't let you!"

"You can't stop me."

His simple statement silenced her childish tirade.

She ground her teeth together, searching for an outlet for her rage. "I don't know how I'll do it," she vowed. "But I do know this. I'll fight you every step of the way. And what's more, I'll win. See if I don't."

Adam cooked their dinner and they ate it in complete silence. Letitia nursed her flame of anger as she pushed her food around on her plate. It was much better than thinking about how completely she'd been betrayed. He had all the answers and she had none. But she'd find a way to outwit him, she would! What's more, she'd find a way to make him pay for what he'd done to her. He'd suffer, she promised herself. He'd suffer much worse than she was suffering now.

"If you're through with that . . ." Adam glanced at her half-eaten meal.

"I'm through," she said. She couldn't hold back her anger any longer. "I'm through with you, through with your horrible food, through with this whole terrible business."

"No, you're not," he contradicted. Then, in a kinder tone, he added, "Go to bed and try to get some sleep. Who knows how this will end?"

Letitia sniffed. She took her blankets and lay down on the hard bunk, resolutely not listening to Adam's slow, even breathing as he lay near the fire, between her and the only door.

In her imagination she acted out all the things she should have said to him, all the things she should have done to bring him, groveling, to his knees, begging her forgiveness. As satisfying as that mental image was, she knew it had no basis in reality.

She knew of only one way to deal with her pain. Grandmama had taught her granddaughter how to survive heartache, if nothing else. The memory of the time with Adam at the desert oasis had to cease to exist. If you can't feel pain, you can't hurt, Letitia told herself. Deliberately, she tried to blank out all sensation, forcing herself to concentrate on what her life would be like when she finally reached Papa. Then, and only then, would she be the cherished one.

*   *   *

Letitia woke abruptly. Disoriented, she looked around the small cabin. Morning light, filtering through the oiled cotton across the window, dimly revealed the Spartan interior. Then she remembered what had happened—what Adam had said. Her stomach knotted with tension.

He was nowhere to be seen, but the twisted pile of blankets on the floor in front of the fireplace indicated where he'd spent the night. The echo of a gunshot reverberated through the chinks in the cabin wall. Maybe someone was shooting at him.

"I could use some luck for a change," she muttered.

She'd tried to come to terms with what had happened to her and failed. She'd let him make love to her and now she was paying the price for a few moments of ecstasy. Why should Adam even think of marrying her when he could have what he wanted from her for free? There was no way to overcome her feelings of guilt and inadequacy.

All she had left to cling to now was her anger. That, and a burning determination that she'd never, ever, no matter what, let herself be seduced by a man again.

She swung her legs over the side of the bunk and gently massaged the small of her back. She wondered what had happened to the mattress the frame had been built to support. Not that it mattered. She wouldn't be staying here long enough to require physical comfort. She'd find a way to outfox Adam.

The door opened and he entered, a pail of water swinging from his hand. He filled the coffeepot and hung it from a hook over the flames. He looked over his shoulder at Letitia.

"I shot a deer," he said, his words clipped and impersonal. "The liver is in a basin just outside the door. Bring it in and I'll show you how to prepare it. Jonas warned me you weren't much of a cook. I reckon it's time you learned."

"I don't cook."

His blue eyes narrowed. "If you don't cook you won't eat."

Her stomach grumbled, the angry sound audible in the tiny room. He grinned. She swore under her breath and flopped back down on the bunk, her arms crossed over her middle.

Their glares met. She would not give in to him. No matter how small the issue, she would not give in, period.

He shrugged, stood, and left the cabin. When he returned, he carried a basin containing a revolting lump of dark scarlet flesh.

This time Letitia did look away. She couldn't bear to watch. Just listening to him slice the liver was bad enough, but when he started to fry it, and the smell of the cooking meat filled the room, she knew she couldn't stay a moment longer.

She fought not to gag as she stalked away. Outside, she gratefully gulped in deep breaths of the fresh mountain air. She wasn't giving in—not at all. She was just showing him that he couldn't torment her and get away with it.

Adam's horse, Buck, grazed outside the barn, his strong, yellow teeth tearing at the tender shoots of the spring grass. She stared at him and wondered if she dared.

Adam was inside, cooking his disgusting breakfast. She could catch Buck, saddle him, and be on her way before Adam could figure out what she'd done. She had no idea where Papa's ranch actually was, but it didn't matter. San Diego had to be to the south and to the west. She could figure it out.

Her plan was foiled before she could put it into action when Adam came outside. He held a full plate of that horrible liver in one hand and a cup of coffee in the other. He sat on the bench outside the door and proceeded to eat and drink.

She crossed her arms over her chest and stared stonily at the chestnut gelding. She felt as if she could kill for a cup of that coffee.

Adam finished the last of his meal, savoring the fresh taste of the meat. He gazed thoughtfully at the rigid set of her slender shoulders. He didn't blame her for her pathetic attempt at rebellion. If he'd been in her shoes, he probably wouldn't have cooperated either.

The way he'd treated her gnawed at him. He hadn't behaved as he should. But refusing to eat was stupid and it only harmed herself, not him. He felt his anger building and welcomed it. It was much easier when he argued with her. It made him forget his guilt.

Their oasis had been but a slice of time out of the normal course of events. It'd been foolish. Wonderful, but incredibly foolish.

That didn't help things now. Mooning over her would only make things worse. He knew what he had to do. With a sigh, he stood and went to catch Buck.

When the horse was saddled and ready to go, Adam returned to the cabin for his hat. She hadn't moved form her position. Her arms were still crossed and she still gazed expressionlessly across the meadow. A muscle in his jaw pulsed and he felt his anger building in his chest. He clapped his hat on his head and pulled the brim low over his forehead. "I'll be back before sunset. Don't even think about trying to escape. We're a good forty miles from your papa's ranch. You'd never make it if you tried to walk it. I don't recommend you put me to the trouble of trying to come after you."

She didn't indicate by a single movement that she'd heard, or even cared, what he said.

He swung into the saddle and touched his spurs to the gelding's sides. "I'll give Ramsey your best regards."

He saw her back stiffen and had the satisfaction of knowing he'd successfully needled her.

Letitia watched Buck lope away, Adam's lithe body swaying with the movement of his horse. Her arms fell to her sides and her hands knotted into fists as she thought of her aborted escape attempt. But she didn't believe what he'd just said about her not being able to survive. She'd endured that trip through the desert, and she'd even learned a thing or two about navigation and survival as she'd watched Adam.

A simple plan formed in her mind. She'd simply walk west until she reached the ocean. Then she'd turn south and follow the water until she reached San Diego. From there she could find someone to take her to Papa's ranch.

She realized Adam would follow her, but that thought didn't deter her. She had to get away, period. Her luck had to change, sometime, and it might as well be now. She'd find someone, some outpost of civilization where she'd be safe until she could get word to her papa.

According to James Fenimore Cooper, Natty Bumppo and Uncas were able to track anyone or anything through the forest, but she doubted such exploits existed outside the pages of fiction. Whenever slaves ran away, it took dogs to track them down. Adam didn't have a dog and he was no Chingachgook. Besides, she'd heard of the tricks the slaves used to elude their pursuers. She figured she could put those stratagems to good use, too.

She returned to the cabin and looted the interior for useful items. She curled her lip at the remains of the cooked liver, but she forced herself to eat it. Then, gratefully, she finished the coffee. She opened the cupboard, searching for staples, amazed when she found Adam's small collection of books. Her fingers brushed the spines as she read the titles, *The Collected Works of William Shakespeare, Leaves of Grass,* and *The Scarlet Letter.* She had no idea what *Leaves of Grass* was about. She'd always wanted to read *The Scarlet Letter,* but Grandmama had forbidden it.

She closed the cupboard door with a thump. When she was safely with Papa she could think about losing herself in novels once again. She dumped the food she'd found into the middle of a blanket and tied the four corners together. She knotted the corners in pairs, making a crude harness to slip over her shoulders.

A battered straw hat rested on top of a barrel. Letitia tried it on and it drooped down over her ears. She'd have to find some rags to line the crown. There wasn't any way she could leave without a hat to shade her face. It didn't matter what she looked like, she needed the protection.

Letitia pulled the door to the cabin shut behind her and walked away from the small building, Adam's compass flat on her palm as she figured out which way was due west. She pulled her rough pack into a higher position on her shoulders and strode confidently across the meadow.

Adam reined Buck to a halt by a gigantic oak growing beside the dirt road that led to Ramsey's ranch. He glanced at the sun, judging it to be early midmorning. A small creek ran in the gully a few yards to the west. This was his prearranged place to meet Swen.

When they'd started their quest, Swen insisted on going to work at the Ramsey ranch so he could try to ferret out additional information. The knowledge that he'd let his little brother ride into the lion's den gnawed at Adam. What if Swen didn't make their rendezvous? What if harm had come to him at the ranch?

He'd commanded men on the battlefield—sent more than he wished to remember to their deaths. He tried to convince himself that Swen was no different from any other soldier, but it didn't work. Damn it, where was he?

A half hour passed with glacial slowness. Buck lifted his head from the patch of grass where he was grazing, his ears pricked. Adam moved silently to his horse's side, his hand resting on Buck's nose to keep him from whinnying. Then he heard what Buck had already sensed—the steady rhythm of a horse trotting on the hard-packed earth of the road.

The hoofbeats slowed and were almost silenced as the rider guided his mount toward the stream. "Adam?" the rider called softly. "Are you there?"

"Over here." Adam hoped his overwhelming sense of relief didn't show in his words.

Swen dismounted and Adam seized his brother's hand in a hard grasp. "It's good to see you."

"You, too." Swen returned the handshake, his face splitting into a wide grin.

Adam looked at him. He was losing that gawky awkwardness that had so characterized him in San Francisco. He must have grown another inch and he'd filled out, too, until he was looking more like a man and less like a sixteen-year-old adolescent.

"Have a seat." Adam squatted down on his heels and stretched his right foot out in a stockman's resting pose. "I've got good news."

Swen copied his brother's movements and said, "That's great because I've had a real stroke of luck, too."

"You tell first then."

"Ramsey's had a bunch of big guns at his ranch all this week," Swen explained. "I recognized one of them —Senator Connoley."

Adam pursed his lips and whistled. "Are you sure?"

"Sure, I'm sure. Connoley had some sort of political dinner at the hotel I stayed at while you were down here buying your ranch. I was even introduced to him."

"Did he recognize you?" Adam demanded.

"Of course not," Swen said. "Who would look for Adam McCormick's little brother among a bunch of ranch hands? But that's not all. I pretended I sprained my left wrist so the foreman put me to work in the house. Even so, I didn't get a chance to see Ramsey and his guests up close, but I did my best to figure out what was happening, because it's pretty obvious something important was going on."

"And?" Adam prompted.

"Ramsey took his guests hunting today. While I was supposed to be cleaning the fireplace in his office I took the liberty of going through his desk." A delighted smile wreathed Swen's face. He reached inside the front placket of his jacket and pulled out a piece of paper. "Here, take a look at this."

Adam unfolded the document, his forehead creasing into a frown as he read. It appeared to be some sort of legal paper—an agreement. He glanced at the bottom of the last page. "This isn't valid until Ramsey countersigns it."

"I know." Swen sighed. "But it does spell out what Senator Connoley, what the government, will do for Ramsey. It's outrageous the amount of land they'll just give him outright for building his railroad. He'll control thousands and thousands of acres on each side of the tracks. I can't even begin to imagine how rich all that land'll make him, but I know it'll make you gold miners look pretty sorry. Worse, he'll be more powerful than ever if this goes through."

Adam nodded. "That's probably an understatement. Ramsey, Connoley, and the others will control the state, and the territory, too, for starters."

"I thought we could release it to one of the newspapers—maybe even back east somewhere. It'd make an almighty uproar and I bet it'd stop Ramsey in his tracks."

"It'll take more than that." Adam considered the best way to use Swen's startling piece of evidence. "I'm not without influence, myself. The money from the Ingrid gives me a certain amount of power, especially with my fellow mine owners. We can do more with this than just give it to some news hound."

Adam refolded the document, still thinking hard.

"Right now, is there any way Ramsey can know you took this agreement?"

Swen shook his head. "No. They won't be back for hours."

"This advantage won't last long." Adam grimaced, and his lips thinned. "Worse, I'm afraid this agreement is worthless unless we can force Ramsey to validate it."

Swen stood. "I guess I didn't do so good after all."

"That's where you're wrong." Adam smiled at his brother. "Things couldn't be working out better if we'd planned them this way."

"Why? What do you mean?"

"I mean I got lucky, too. You know I've got the Bickles working on uncovering the New Mexico Territory side of Ramsey's business."

Swen nodded.

"When I caught up with them they had Ramsey's daughter, Letitia." Adam paused. Swen didn't know what dedicated crooks the Bickles were and Adam had to decide just how to edit his story.

Swen squatted down again, eye level with his brother. "I didn't know Ramsey had a daughter. No one at the ranch has ever said anything about her."

"She's been living in Kentucky. She left when her Grandmother died so she could join her father—Ramsey," Adam said. "There'd been an accident to the stagecoach she was traveling on so I offered to bring her the rest of the way to her 'dear papa.'"

Swen glanced at his brother. "How old is Ramsey's daughter? Ma wouldn't like it if you misused a child—especially a little girl."

Adam ground his teeth together. "Letitia's not a little girl—she's twenty-three."

"Still, Ma always said a woman—"

"It was Ma who got us into this in the first place!" Adam didn't realize he'd shouted the words until Swen looked away uncomfortably.

Adam watched as his brother ripped a blade of grass from the ground and twisted the green length around his finger. He tried to modulate his voice and contain his anger. He didn't need Swen telling him how to treat Letitia!

"I'm planning to ransom her to Ramsey," he said. "I haven't hurt her."

Sure you haven't, his thoughts mocked him. "I was going to use her as my way of getting past his guards so I could confront him. Now, with your agreement, I'll force him to sign it to get his daughter back. It's easy, really. We'll have the proof we need to break him, and we'll have done what Ma wanted."

"It's simple enough," Swen agreed. "So your plan should work. Except for one thing. You'd think I'd have heard something about it if they were expecting Ramsey's daughter."

Adam frowned, staring at the bushes growing on the other side of the gully. "Letitia's no liar. She's Ramsey's daughter, all right. She said he wrote asking her to come to California. He's probably keeping quiet about her for some deep reason of his own."

"That's possible."

Adam pulled a small notebook and a stubby pencil from his vest pocket. "I'll write the ransom note and find a way to deliver it."

"I can deliver it," Swen said.

"Unh-uh." Adam shook his head. "What do you think will happen to you once Ramsey discovers his agreement is missing? I don't think much of the odds."

"Well," Swen countered, "What do we do? Seems to me as if this plan of yours hinges on the delivery of that ransom note and you know you won't get past the guards. I can."

Adam frowned. "You said Ramsey and his big spenders are out hunting?"

"That's right."

"When are they due back?"

"Sunset, more than likely. I don't think it will be much earlier, but it sure won't be much later than that. I can't see any of them spending a night away from their beds."

"Then there's time to deliver the note to someone who can be trusted to give it to Ramsey this evening. But that someone has to be a person who trusts you, too," Adam decided. "I'm not letting you go back into that snake pit unless we've worked out a foolproof way to assure your safety."

"I'll give the note to Consuela, the housekeeper," Swen said. "She likes me. When I told her I was fed up with being a butler, she told me to take the rest of the day off, since Ramsey wouldn't be around. Otherwise, I'm not quite sure how I would have made our rendezvous, unless I just rode away."

"Here's what you're going to do," Adam ordered. He wrote his note quickly, ripped the piece of paper from the pad, and folded it. "Give this to Consuela." Adam handed the paper to Swen. "Grab your gear and leave immediately. Be sure to hide your trail the way I showed you."

Swen nodded.

"Then head north to Temecula and see Fred Barlow, the stagecoach agent. He runs a small general store, and you can load up on supplies. I'm running low on food, now I've got Ramsey's daughter to feed, too. On your way back, be sure you approach my ranch from the north side. If things go wrong and Ramsey figures things out, he'll come from the south."

"If things go wrong—!"

"They won't." Adam smiled. "It'll all run like clockwork, see if it doesn't. Ramsey won't be able to start out until first light tomorrow, at the earliest. You'll have a good lead on him."

"It should work," Swen said slowly. "That is, it should work if you're sure the woman you've got is really Ramsey's daughter."

Adam's jaw tightened. "Letitia's no liar. Maybe that grandmother of hers kept her away from Ramsey all this time—who knows? What I do know is if I was Ramsey I'd move heaven and earth to get my daughter back. He'll do what he's told. He's willing to risk a lot, but he won't risk his daughter. He won't take chances with Letitia."

The westering sun sent its light directly into Letitia's eyes. She put up a hand to shade her face and continued to trudge through the rugged terrain. Heavy stands of chaparral seemed to grow everywhere, and she'd exhausted herself pushing through the dense bushes. Where the chaparral didn't grow, the ground was littered with huge boulders, the outcroppings of rock treacherous underfoot.

She'd found a small creek earlier. She'd waded down it for at least a mile, hoping the subterfuge would put Adam off her trail. Even though the water headed steadily southward, she'd decided to abandon it and strike out west again, in keeping with her original plan.

Still, she'd made steady progress and she hoped she'd come more than ten miles. She feared it was much less. It seemed as if she'd climbed as many hills as she'd slid down. The bushes thinned and Letitia paused, her attention caught by a shining ribbon of water cutting its way through the valley floor below her. Heartened by the thought of a fresh drink, she carefully made her way down the steep mountain side.

The precipice was only a few degrees less steep than the ravine she and Greedy had tumbled down. Swiftly, she blocked out that image. She could endure what was happening to her only as long as she concentrated on the present and ignored all her memories of Adam.

Letitia pushed her way through the bushes, her gaze fixed on the oak trees growing thickly on each side of this new stream. When she finally reached the water, she bent to drink the cool, fresh liquid. Then she collapsed gratefully on a convenient boulder. Sunlight filtered through the trees, the elongated shadows indicating how quickly the day was slipping away.

Letitia sighed. She couldn't keep sitting here. She had to make a camp and build a fire. Actually, she knew a fire might be dangerous. What if Adam saw it or smelled it?

He had to be on her trail by now. But that didn't mean she intended to let him catch her. She shivered in the gathering gloom. Without continuous exercise to warm her, she felt the cold. She decided to at least collect some wood. If it froze tonight she'd die without some sort of warmth.

She pushed herself back onto her aching feet and bent to collect the fallen branches scattered underneath the oak trees. She worked her way around a stand of scrub, her eyes on the earth, searching for likely sized pieces of wood.

A rough sort of a *woof* that didn't sound at all like a dog made her look up. A huge brown bear reared up from a patch of scrub not fifteen feet away from her. He raised his nose to the sky and twisted his head on a massive neck, scenting the air, searching for his prey.

She screamed, the wood dropping from her suddenly nerveless fingers. She didn't stop to think, she only reacted, racing for the nearest oak tree. Over the frightened pounding of her heart and her gasping breath, she heard the sounds of pursuit as the bear chased her. Panic gave her the added speed she needed. With a leap, she hit the trunk of the tree, clawing her way up the armlike branches.

She went up the tree like a cat, her senses coming back only when she realized she couldn't reach the next branch above her head. The treetop swayed dangerously under her weight. Cautiously, she turned her head and looked down over her shoulder.

She whimpered involuntarily with fright. She'd climbed perhaps twelve feet. God, how she hated heights. She could hear the bear moving around the base of the tree, his whoofing grunts indicating his frustration. The bear reared up and stretched his length up the trunk, one paw waving as he tried to snag Letitia.

She moaned and clung all the tighter to her branch, unable to tear her gaze from the bear's piggy, feral eyes.

With a shake of his head and another of those odd *woofs*, he dropped down on all fours and circled the tree. Letitia's palms were smarting from the scrapes she'd inflicted on herself as she'd swarmed up the tree. Perspiration made the cuts sting, but she clung as tightly as she could to the rough bark.

The bear discovered her small bundle. He knocked the blanket open with a single swipe of his paw, and his nose tested the contents. He consumed Letitia's small store of jerky and then lost interest in the bundle. Apparently salty meat made bears thirsty, because he ambled over to the stream and gulped down what seemed to Letitia to be several gallons of water.

She watched the bear drink and prayed he would go away. Should God spare her to make it back down this tree, she intended to light a fire to keep the rest of the wild beasts in this benighted wilderness at bay. It didn't matter if Adam saw the flames or not.

The bear wandered back to the base of the tree. She peered uneasily down at him. It was close to sunset now, but that fact didn't bother the bear. He squatted back on his haunches, pointed his nose at her, and licked his chops.

To Letitia it seemed as if a silly grin wreathed the bear's mouth as he waited her to fall from the tree, just like a piece of ripe fruit.

"Shoo," she said weakly.

The bear growled, the sound low and menacing.

8

Adam reined Buck in and looked across the meadow at the cabin. The door was shut and no smoke rose from the chimney. The place had an uncanny look of desertion.

He spurred his horse forward. He'd never stopped to think that Letitia might just simply walk away. His ranch was too isolated, too far from any outpost of civilization to encourage anyone in his right mind to try to leave on foot.

"Damnation!" If he'd stopped to think he would have realized Letitia was so angry with him that she'd discount all the dangers of the wilderness in favor of an escape attempt.

He yanked the cabin door open and swore again. The cupboard doors hung open and the blanket he'd left neatly folded on the hearth was missing.

He stepped inside, checking to see which supplies were gone, thinking hard. She'd taken the compass. He rued the day he'd taught her the principles of navigation. Still, it would make finding her easier. At least she'd be heading in a straight line, not circling around like a lost tenderfoot.

He stepped outside. His trained eyes noted where she'd walked across the meadow, heading due west. He picked up the horse's reins from where he'd left Buck ground tied and swung back into the saddle. He was running on a pretty damn tight time schedule as it was. Now he'd have to go and rescue the silly woman, again.

He followed her trail until it ended at the edge of a creek. He grinned to himself when he realized she'd taken to the water in an effort to throw him off. He wondered how long she had stuck to wading through the chilly stream. He reined Buck to the left, following the rushing water.

She'd waded longer than he'd thought she would. Still, a mile from where she'd entered the stream, he could see the faint, unmistakable sign where she'd left the creek and headed due west again.

He turned his horse and pulled his hat brim lower, shading his face against the late afternoon sun. He knew he wasn't far behind her now. Her trail led along a steep escarpment. To his left, in the valley below, he could see a stream meandering its way to the west.

It was almost sunset when Adam heard a scream, a woman's scream. Letitia! The sound was loud and piercing and echoed across the valley. He reined Buck to the south. A sane man would cautiously coax his horse down the almost-perpendicular slope. The last echo of the scream died. So much for sanity, Adam thought as he ruthlessly spurred his gelding toward the edge.

Buck leaped forward. Adam looked past the drop as it yawned before him. He felt Buck's muscles tense as he tried to stop and Adam mercilessly applied his spurs again. Buck snorted in protest and jumped out into space.

Adam leaned back in the saddle. If he let gravity force him almost parallel to the horse's hindquarters, he'd retain his balance. With a little luck, they both might just survive this wild ride.

Buck landed on the steep hillside. The force of the descent made Adam feel as if his spine were being driven straight into his skull. The horse galloped gamely downward. With his left hand, Adam clung to the reins as a drowning man seizes a lifeline. His right hand flew straight back. His feet drove deep into the stirrups until his boot heels were wedged against the wood.

The horse plunged on, his ears plastered to his skull, his breathing a frightened rasp. Small stones broke away and rolled ahead of them, and dust rose up to cloud Adam's vision. It felt as if he and Buck had just been fired from a gigantic cannon.

The gelding barreled on like a runaway freight train. Somehow, he was still on his feet, with his rider on his back, when they made it to the bottom. Adam forced himself to ignore Buck's tortured breathing and ruthlessly applied his spurs. The horse bounded forward.

When they reached the trees growing by the stream, he reined the gelding to the west, urging him to a faster gallop. In the gathering gloom, Adam saw the bear only when it swung its heavy head to glare at the horse and rider. The gelding scented the other animal and slid to a halt, tossing his head nervously.

With a single fluid movement Adam pulled his Enfield rifle from its scabbard, cocked it, lifted it to his shoulder, and fired. The bear grunted at the pain of the bullet's impact. He roared in anger before he heaved himself to his feet and charged.

Adam recocked his rifle, the motion of his hands blurred as desperation drove him to a greater speed than he believed possible. He fired again. In midcharge the bear exhaled, the sound a tortured grunt, and crashed to the ground.

Adam soothed the horse with quiet words and a gentling hand. The gelding snorted, and danced nervously. Finally Adam managed to guide his horse past the bear's massive carcass, checking to make sure the animal was definitely dead. He stopped the gelding at the base of an oak tree and craned his neck to search the foliage. The bear had something up that tree. He prayed it was Letitia.

She stared down at him, her face ashen under smudges of dirt and a livid scratch that ran the length of her cheek.

"Thank God," he muttered. He wanted to yank her from that damn tree and hold her securely within the shelter of his arms. He wanted to curse her for the fool she was and cherish her and keep her safe always. He wanted to shake her silly and he wanted to kiss the fear from her lovely, drooping mouth and erase the strain from her frightened eyes forever.

He wanted to do so much, but he couldn't do any of it.

He gazed up at her. "Treed, by God," he said.

She stared down at him, saying nothing. The

ground started to spin in ever-widening circles. She shut her eyes tightly against the sensation and clung to the bole of the tree. She concentrated on the feel of the jagged bark beneath her cheek and hands, fighting the sick, shaking tremors sweeping through her and threatening to weaken her grip. She clung all the tighter to the trunk, knowing Adam was speaking to her, but unable to discern his words.

His voice rose in volume. The sound penetrated her dazed senses.

"I said," he yelled, "are you going to crawl out of your perch?"

"I can't." It felt as if her knees were going to give way at any second.

"Just like a damn kitten."

He swore at great length, even as he swung from Buck's back to one of the lower, stronger branches of the tree. His face was on a level with her ankles when he reached up and placed his hands on her trembling calves. "I've got you now. There's a branch just about six inches below to your left. It's a little to the side. Can you step down to it?"

She nodded and forced herself to put her foot out into space. If it weren't for the comforting strength of Adam's hands as he helped guide her faltering movements, she'd never have accomplished even that small task.

With infinite patience, he helped her down until they both were standing on the ground. He let her go and she slumped back against the tree, once again depending on its trunk for support.

"Well," he said, his arms crossed across his chest, his jaw jutting out, "that wasn't very bright, was it?"

She pushed away from the tree, solely intent on

somehow getting away from his fault-finding expression and hurtful words. In the dusk the bear's body loomed up in front of her. She stumbled, nearly tripping over the carcass, the smell of its blood sickening in the still air.

"Oh, God!" she cried, swinging away from the bear. She tripped and fell heavily to her knees, unable to fight the sobs tearing at her chest, the tears pouring down her face. She didn't think, she only felt the raging pain tearing at every fibre of her being. She collapsed to her side and pulled her knees up to her chest, curling into a tight ball of complete misery and utter desolation.

She didn't realize Adam had been moving about the clearing, kindling a fire, until she heard a piece of wood snap, the sound almost as loud as a pistol shot. She sniffed miserably and wiped the backs of her bruised hands across her cheeks. She wanted nothing more than to have Adam take her into his strong arms and comfort her. It didn't matter that he'd betrayed her, and for all she knew, intended to murder her Papa. What she wanted right now was the reassurance that he cared for her.

He sighed heavily and said, "Are you hurt?"

"N-no." Letitia hiccuped and put her smarting hands behind her back.

He walked over to his gelding, led the animal into the firelight, and ran his hands down the horse's front legs. "It's a miracle that Buck survived that wild ride, unscathed."

Letitia sniffed.

"As soon as the moon is up, we're leaving. I don't fancy spending the night with a dead bear," Adam said.

"No."

She'd argued with him, fought with him, run away from him. Would begging help? She bit her lip and forced herself to be humble. "Please, Adam. Please let me go."

She watched his face, struggling to make out his expression as the firelight shadowed his features. It seemed as if his face softened, but it must have been a trick of the flames, for his lips thinned until his expression was a harsh sneer. "No," he said simply. "Not until I've done what I have to do."

"Why, Adam?" Letitia cried. "Why?" She had nothing left, not even her pride. "I don't understand. In the desert—at our oasis—you—"

"Don't!" Adam shouted.

He faced her and she could see pain in his eyes. Or was it just the flickering of the firelight? Still, she pressed him. "Please, just make me understand."

"Because you were there. Because there was nothing . . ." He intended to say *Because there was nothing better to do,* but he couldn't force the words out. He couldn't keep up this cruel facade. He couldn't do it, not to Letitia. "Because there was no way in the world I could stop myself," he finished honestly.

"Then why?" she pleaded. "Why do you want to use me to hurt Papa?"

"Because I have to."

"Oh, Adam. What sort of answer is that?"

"The truth."

The need to tell her everything tore at him like a wild thing trapped inside his chest. But if he told her about Ma's last wish and convinced Letitia of her father's perfidy, then what?

Right now, he had Ramsey exactly where he wanted

him. With Swen's startling document about the railroad and Letitia, Ramsey's ambitions would be thwarted forever. Ma's request would be fulfilled. Plus, Letitia would never need to know her idolized papa had lived a thoroughly villainous life. When this was all over, she could go to him, live with him in a life of obscurity, safe and secure on that ranch of his.

It was the life she'd been bred to, the life she deserved.

A pale glow filtered through the oak trees as the moon rose above the mountain tops. Adam glanced up.

"It's time to ride."

He looked down at her tired, tearstained face. No woman could be beautiful under those circumstances, but he wanted her . . . wanted to tell her . . . No! His hands tensed as he fought back an overwhelming urge to take her into his arms and damn the consequences. All he wanted was to kiss away her pain, her fear, and regain the perfect satisfaction of their desert idyll.

"I can't explain any more," he finally said. All the bumps and bruises he'd collected from his wild ride down the mountainside started to throb, each with a savage life of its own. "I have to do what I have to do. You've got to accept things as they are. Even if I wanted to, I can't swerve from my chosen path."

"You mean you won't!" she cried.

"I mean I can't," he said, with awful finality. "I can't and I won't."

"Oh, Adam."

He could hear the tears in her voice. Her obvious pain clawed at him.

"What I'm doing . . ." He paused, searching for a

way to make her understand. He couldn't find the words—they just didn't exist. "Ah, hell! There's no way to explain this," he said. "Someday, though, you'll realize it's for the best."

Letitia glanced around the Spartan interior of the cabin and sighed. She scrubbed at the beans stuck to the bottom of the fry pan. Jonas had been right. She wasn't much of a cook. She rubbed and rubbed, wishing she could clear the confusion from her mind the way she scraped aside the burnt food.

They'd returned to the cabin two days ago. Since then Adam had barely spoken to her, or she to him. They'd used only the merest words necessary for basic politeness. Yet he wanted her. She could sense it in the smoldering, unspoken tension. If she could only figure out what it was that drove him. Then, perhaps, she could find a way to free him and save herself.

He'd revealed very little the night the bear had chased her up the tree. Yet she felt a measure of relief from that encounter. Somehow, his sketchy explanations had made her feel not quite so abandoned and had eased some of her pain. If only . . . if only . . .

She sighed and rubbed her hands dry on a rough piece of sacking. She picked up the basin full of dirty dishwater and carried it outside. She flung the contents on the ground and straightened, watching Adam as he repaired the rude corral at one side of the barn.

She sighed again, trying to banish her thoughts, which were running around in circles like a horse circling on a lunge line. She looked around the meadow. With unbelievable swiftness, spring had blossomed in the mountain fastness. Already, the hillsides were a tender green and three of the cows in the small herd had dropped their calves.

She rolled up the sleeves of the shirt she'd borrowed from Adam and used the tail to wipe her hot face. Who would have believed it could get this hot so early in the spring?

She watched Adam moving about the corral. He'd coped with the heat by removing his shirt. She knew she shouldn't be so weak, but she couldn't keep her eyes off him as he wrestled to nail the poles in place. Her mouth went dry as she watched the play of muscles in his shoulders.

From this distance she couldn't see the scars that crisscrossed his back from his stepfather's belt, but she could remember the tough ridges under her fingertips. She forced herself to harden her heart. Just because he'd been abused, that didn't make what he intended to do right.

No matter what he'd said, she had to find some way to escape, some way to warn Papa. As hard as it was, Adam had made that choice for her. If nothing else, she owed Papa her loyalty. Except Adam watched her like a hawk. This time, when she made her getaway, she'd manage to be the one on Buck. With a horse, she knew she could make it.

The gelding lifted his head and neighed. Another horse galloped around the huge pile of boulders at the entrance to the meadow. Adam reached for the rifle that never left his side these days. When the horse and rider came close enough to recognize, he laid the gun aside and walked to meet the visitor.

The man dismounted and the two shook hands. They turned and walked toward the cabin.

Letitia straightened her shoulders. How embarrass-

ing to meet a newcomer when she was dressed in
Adam's cast-off clothing. Worse, it was obvious that
she'd been living with him. Anyone would think she
was his woman.

The stranger was younger than Adam by a good
fifteen years. He was also much taller, at least by four
inches. As the two came closer she was struck by the
similarities between them. They had the same blue
eyes, square jaw, and long, straight nose.

"Letitia," Adam said, "I'd like you to meet my
brother, Swen."

"Ma'am." Swen awkwardly touched the brim of his
hat.

Summoning all the poise of Miss Ramsey of Bellewood, Letitia offered her hand graciously, and said,
"I'm pleased to meet you, Mr. . . . ?"

Swen reddened.

Adam said, "Mr. McCormick. Swen's last name is
McCormick, the same as mine."

"Then I'm pleased to meet you, Mr. Swen McCormick." She lifted her brows haughtily. Now she knew
Adam's last name. So what?

"Adam," Swen said in an urgent undertone. "We've
got trouble."

Instantly alert, Adam's eyes narrowed as he faced
his brother. "I thought as much when Ramsey didn't
follow up on my ransom note. What's happened?"

Swen gestured awkwardly at Letitia, her presence
obviously affecting his ability to speak.

"Say what you've got to say. Letitia's intimately involved in this, so to speak. She may as well hear it all."

"I'd better take care of my horse first." Swen pulled
the bridle from his horse's head, tugged the saddle free,
and affixed hobbles to his mare's front legs. He

slapped her on the rump and she hopped off to join Buck.

Adam pulled the single chair from the house for Letitia. He drank thirstily from the barrel of creek water he kept covered with a damp gunnysack and then gave the dipper to his brother, who drank his fill of the cool liquid.

When he offered the dipper to Letitia, she shook her head no. Then she wished she hadn't refused the drink. Her throat felt dry with tension.

Swen sat on the bench, his long legs sticking out, the heels of his boots digging into the soft dirt in front of the cabin.

Adam faced the younger man. "Well?"

"I gave Consuela the ransom note like we discussed and then I lit out of there. Except before I left Barlow's a rider showed up with a message for you from Ramsey." Swen fished a piece of paper from his pocket glanced uneasily at Adam. "I figured I'd better read it —so I could find out what he was up to."

"Of course," Adam agreed. "And?"

"This note says Ramsey isn't going to pay the ransom because . . ." Swen glanced at Letitia and then focused his attention on the dirty toes of his boots. "Because he hasn't heard of any Letitia Ramsey, because he doesn't have a daughter. He says the woman we're holding must be an impostor."

"What?" Letitia leaped to her feet, her hands knotting into fists at her sides. "What do you mean, Papa doesn't know who I am? He *sent* for me, he . . ." Letitia's voice broke.

She remembered Grandmama's funeral and thought hard about all that had happened that day. Could the letter from Papa have been a hoax, perhaps perpetrated by Cecily? She wrote a beautiful copperplate hand, just like his.

Letitia couldn't deny it'd been a coincidence when the letter had come so soon after Grandmama's death. Yet even if the letter was a hoax, there was still a Hunt Ramsey living near San Diego. There couldn't be two men by that name, could there? Even if he hadn't sent for her, he *had* to know who she was!

"You told me Ramsey is your father," Adam demanded. "Is that true?"

Her hand went to her throat. Papa wasn't her father, but she couldn't explain their correct relationship to Adam. After all that had happened between them, she just couldn't bear if he knew the ruinous truth of her illegitimacy. She nodded and said in a flat, little voice, "Hunt Ramsey is my papa."

"I reckon Ramsey sent for Letitia, all right." Adam leaned back until his shoulders touched the side of the cabin. "I also reckon he doesn't intend to pay to get her back. However, that doesn't mean he doesn't want Letitia. He's bluffing."

No one said anything.

"Damnation!" Adam broke the silence. "I can't believe the bastard would put his only daughter in this sort of danger. He can't know our intentions toward her are honorable. Ma didn't know the half of it when she sent us out for revenge."

The silence drew out again. Letitia shifted uncomfortably. She didn't have Adam's confidence that Papa would come hunting for her. What should she do? What could she do?

Adam turned to Swen. "Did anyone follow you?"

Swen shook his head no.

"Not that it means a lot. Hell!" Adam swore again,

his voice low and forceful. "Unless you approach this valley from the east, it's pretty well hidden. We've both been careful not to let anyone know where we're holed up. Still, Ramsey's probably figured it out already."

"We'll just have to be ready for him when he comes," Swen said.

"This isn't your fight," Adam said.

"She was my ma, too."

Letitia watched the two men and tried to make some sense of their comments. What could their mother have to do with this? Adam was so certain Papa would come, but would he? She tightened her lips and fought back her feelings of inadequacy. Why should Papa want to pay for her? Why should he want to fight for her? No one else ever had, except Shelly.

Adam and Swen discussed ways to fortify themselves from the attack they expected. Every idea either one proposed seemed to have a flaw.

Finally, Adam said, "It just won't work. We're too exposed here. Worse, there's only the two of us. Ramsey'll have his men out looking for us. That's a sure thing."

"So what do we do?" Swen asked.

"We need a more protected place, for starters," Adam decided.

"It's your ranch."

Adam looked at the thick forest that circled the meadow. "I recommend we make a camp under the cover of the trees. The spring that feeds our stream is up there, so we'll have water. There's a cave farther back that will shelter us and hide our fire."

He turned and looked at Letitia. "Seems as if we're on the move again. When Ramsey's men get here I want this place to appear to have been deserted for years."

Under Adam's direction, she and Swen cleaned out the cabin. She tried to think of a way to leave a message for Papa, a way to let him know she'd been at the cabin. But Adam watched her like a hawk and she still hadn't hit on any ideas by the time all Adam's meager possessions were loaded on the horses. He led them to the cave that was almost a quarter of a mile from the edge of the forest. An apron of jumbled rock led to the opening, which was less than six feet tall. The entrance yawned unpleasantly, reminding Letitia of a greedy mouth. To the left, the spring Adam had mentioned flowed from a fissure between the rocks.

Game obviously came to drink the water. Their feet had beaten back the undergrowth to form a small clearing.

"This'll do," Adam said. "We'll set up a picket line for the horses on the other side of the cave from the spring. There's plenty of cover all the way back to the meadow. We'll establish a couple of observation posts there. When Ramsey and his men try to ride into this valley, it'll be like shooting ducks in a pond."

"There's only two of us," Swen said.

Adam smiled unpleasantly. "When we have our defenses prepared to my satisfaction, that's all it'll take. There's no reason for it to happen—but one man could do the job in a pinch. Let's get this stuff unloaded so we can finish up at the cabin."

Finally, Adam set Letitia to work smearing mud on the new boards he'd used to mend the barn, while he and Swen dismantled the half-completed corral. Letitia continued to try to think of a way to leave a clue for

Papa's men. One that would tell them she'd been here yet would be overlooked by Adam's eagle eyes.

She reached for another fistful of earth and slapped it on the pale new wood. A splinter pierced her fingertip. "Ow!" she complained, while thinking hard.

The end of the new board didn't match up evenly to the other, older wood. As she stared at the small cavity, a thought formed in her mind. She fumbled for the piece of rag she used as a handkerchief, stuffed it into a crack, making sure it was snagged on a splinter, and slapped wet dirt on top of the fabric.

She made sure the mud was thickly plastered, and prayed that when it dried, the weight of it would cause it to fall to the ground, revealing her handkerchief. It wasn't much, and probably wouldn't work, but it was the best she could think of under adverse conditions.

It was midafternoon before they'd removed all traces of recent occupancy from the meadow. Adam stood by the door to the cabin, fingering the rough wood.

"I can't decide to leave this ajar or not," he said. "Certainly if it was open it'd add to the deserted appearance of the place, yet, with my luck, a family of skunks would decide to take up residence."

Letitia wrinkled her nose and opened her mouth to make the obvious comment.

"Don't bother," he said. "The skunk in this piece is clearly your papa."

Letitia was half-tempted to agree. After all, Papa had refused to pay her ransom. Yet her innate honesty stopped her. What made Papa responsible for her? Nothing, actually. They didn't share ties of blood, even though he'd been forced by Grandmama to lend a semblance of respectability to Letitia's birth. Perhaps, too, he'd somehow divined Adam's lust for revenge.

She shrugged and went to mount Buck. It was up to her to save herself. Depending on others wasn't the answer. They always let you down.

Using a leafy branch, Adam brushed away their footprints from the dirt in front of the cabin. He tossed the makeshift broom aside and swung onto Buck's back, behind Letitia.

"Let's go," he said.

His hard arms circled her waist. The warmth from his body enveloped her. She leaned away from him, giving Buck the signal to walk. The gelding stepped out, his head bobbing up and down in an unhurried rhythm.

Adam's hands pressed into her middle. She glanced down at his interwoven fingers. The nail on his left thumb was bruised. He must have hit himself with his hammer. Uninvited, the memory of his hands caressing her breasts while they made love beside the palm-ringed pool crept into her mind. She wriggled uncomfortably.

"What's wrong?" he demanded.

His breath tickled her ear, starting a chain reaction of sensation down her neck. She couldn't twist away, trapped as she was in the saddle and his arms.

"Nothing."

"Uh-hunh."

Another soft gush of air tickled the sensitive skin at her nape. She could sense his lips hovering just behind her earlobe. *Don't!* she silently screamed. *Don't touch me.* She couldn't bear it if he did.

His hands dropped away to grasp each side of the

cantle. Illogically, she felt let down, abandoned, bereft. *Oh, Adam,* her thoughts cried. *Why?*

She could feel him, sitting behind her, his body swaying to the rhythm of his horse's walk, his hands braced on the saddle. He might as well be a rock, she thought bitterly. Well, she'd fix that!

She moved her weight to the left side of the saddle, dug her heels into Buck's sides, lashed his withers with the reins, and whooped at the top of her lungs. The startled horse jumped forward in a headlong gallop. She shifted her weight in the saddle and pulled hard on the right rein. As she'd planned, the well-trained horse executed a tricky little dance step with his front feet with enough force to dislodge his second rider.

Instead of falling off, as he should have, Adam encircled Letitia with his arms, his firm hands grasping the reins above hers. Within a matter of seconds, he pulled the horse back to a bouncy jog trot and then a walk.

"Nice try." His breath brushed her ear, his voice indulgent and amused. "But no cigar."

"Grrrr." Until she did it herself, she'd never known human beings could actually growl.

Adam pulled Buck to a halt where she and Swen had dumped the contents from the cabin. She breathed a sigh of relief when Adam slid to the ground. She had to keep away from him, for pride's sake if nothing else. Yet he drew her the way a magnet draws iron filings. How could she fight that?

Somehow, she'd find a way. She dismounted and tried to lead the gelding toward the picket line.

Something spooked the horse. His eyes rolled, the whites showing at the edges of his normally gentle brown eyes. He snorted, his head tossing up and down.

"Easy, Buck," she soothed. She tightened her grip on the bridle and patted the horse's warm neck. "What's the—"

She never finished her sentence. A low rumbling filled her ears and the earth shook in a most peculiar fashion under her feet. Trees swayed and Buck neighed trying to jerk away from Letitia's hold.

She clung to the reins, her feet spread wide apart as she balanced against the violent shaking. The earth rolled the way full-grown wheat undulates in a field when the wind blows. For a second Letitia stood on a crest, looking down at Buck in the trough, and then their positions were reversed. Her arms were nearly ripped from their sockets as she fought to retain her grip on the leather straps. She fell on her knees. The earth gave a final, violent, twisting kind of jerk and stood still.

Adam helped Letitia back to her feet and took the gelding's reins from her. The horse quieted under his touch.

"What happened?" Letitia's shrill voice reflected her fear.

"It was an earthquake!" Swen exclaimed.

"That's right." Adam secured Buck to the picket line and took Letitia's hands between his own. "They're fairly common around here. Are you all right?"

"Yes." She pulled her hands free and brushed distractedly at her hair. "I've heard of earthquakes, but I've never felt one. That horrible, rumbling sound. It seemed to go on forever."

"It always seems that way." Swen grinned. "Actually, they never last *that* long. Although, I must say this was the longest shake I've ever been in. How 'bout you, Adam?"

He returned his brother's smile. "I have to admit it ranks right up there as one of the biggest. We're lucky we were in the open. Quakes like this can do a lot of damage to adobe homes."

Letitia couldn't share the brothers' sense of exhilaration. What had just happened was terrible. The idea that the earth could shake even worse than it just had was horrific.

"How . . . how often does this happen?"

"It depends on where you are. Some places in California are more prone to earthquakes than others. Usually, when you get a bad jolt, you get a series of little quakes in the next couple of days or weeks. I don't think this one was that much, but you never know. I recommend we stay away from the cave tonight. I wouldn't like to be inside it should the earth start dancing around again."

She shuddered. The idea of being trapped inside the living earth while it twisted and shook was perhaps the most awful possibility she'd ever contemplated.

"Wonder if it did much damage?" Swen asked. "Hunt Ramsey, he lives in one of those adobe houses. If it came tumbling down on top of him it'd put paid to all our plans."

Adam nodded, his face grim. "I doubt that's the end Ma envisioned for him. Still, I don't reckon we should go see, do you?"

Swen nodded his agreement.

Letitia bit her lip, unable to shake the awful fear that the dreadful shaking might start again. What if Papa had been buried alive as Adam said? Had she come this far, lived through so much violence, only to have Papa die before she could reach him?

No matter what was happening now, Papa had been good to her when she was a little girl. He didn't deserve to be buried alive. He didn't deserve to die.

9

Letitia tried to recall where she'd been the last time she'd seen it rain. Texas? Maybe. She couldn't remember for sure. All she knew was each day since then had been filled with sunshine, the sky blue and cloudless. Today though, high gray clouds obscured the sun. The sky looked as if it might erupt at any moment.

She watched Adam and Swen use a complicated arrangement of ropes to booby trap the tree that arched over the trail leading from Adam's meadow to the south. When they were through, the two stepped back to admire their handiwork.

"Where did you learn to do this?" Swen asked.

"During the war. It's a skill I hadn't counted on needing again."

His grim face effectively quieted his younger

brother. In the silence that followed, the steady clip-clop sound of a horse traveling on the hard-packed earth of the path reached her ears.

"Hell!" Adam swiftly jerked up his rifle, herding Letitia, Swen, and the horses into the trees lining the trail.

"Ramsey?" Swen whispered.

"Wait here," Adam ordered. "Keep Letitia and those horses quiet. I'll go see."

He disappeared into the forest. Horrified, Swen glanced from their mounts to Letitia. She could read his expression easily. How could he silence her and the horses at the same time?

"I'll do what I have to do," she hissed, not even stopping to wonder why she was whispering.

"Please." Swen's hoarse voice revealed his dilemma. "Don't make me do something we'll both regret."

She sucked in her breath to yell. Swen's left hand clamped over her mouth. His right arm circled her shoulders, subduing her struggles at birth.

Adam suddenly materialized beside them. "You can let her go. It's the Bickles."

Swen's arms dropped to his sides. "Who?"

At the same time, Letitia exclaimed, "What?"

Adam ignored them both. "Bring the horses. Jonas's been shot. They need our help."

The Bickles? Letitia'd almost forgotten the nefarious clan and their connection with Adam. The way Jonas had treated her, and especially the way Walt had fondled her, flashed through her memory. She definitely didn't want to see any of the Bickles ever again. Clearly, it'd been a public-minded citizen who'd shot Jonas.

Still, Adam had said the Bickles needed help. It

didn't matter if she wanted to assist Jonas or not. She couldn't refuse to give whatever aid was within her capabilities. Her conscience required that she do what she could.

"What can I do?" she asked.

"No matter how those crooks treated you, I knew you'd back me up," Adam said, his smile of approval warming his eyes.

She felt a glow spreading through her in response to his praise. She'd always tried to do what was right, but until Adam, no one had cared if she followed her personal code of honor or not.

Letitia and Swen followed Adam back to the trail. A bay stood patiently, his coat roughened with sweat, its head drooping until its chin hung a few inches above the ground. Billy, his young face frightened, his shoulders sagging with tiredness, stood by the horse, gazing anxiously at the rider—Jonas. He slumped over in the saddle, his dirty hair straggling around his face, his hands hanging down limply.

"What happened?" Letitia exclaimed.

"A couple of men—they must have been Ramsey's —jumped them," Adam said. "Jonas was shot while he and Billy were trying to get away."

Adam stepped up to the injured man. "Can you hang on a bit longer?"

Jonas lifted his sweat-streaked face and nodded.

Adam picked up the bay's reins. "Swen, you and Letitia ride ahead to the campsite. It's closer than the cabin. Besides, what few medical supplies I've got are at the cave. Billy and I'll bring Jonas."

"No . . . medicine . . . can save me . . . now," Jonas panted. "I been . . . gut shot."

Letitia gasped. She turned to Adam, horrified. He

nodded, confirming Jonas's statement. "Go on," Adam said gently.

Swen mounted his mare. He leaned down and crooked his left arm. Letitia grabbed his sinewy forearm and he helped her leap onto the horse's rump. He urged the mare into a gallop and they raced back to the cave.

Swen pulled the horse to a halt in the small clearing. Letitia slid to the ground and looked up at him. "Adam will expect us to have things ready for Jonas. What do we do?"

Swen pushed his hat to the back of his head and blinked. "Don't ask me. I helped Ma some when she was sick, but I don't know nothing about gunshot wounds."

"Neither do I." Letitia gazed helplessly around the clearing. It was all so primitive. What could they do? "Let's try to be practical, at least," she decided. "It'll hurt Jonas terribly if we try to carry him into the cave. There are too many rocks in the way. I think we should bring some blankets out here for him to lie on. Besides, Adam will need the best light he can get."

"That makes sense," Swen agreed. "I'll tie up my mare and—"

"I'll get the blankets if you'll build up the fire," she interrupted. "We don't have any time to waste. Adam'll want hot water."

She and Swen were ready and waiting when Adam rode into the clearing. The Bickles' horse followed dispiritedly. Billy rode behind his father, holding Jonas in the saddle.

Letitia looked at the old man and gasped in horror. "Is he dead?"

Adam gently drew Jonas from the exhausted bay

and laid the elder Bickle on the blankets Letitia had prepared. Adam's steady gaze registered his approval of her preparations while his fingers searched for Jonas's pulse.

"He's still with us," Adam said.

She grabbed a rag and moistened it in the pot of water warming over the fire. She bathed Jonas's face. "What can I do?"

"Make him as comfortable as you can. I'm afraid that's about all we can do." Adam looked at Billy. "Where's Jonas's home brew? It'll help."

Billy gazed despondently at Adam. "When those men jumped us, they shot Pa's horse out from under him. That's where the whiskey was."

"Swen," Adam ordered, "bring me some of our rum." He knelt beside Jonas. "Sorry. My stuff isn't up to your usual standards."

"Just . . . give it . . . here." Jonas gasped.

While Adam carefully raised Jonas's shoulders, Swen ran to fill a tin cup with liquor. Letitia took one look at his frightened face and said, "Give me the rum." She held the cup to Jonas's lips and he sucked greedily.

"Careful," Letitia cautioned. "You don't want to start coughing."

"Bickles . . . can . . . hold . . . their . . . likker."

When the cup was empty, Adam lowered Jonas back to the ground. "Swen, is that water hot yet?"

"Almost."

To Jonas, Adam said, "I'm going to take a look and see if I can do anything."

"You cain't." Jonas's voice grew stronger as the alcohol entered his system. "I'm a goner for sure, boy."

"That remains to be seen."

Jonas's hand grabbed Letitia's, his grip bruisingly tight. "Sorry, Missy."

"For what?" she asked, surprised.

"For taking you from that stagecoach." His voice faded and his breath rasped in his throat. "For . . . making you . . . bury your friend."

Caught off guard, Letitia bit her lip.

How could she respond? She couldn't lie, couldn't make herself tell him it didn't matter, for it did. Nothing, not even time, could truly erase the pain and terror she'd suffered at the hands of the Bickles. They'd started a disastrous chain of events that nothing could undo.

If it hadn't been for Jonas, she'd be safe and secure with Papa right this minute. She wouldn't be trapped in the wilderness, holding this ruffian's hand, helplessly watching him die. She wouldn't have met Adam, wouldn't have behaved so irresponsibly, wouldn't have gotten caught up in his personal battle with Papa.

In spite of all her regrets, pity for Jonas swept through her. If it hadn't been for Papa, Jonas would still be hale and hearty, doubtlessly committing a crime somewhere or the other. She couldn't condone his misdeeds, but she didn't believe that he deserved to die for them, either.

Swen lifted a large pot from the water. He and Billy carried the steaming container the few steps it took to reach the injured man's side.

"Okay." Adam carefully pulled Jonas's blood-stained vest and shirt away from the wound in his left side. The skin was bruised purple and caked with dark, gelatinous matter. A fresh trickle of bright red blood oozed from the black-rimmed hole.

Letitia bit her lip as she gazed at the unsightly mess. Her stomach heaved. She forced her gorge back, hanging onto Jonas's hand as tightly as he grasped hers.

Billy made an odd, gasping kind of moan and fainted dead away. His body crashed to the earth with a heavy thud.

Harassed, Adam glanced at Swen. "Get Billy on his back. I reckon he's just passed out. Even so, make sure he's still breathing. If he is, don't try to revive him. He'll come around soon enough."

"But, Adam . . ." Swen protested.

Adam twisted around to look at his brother. "I know it sounds heartless, but trust me. A lot of men faint at the sight of blood. It'll be better for Billy if he doesn't have to watch this."

Adam completed his examination of the wounded man. He rocked back on his heels and faced Letitia. "Bickle's right. There's nothing I can do for him. I don't think a doctor could help, either. The bullet's still in there and there's no way in hell anyone can dig it out without killing Jonas in the process. What amazes me is the fact he's lasted this long."

"It . . . takes a lot . . . to kill . . . a Bickle," Jonas wheezed.

"Don't try to talk," Letitia said in a soothing voice.

"Why?" Jonas demanded. "Gonna die . . . anyway. Gimme likker. Got something . . . say."

Adam raised Jonas's shoulders while Letitia refilled the cup. Together, they helped the old man drink. Distracted by a rustling sound, Letitia noticed Billy stirring. Swen helped the younger Bickle to sit up. Billy, his face white and strained, gazed blankly at his father.

Jonas finished the second cup of rum. His pale blue eyes appeared glazed. Letitia wasn't sure if it was the liquor's effect, or the fact that he clearly didn't have much longer left to live.

"Better?" Adam asked.

Jonas nodded carefully. He twisted his head to gaze at Letitia. "You believe in God, Missy?"

"Yes. Of course."

"My Pearl, she did, too." Jonas lifted his hand a few inches from the ground. His voice grew stronger. "Billy. Your ma always said I'd come to a bad end. Don't be like your pa, son. Pearl, she said something when our baby girl died." He moaned, unable to continue.

"A prayer?" Letitia asked.

Jonas's faded blue eyes pleaded with her silently. His breath rasped as he fought to form a word and failed.

"What prayer?" She racked her brain, trying to think. The Lord's Prayer, perhaps? Everyone knew that. But was it the comfort a dying man sought? No, she didn't think so. A prayer for a dying child, a prayer to comfort a grieving mother. She decided on the psalm that always comforted her the most.

"The Lord is my shepherd," Letitia began. "I shall not want."

Jonas's hand tightened around hers. A single tear crept down the side of his lined, grizzled cheek.

"He maketh me to lie down in green pastures," Adam continued the psalm, his voice low and hoarse.

Together they finished the words. "Amen," Letitia whispered. Jonas's fingers slipped from hers and fell limply to the ground. Adam leaned forward and closed the old man's eyelids, covering the sightless gaze.

Letitia tried to swallow the lump in her throat, tried to convince herself Jonas didn't deserve her tears. He was a crook, a thief, a murderer. He'd come to the end he richly deserved. That being the case, why did she want to hide and bawl her eyes out?

Adam swiveled away from the body and faced Billy. "I'm sorry," he said.

He helped Billy up and guided him toward the cave, away from his father's still body. Swen followed. Letitia crossed the dead man's hands over his chest. "Lord, have mercy on thy servant, Jonas," she said.

Perhaps the Lord would. In dying, Jonas had turned to God for comfort. Wasn't that what Christianity was supposed to be about? Not justice, not vengeance, but simple charity, understanding, and forgiveness.

"I'll never forget you, Jonas," she said softly. She sniffed and forced herself to stand and join the living.

"It hasn't been much of a month for the Bickles." Billy sat on a low, flat rock, his knees pulled up to his chest, his arms wrapped around his knees. "You sent us sniffing around those banks of Ramsey's in the territory."

Adam nodded.

"Well," Billy continued. "Walt got the idea we oughta rob the one in Yuma. Pa was all for it. And me," Billy laughed derisively. "I don't never get no vote. They reckoned you wouldn't know nothing about the robbery, so the money'd be all ours. What they hadn't reckoned on was the fact that those bank guards meant business. One of 'em kilt Walt."

Letitia remembered Walt's snakelike eyes and what he'd wanted to do to her. She shivered. Somehow, she couldn't feel the compassion for him she'd experienced for Jonas. But, maybe that was because Walt hadn't held her hand while he died. How had things gotten so confusing? Why couldn't they be black and white—simple?

"Walt was a loaded gun. He was always looking for trouble." Adam gestured helplessly. "What can I say?"

"I reckon it was better than swinging from some tree." Billy shrugged his shoulders. "Walt would've hated that. Anyway, we had to get out of the territory, fast. We had a posse after us. We dodged down Mexico way and lost them. Pa, he decided we'd come find you. After all, you owe us money for what we've been doing."

"So I do," Adam said. " 'Course what Walt and Jonas decided to do in Yuma has nothing to do with me."

"Yeah, I know." Billy hung his head. "Seems like I've been listening to those two for so long I hardly know right from wrong."

"We'll talk about the money later," Adam said. "How did Jonas get shot?"

"This morning we ran into two men." Billy laced his fingers together. "They stopped us—"

"Were they Ramsey's men?"

"I dunno who they were working for. They could have been following us from that robbery back in the territory. Still, Pa reckoned we oughta jump 'em first and ask questions later. So we did. It was all pretty mixed up, what with the shouting and all the bullets flying around, but I remember seeing Pa's horse go down. When it was through, Pa was shot and one of the other men was dead. I think another was wounded, but I don't know how bad, 'cause he lit a shuck outta there. I could tell Pa was real bad, so I loaded him up on my horse and went looking for your ranch. I didn't know what else to do."

"You did the right thing," Adam said. "Those two men. What did they say?"

"Not much. They wanted to know if we knew you, wanted to know if we had any idea where you are. You've sure lit a fire under Ramsey's tail, Adam. What've you done to him?"

"Not enough," Adam said grimly.

Letitia seized on the one piece of information vital to herself in all Billy had communicated: Papa hadn't died in that earthquake. Better yet, he had his men out looking for her. He did want her after all!

But at what cost? Two men were dead, maybe three. Papa's men weren't murderers. If Jonas had cooperated, he'd be alive right now. So would the man they'd killed.

She gazed at Adam. Even if he hadn't done the actual killing, he was responsible for starting the chain of events that led to three deaths. Letitia didn't even know why he was doing what he was doing. It didn't matter any more. She didn't need to know. Nothing could justify death.

They buried Jonas at the very edge of the clearing, at the opposite end from the spring. Billy gazed down at the fresh mound of earth. "Ma always said Pa'd come to a bad end. She said none of us would live to a ripe old age." A bitter smile twisted Billy's face. "Pa now, he could be pretty ripe—"

"Take it easy." Adam placed his hand on Billy's shoulder. "You're welcome to stay with us as long as you want while you sort out what you want to do."

"Thanks."

"If I were you, I don't think I'd thank me for that offer." Adam rubbed his hand over his face. "Ramsey's out for blood, my blood preferably. I'm not a very healthy man to be around right now. It might be smartest for you to take the money I owe your pa and head out of here."

"Head where? Do what?"

Adam didn't have an answer.

Billy shrugged. "I reckon I'll stay awhile. I don't have anything better to do. Not yet, that is. One thing's for sure. I'm damn well not going to live the sort of life Pa and Walt did. I'm going to settle down and make something outa myself. Pa always said Bickles were the best, but I reckon that was just bluster on his part. Me, though, I'm gonna make it come true. This Bickle's going to amount to something."

Adam offered his hand to Billy. "I'm glad to hear that. If I can help you in any way, you just ask. In the meantime, I'm glad you decided to stay. You're a good man to have around."

They turned and walked away from the grave. A few drops of rain splattered down. Swen followed Adam and Billy, but Letitia lagged behind. She felt so tired, and dizzy, too. She angled off toward the cave, barely making it to where the rocks jumbled around the entrance.

She felt awful. Queasiness assailed her. She shut her eyes, fighting the sickness within her. Suddenly, she bolted for a bush and emptied the contents of her stomach, still retching even when there was nothing left. She heard someone moving through the brush.

"Letitia!" Adam knelt beside her. "What's wrong?"

"What's wrong?" She rounded on him. "What could possibly be wrong? I just held a man's hand and watched him die. That might be a common, everyday occurrence for you, but it's not for me. It's no wonder I'm sick."

"All right. I know this hasn't been easy—"

"Easy!"

"Just calm down, will you." He reached for her hands. "It'll be over soon.

She pulled away. "And by then how many more men will have died? Let me go, Adam. Whatever it is you want, it's not worth it. Nothing could possibly be worth it."

"I told you, you don't understand."

"Oh, I understand. I understand all too well."

She forced herself to her feet and stalked away. She would not let him see how tired she was, how sick to death she was of all this. You just couldn't reason with the man.

Dinner was a depressing meal. The sky, which had been threatening and overcast all day, finally began to drizzle steadily. Swen took his slicker and went to stand guard duty at the edge of the clearing. Adam, Billy, and Letitia sought shelter in the cave. A fire burned just inside the entrance, but it did little to alleviate the chill from the clammy rock.

Letitia tucked her blankets securely around her shoulders and tried to sleep. But who could sleep with Billy snoring like that?

Exhaustion seemed to ripple through her arms and legs. Her mind whirled, with flashes of the dreadful day she'd spent firing across her memory in quick succession. The awful nausea attacked her again. She knew she was going to be sick. She darted around the fire and groped her way toward the darkness beyond the flames. She reached the bushes just in time for her stomach to return its meal once again.

"Oh, God," Letitia moaned. Were those tears on her face, or was it the rain? She felt tired, so tired. If she could just get warm and get some sleep, she'd be fine. She'd be even better if she could get away from this terrible place. It was all Adam's fault. But for him, she'd be with Papa, safe, secure, warm and, most of all, well.

Adam joined her. His voice penetrated the dark. "What's wrong? You've been sick again, haven't you?"

She gritted her teeth and forced herself to admit the truth. "Yes." The silence stretched out between them, fraught with tension. She tried to explain, as much to herself as to him. "It must be because I'm so upset. That's the only thing that makes sense."

He breathed a sigh of relief. "You'll be better in the morning."

She snorted. "A fat lot you care."

"What do you mean by that?"

"How should I know?"

He peered at her, trying to make out her expression while they stood at the very edge of the circle of firelight. "Don't play games with me. What is wrong with you?"

"I'll tell you what's wrong!" Letitia spat. "We both know I'm no Helen of Troy. Yet you and Papa are fighting over me as if I were . . . as if I were a piece of property. How do you think that makes me feel? It makes me sick. That's what it does. Because of your . . . your . . . !"

Her fists clenched, her nails dug into the soft flesh of her palms. He tried to speak but she rushed on. "Because of your . . . your mysterious crusade, one innocent man died today and another's been wounded, perhaps mortally. Jonas certainly was no innocent but he didn't deserve to die, either. If you hadn't decided to hold me for ransom, all those people would still be alive. It's all due to you, Adam. You may not have pulled the trigger, but you're a—"

"Don't!" His hands flashed out to seize her shoulders. "Don't say it."

"Murderer! Why shouldn't I? It's the truth, isn't it?"

He flinched. In the flickering light, his face was pale gray, his eyes unreadable. "Is that what you think of me?" he asked, his voice low and furious. "Is that what you think?"

She stared up at him, tears pricking at the backs of her eyes. Her lips trembled. "How do you expect me to react? Aren't you a murderer?"

His hands fell away from her shoulders and he disappeared into the shadows beyond the fire.

"No, Adam," she said softly. "I don't really think you're a murderer." She strained to see him in the dark. "It's just I'm so frightened I might end up helplessly holding your hand, watching you die, just the way I did today when I watched Jonas die. Please, please end this . . . this whatever it is. Not for my sake, but for yours . . . before you really do become a murderer."

She paused. Had he heard her? The wind rustled the leaves in the trees, a precursor of a heavy blast of air. The heavens opened, rain gushing down in a hard, fast torrent. Letitia ran back to the cave for shelter and crawled between her blankets. Where had Adam gone?

Swen ducked inside the mouth of the cave, water cascading from his slicker. He shed the garment and knelt to warm his hands at the fire.

She raised herself up on one elbow. "What happened to Adam?"

"He came to relieve me." Swen grinned, his teeth a white flash in the gloom. "Personally, I don't think a sentry is necessary tonight. The way it's raining right now, I wouldn't be surprised if the animals started lining up, two by two. But he insisted. He won't leave anything to chance. Not my brother. Ramsey'll be dog meat by the time Adam is through with him."

"Why is he doing this?" Letitia questioned.

Swen turned to stare into the flames. "Don't ask me questions I can't answer."

"You mean won't," she flared.

"Can't, won't." Swen shrugged his shoulders. "It's the same thing, as far as you're concerned."

The weather remained stormy for the next two days. Letitia began to think Swen's quip about forty days and forty nights might be prophetic. The heavy weather made it impossible to stay outside. The smoky, sullen fire at the mouth of the cave seldom challenged the damp chill that seemed to penetrate her very bones. She thought she'd never been so miserable as she battled both the wretched weather and her persistent nausea.

On the third evening she listened gratefully to the silence—no more rain. By sunrise the sky was clear, except for a few lingering clouds to the east. She climbed out of the cave and sat on a handy boulder next to the pocket campfire at the mouth of the cave. She nursed a cup of coffee while her stomach roiled at the thought of actually sipping the bitter liquid.

Fatigue tugged at her shoulders. Since their fight by the fire, Adam had studiously ignored her. She still felt positively awful, but luckily she'd been able to conceal her sickness from him. She didn't want him to see how badly he'd upset her with his lust for revenge.

She had no concept of the number of days that had passed, but she knew it'd been a long time—time enough for her body to follow its normal monthly cycle. She tried to count the days since her idyll with him at the desert oasis. She had to accept the fact that her monthly flux was severely past due.

She'd never been regular, but she couldn't attribute her state to all she'd experienced since she'd left Kentucky. Now, as she bit back the ever-present nausea, she had to accept the fact she'd refused to consider. She was pregnant.

The thought frightened her. What could she do?

Adam seemed so sure Papa and his men would appear. But they hadn't, in spite of what Billy had said the day Jonas died. The waiting wore everyone down, especially Adam. He seemed to be in a constant state of bad temper. It served him right, she thought, that Papa wouldn't dance to a tune of Adam's piping.

But what would she do, unmarried and pregnant, if Papa claimed her now? Would insist on her marrying to legitimize her baby? She knew firsthand what happened when a man was coerced into a marriage to give an unborn child a name.

No matter what, she didn't intend to force her baby into the sort of life she'd lived. Better for him to be born knowing his mother loved him than to be born with an indifferent father, or even worse, a father who didn't want a child and wouldn't help him in times of trouble.

She'd heard tales from the slaves about voodoo women who could get rid of a baby. She had no idea if women like that even existed in California. She prayed they didn't and promised herself no one would make her seek out the services of such a person.

She'd never wanted to be pregnant with Adam's child, but it'd happened. Her life would be immeasurably easier if she weren't pregnant, but the knowledge that she was carrying a child filled her with awe and wonder.

How could she possibly tell Adam? She simply had to find a way to escape. But with Swen and Billy always around, and Adam glowering at her when he deigned to notice her, she had no idea how she could get away.

Swen and Billy walked up to the fire. Swen poured each of them a cup of coffee and gestured with the pot toward his brother.

Adam held out his cup, saying nothing.

"We're running low on supplies," Swen said.

Adam nodded. "That, and we've made serious inroads on the game around here. We could always butcher another steer. Thing is, the meat goes bad before we can eat it all. I hate waste like that."

"What do we do for coffee and flour and sweetening?"

Adam didn't have an answer.

"One of us will have to make the trip." Swen glanced at Letitia. "I guess I'm elected."

"I'll go with you." Billy shuffled his feet awkwardly. "I'm one of the reasons you all are low on food. It'll be safer if two of us go together."

"I can't let either of you go," Adam said. "It'll be dangerous. Ramsey must have his men out searching for us. What if you cross paths with them?"

Swen turned to face Adam. "What if Ramsey's men show up while we're gone? No matter what you said when we were setting all those booby traps, you can't hold them off alone."

Adam frowned. "One man is all it'll take. I'm ready for them." He wasn't boasting, he was merely stating facts. "It's safer here than it'll be out on the trail."

Swen snorted. "Safety's no good when there's nothing to eat. Billy and I'll be careful."

Adam rested his hand briefly on his taller brother's shoulder. "Damn, but this sitting around wears a man out. Why won't Ramsey come? I know he's waging a war of nerves, just waiting for one of us to appear. He has to know we're holed up somewhere in these mountains. I reckon his strategy is to lie back and let us make the first move. You two heading out will be the first move. It's sheer stupidity to play into his hands."

"Starving to death isn't very smart either."

"We won't starve to death. We may have to work at it, but there's enough game."

"And plenty of nothing else." Swen looked earnestly at Adam. "Someone's got to go for food. I, for one, see no need to go without coffee when it's not necessary. Billy and I can get the supplies and be back here in a couple of days. We'll be fine, honest."

Adam was silent, considering. At last he said, reluctantly, "Okay. You win. We do need food. But you'll go north, and loop back around to Temecula. It'll take a while longer but it'll be safer. Even though that ranch of Ramsey's is a good ways north of San Diego, it's still his town."

"We'll be fine," Swen said. "Don't worry."

Adam frowned. "I don't like it, but as you pointed out there aren't a lot of choices. For God's sake, don't take any chances."

Letitia watched Swen and Billy guide their horses

away from the primitive campsite. Adam stood beside
the dying embers of the small morning fire, his shoulders rigid, his face grim. He turned, and snatched up
his Enfield rifle. "You can come with me," he told Letitia. "I want to check the trap lines and see if Ramsey
or any of his men are stirring around."

"I won't run away," she said a trifle too hastily.

"That so?" The glint in his blue eyes reflected his
uncertain temper.

She felt herself blushing under his skeptical regard
and tried to think of a way to keep the betraying color
from her cheeks. She bent and fiddled with the buttons
on her boots. That would give her an excuse for her
red face.

"It'll do you good to get some exercise," he pointed
out. "Ever since Jonas died, you haven't been past the
clearing."

"Whose fault is that?"

"Ramsey's."

"Oh, all right." She stood, feeling lightheaded from
her sudden movement. "But don't expect me to help
you slay whatever it is you intend to catch."

"Fair enough."

She fell into step behind him as he led the way
through the still sodden forest. In the leafy gloom, his
broad shoulders and narrow hips were silhouetted before her. She couldn't help admiring the economy of
his movements as he stealthily made his way along the
game path. She rushed to keep up with his effortless
stride. At least she felt better, moving. The nausea
wasn't so bad. Even though she carried her exhaustion
like a burden on her back, she felt almost at peace as
she absorbed the gentle quiet of the forest.

He stopped, turned, and pantomimed extreme caution before he took her hand and guided her to stand next to him. He pointed. She looked through the trees at a tiny clearing.

A doe bent her head and licked at her tiny fawn as he lay on the ground. The small creature's ears twitched. The deer butted her baby with her head. He struggled convulsively, his fragile legs failing for a few moments. The doe made an encouraging sound, a sort of a bleat, and licked her fawn again. His head bobbed and this time he managed to get his legs under control and heave himself into a standing position.

The doe bleated again. The fawn's legs splayed out. He wobbled from side to side, almost collapsing when his mother licked him again. With a nudge from her nose, the doe managed to guide her baby to her udder. The fawn sucked thirstily, his tiny tail twitching from side to side.

The doe looked up. It seemed to Letitia as if the deer stared straight at her. She glanced at Adam, her mouth suddenly dry. They'd come into the forest, hunting. Meat from a deer would feed them for several days. She knew firsthand the rigors of survival in this deceptively beautiful but dangerous land.

Adam's rifle still hung from his hand. He made no motion to lift it to his shoulder. Instead, he took Letitia's hand and led her away from the peaceful, sun-dappled clearing.

When he was sure the doe wouldn't hear them, he stopped. "I think what we saw was that baby's first meal."

She nodded, wordlessly.

He smiled. "There is something to be said for living in a city and having your food come to you already cooked."

"I'm glad you didn't kill her," Letitia said softly.

"I couldn't," he admitted. He hefted his Enfield. "Of course, if the rest of the snares are empty we'll be reduced to eating berries or butchering another one of my steers. If I had my druthers, I'd just as soon not do either one."

"Even if it is berries, I'll still be glad."

"That's good."

He looked down at her, fighting the familiar longing to take her into his arms. He'd let her words get under his skin the night they'd fought. He'd let her drive him away and as a result he'd stupidly stood too long in the rain. His throat felt scratchy. That was all he needed— a cold on top of everything else.

What she'd said gnawed at his soul. There was a measure of truth in her accusation. He hated it, but he couldn't deny it. Where in the hell was Ramsey? What did the man think he was doing? How could he treat his daughter so?

She and that fawn, innocents both, were at the mercy of men who indiscriminately murdered whatever lay in their paths as they chased after success. Adam forced himself to recall his mother's letter and her worn face the last time he'd seen her. His memories lacked the necessary power.

He swore viciously, destroying the fragile moment of understanding between him and Letitia.

She stared at him. It seemed to him as if her eyes were as wild and as frightened as that doe's might have been if she'd seen them. Yet Letitia's words were at odds with her appearance.

"Do the berries you mentioned really taste that bad?"

He smiled, his lips parting with genuine humor.

"Worse." He turned and looked back over his shoulder. "Come on. We've still got ground to cover."

In the next snare Adam found a rabbit. She spun around so she wouldn't have to witness him dispatching the animal. She knew they had to eat, but the thought of consuming another gamy rabbit was just too much. She fell to her knees and tried to control her stomach.

"Letitia!"

She tried to stand and run away from him but didn't have the strength to go more than a few stumbling steps.

His strong hands held her back. Another spasm racked her body and he knelt with her, cradling her, his hand on her forehead. When she was through he pulled her onto his lap, wrapping his arms tightly around her. He brushed her hair away from her clammy face.

She buried her head in the curve of his shoulder. What heaven to be close to him, secure within his arms, breathing in his masculine scent, absorbing his strength.

"What's wrong?" he asked gently.

"Nothing," she mumbled.

"What?"

"Nothing," she repeated in a stronger voice.

"That's right, nothing," Adam echoed, an ironic edge to his tone. "You've been throwing up pretty regularly since Jonas died. I know that's enough to upset anyone, especially someone who's been as sheltered as you have. But you should be getting over it. Do you hurt anywhere?"

She looked up at him and shook her head.

"What about a headache?" His hand rested on her forehead. "Have you been running a fever?"

There wasn't anything seductive about his gesture, but she couldn't maintain her equilibrium with his fingers on her flesh. She twisted away. "I'm fine, honestly."

He let her slide off his lap and reached for the canteen lying on the grass by his side. "I haven't anything to offer but water."

She concentrated on watching his strong, brown hands uncork the container. It'd been heaven resting in his arms. She knew she'd done the right thing, moving away from him. The knowledge didn't make her feel any better. She wished she could turn back the clock and regain the peace of just a few moments ago.

"Do you want a sip?"

She nodded. He guided the canteen to her lips. "Rinse your mouth out, first."

She complied and then drank the water. Again, he pulled her across his chest. Just for a moment, she promised herself as she luxuriated in his nearness.

"I'll be fine." She knew she was reassuring herself as much as she was reassuring him. "I didn't think you'd noticed I'd been sick."

"I notice everything about you."

His arms tightened around her and he gazed down at her brown head nestled against his shoulder. In a sudden flash of revelation he accepted the fact that all his scheming might not work. Damn it, maybe the whole thing had been a bad idea from the very beginning.

He knew his mother had seemed unbalanced in the last years of her life. Yet he'd foolishly taken her cause for his own. Now he'd inextricably involved Letitia in his convoluted plotting. Worse, she'd become ill.

He had Ramsey by the tail like a tiger, and Adam couldn't let go. Yet he knew he must. He had to abandon his pursuit of Ramsey, at least temporarily, for Letitia's sake. Hers was the greater need.

She'd denied any pain, but she was so fragile. The idea of stomach fever caused his insides to knot with fear. Whatever she had, and he prayed it wasn't something fatal, she clearly needed the attention of a doctor.

Hell, he didn't feel all that great himself. His throat hurt and his chest felt tight. Standing out in the middle of that storm hadn't been one of his wisest moves. What can't be cured must be endured, he reminded himself. Or, failing that, ignored.

His mind made up, he rose to his feet, Letitia still cradled in his arms. A smile touched the edges of his mouth as her arms went around his neck. No matter what she'd said that night, she did trust him, by God. The decision to leave was easy—pure and simple and surprisingly painless. Ramsey could wait.

She struggled in his arms. "What are you doing?"

"Taking you back to the camp," Adam said.

Treacherous thoughts invaded her mind as she remembered their time together in the desert. She had to be strong. She couldn't let herself be seduced again. "Put me down. I can walk."

"I don't think you can."

"Of course I can." She had to free herself from this exquisite torture. "Besides, you can't carry me all that way."

He smiled tenderly at her and echoed, "Of course I can."

She wriggled, fighting the tantalizing touch of his hands, as traitorous impulses raced through her blood, tempting her to give in to seduction once again.

He paused, tightening his hold on her. "At least, I could carry you if you'd stop thrashing around."

She struggled all the harder. He swore and lost his grip, and her feet touched the ground. She backed away, gulping in mouthfuls of reviving fresh air.

"Honestly, I'm fine." She tried to convince herself as much as him. "I can walk back to the camp."

He gazed down at her, his blue eyes reflecting his concern. "Are you sure you're okay?"

She didn't answer him because she couldn't. She didn't have an answer. She only knew she had to get away from him before she gave in to temptation. She forced herself to stride away, following the game trail.

He watched the seductive sway of her hips as she walked away, her undulating shadow elongated by the rapidly setting sun.

"Hell!" he swore. The light would be mostly gone by the time they got back to Buck and the cave. The moon was less than a quarter and rising late. There wouldn't be enough light to travel safely at night. They'd have to wait until sunrise.

He didn't believe much in prayer but he sent a silent thought upward to whoever might be listening. "Please, let her be okay."

She did feel better, too, until that evening when Adam cooked the rabbit. She gritted her teeth and tried to endure but the smell of the meat seemed to twist her stomach inside out.

He found her crouched behind a boulder.

"That's it!" he exclaimed. "Why are you so damned bullheaded? I don't care if there isn't any moon tonight. As soon as I can get Buck saddled we're leaving. You need a doctor."

"I don't!" The last thing in the world she needed was a doctor. He'd tell Adam she was pregnant and then what would she do? "Don't make me go!"

He shook his head from side to side with awful finality. "You need medical attention and that's all there is to it. You could die if you don't get help."

"I won't die," she said flatly. At least not yet, she amended to herself. Women did die in childbirth, but she'd never heard of anyone dying just because they were pregnant. "I know what's wrong with me. No doctor can cure it."

He grasped her shoulders, his hands curling tightly around her shoulders. "Okay. What is it that can't be cured?"

Stricken, she stared up at him. She'd almost told him. If she wasn't careful, he'd figure out what ailed her. She gestured helplessly. "It's just the steady diet of wild game. It doesn't agree with me. When Swen and Billy get back with the supplies—when I can eat normal food, I'll be fine."

Adam looked at her, his eyes narrowed to thoughtful slits. "I don't believe you. You're lying. I have no idea what you're trying to hide, but it isn't going to work. We're leaving."

"W-what about your ransom? What about Papa? You've kept me for weeks and weeks. Now, just because I've got a little stomach upset, you're wild to get rid of me. I don't understand."

He glared at her. "You don't understand? I don't understand. I thought you'd be wild with relief at a chance to return to civilization."

"Well . . ." Letitia crossed her arms across her

chest and thought furiously. "Of course I am. But you know I'll try to escape. In a town, my chances of getting away are much better."

"Don't count on it."

"I am." She tried what she thought was a very convincing laugh. "If I thought a little nausea would've persuaded you to take me away from here, I'd have gotten sick weeks ago." She shut her eyes and swayed theatrically. "I don't feel very good."

She peeped through her lashes at him, wondering if she'd managed to convince him of her good health. She increased the angle of her sway.

"Stop playing around." He grabbed her arms and shook her. "Pardon my bad manners, but I've got irrefutable evidence that you're ill. Sit down and don't move. We're leaving!"

What could she do? And what would she do when Adam found out she was pregnant?

10

Letitia watched Adam stalk away and duck to enter the mouth of the cave. Her thoughts raced furiously as she wondered what to do next. If she did see a doctor, could she convince him not to tell Adam? And even if she could, if Adam didn't let her go soon, he'd find out anyway. Pregnancy couldn't be disguised for long.

She started rehearsing arguments in her mind while she watched him come back into the clearing. As he straightened, the earth started to shake. Her thoughts centered on gauging the movement as she tried to decide if this earthquake was going to be worse than the last one. She had her answer when a tremendous jerk twisted the earth violently, throwing her to the ground.

She rolled helplessly, and dug her fingers into the

dirt to stop her wild slide, and hung on, too witless to even think about praying for deliverance. Stunned, she stared across the clearing at Adam as he fought to keep his balance. His feet were spread wide apart, his arms outstretched, as he rode out the earthquake. She imagined that a man balanced on the deck of a ship while riding out a wild storm at sea would look just the same.

As she watched, one of the rocks balanced on the hill above the cave broke away and tumbled down the slope. It seemed as if her scream had lodged tight in her chest, but somehow she managed to shriek over the sickening rumble of the earth, "Adam! Watch out!"

She saw him react to her cry. Yet it took several precious seconds before he comprehended her warning and twisted his head to follow her pointing hand.

Several more boulders broke loose and started to roll. Adam leaped back and flattened himself against the bare rock at the opening to the cave. The avalanche started with agonizing slowness and then gained speed with incredible swiftness, rushing down the mountainside above the cave. The rush of tumbling, turning stones drowned out the incessant groaning of the tortured earth. The landslide slowed to a steady stream of debris, but the quaking of the earth continued relentlessly. More stones rained down, and an anvil-sized rock thudded against Adam's left shoulder.

She couldn't hear if he made any sound over the cacophony of the earthquake. But she could see his pain, and her body tightened in an agonized reflex just as his did. He fell, hidden from her sight by a steady stream of rocks, dirt, and other debris that marked the tail end of the avalanche.

Heedless of the still-quaking ground, the horrible groaning of the earth, and the rocks tumbling all around, Letitia struggled to her feet and tried to run. The earth heaved viciously and she fell to her knees. Reverberations from the quake filled the air. More rocks rained down. She feared Adam would be buried alive. She tried to stand but she couldn't find her balance as everything twisted and jerked until she felt as if she were a drop of water skating across a sizzling-hot griddle. She crawled on her hands and knees, intent on only one thing—reaching Adam, helping him.

Then, as quickly as it'd started, the earth stood still.

She propelled herself forward, racing toward him. As she came closer, she could see he'd been knocked flat on his back. Luckily, the rocks that had landed close to the cave had built a small protective cairn around him.

Letitia looked down at his still form, at his dust-coated features. She shuddered involuntarily and twisted her hands together.

Then her fingers stilled. She stood, stunned for a moment, struck by the knowledge that this disaster had freed her. There was nothing, no one to stop her from saddling up Buck and simply riding away. She could go anywhere she wanted. She could do anything she wished. The idea of complete and total freedom overwhelmed her, took her breath away.

The idea of escape was paramount in her mind. From the hillside above, a rock the size of a lump of coal broke loose and rolled away. Startled, she twisted back to watch the movement. The rock came to rest not far from Adam.

She realized there was one thing she couldn't do. Call it conscience, honor, duty, or whatever. She couldn't leave him lying there, helpless, probably injured, perhaps dying. She just couldn't do it.

Letitia yanked at the first stone she could reach, and the pile shifted. She heard him moan and her hands stilled.

"Careful," she whispered. One false move and the rocks could bury him. She forced herself to look critically at the heap of stone, dirt, and rubble. The larger boulders had rolled further down the hillside, miraculously missing her, Buck, and the stream. One of the huge rocks had stopped above Jonas' grave, an impromptu headstone.

She sent a small prayer skyward and pulled at the top rock. It came free and a shower of pebbles rained down on Adam.

"What the—" he sputtered. Then, on a sharply indrawn breath, he groaned and bit off the rest of what he'd intended to say.

"She pulled at the smaller pieces, flinging them behind her, digging away like a terrier chasing a rat, until she managed to clear away enough rubble to reach him. One wheel-sized boulder rested only a hair's breath from his head. She breathed a silent prayer of thanksgiving. An inch more to the right . . . She shoved at the heavy rock trapping his left side.

The stone moved. Adam groaned, his muscles tightening as he fought his pain.

"Merciful heaven. What is it?" She touched his hand. "Please, God," she said. "Make him be all right."

Adam's eyelids opened to narrow slits, barely allowing her to see his blue irises. "Shoulder." He gasped. "Dislocated. Happened . . . before. Help me . . . stand."

"I'll do no such thing!" Letitia exclaimed. "You're hurt. You can't walk."

"I can do . . . what I have to do."

She wiped her damp palms down the front of her pants legs. He was right. He couldn't lie there amidst the rubble. She had to do something.

"I know what to do." His words were all run together as if he didn't have enough breath to fight the pain and talk at the same time.

She grabbed his right arm and struggled to pull him into a sitting position. He bit back an exclamation of pain, but she ignored it.

"I have to get you away." She glanced at the hillside. The remaining boulders looked ominously unstable. She shoved her shoulder under his good one. "You're right. You've got to move away from here. Please, Adam. Help me help you to stand."

He nodded, his jaw tightly clenched.

Letitia shoved and he struggled to his feet. She wrapped her left arm around his waist, supporting his heavy weight the best she could as they stumbled away. They covered less than ten yards when he tripped and went down to his knees, his right hand supporting his left elbow.

"Far . . . enough," he gasped.

She helped lower him to the ground, panting as if she'd just run a mile at top speed. Adam might not be as tall as his brother Swen, but he was solid muscle. She knew she never could have moved him if he hadn't helped her make the effort.

She gazed down at him. He lay flat on his back, his face streaked with sweat, the lines that ran from his beaky nose to his mouth transformed into deep grooves. His mouth was compressed into a straight line, his eyes tightly shut, his body rigid.

She had to find a way to help him. She couldn't just leave him stretched out on the cold earth. She rushed toward the cave, avoiding the fresh rock fall littered about the entrance, intent on retrieving the blankets and Adam's medical supplies. Almost as if she'd run into a solid barrier, she stopped dead in front of the debris-strewn opening. What if another earthquake started while she was in there? What if she were buried alive? What if . . . ?

She glanced over her shoulder at Adam's still form, gritted her teeth, and dashed into the cave, snatching up blankets and his saddle bags. She ran back through the opening into the fresh air, breathing a heartfelt sigh of relief. She knew she'd never feel comfortable in a confined space again.

She dropped to her knees by his side, rolling a blanket into a pillow for his head. He stirred and squinted at her.

"Find some . . . rope."

"What for?"

"Damn it! So I can put . . . this arm back."

"I'll do it." Her stomach lurched at the thought of causing him physical anguish. "I saw the head groom at Bellewood fix a jockey's shoulder when he fell off a racehorse last year."

Adam's lips twisted. "Better . . . let me take care . . . of it. You won't . . . enjoy doing it."

"No matter who does it, I can guarantee you won't enjoy it either," she said.

He looked up at her, his eyes bright with pain. "Go

ahead," he ordered. His lips tried to form a semblance of his normal cocky grin. "Do your worst."

She forced herself to block out everything except the necessity of remembering what she'd seen the head groom do. She twisted around, placed her foot in Adam's left armpit and grasped his flaccid left hand.

"Don't be frightened," he said.

Frightened? Images of the Bickles dragging her across the desert, Greedy crashing down the ravine, the bear chasing her up the tree crowded in her memory. Each time she'd thought she'd been scared witless, but none of those experiences could compare with the horror of deliberately causing pain to the man . . . to the man she loved.

She didn't want to love him, didn't want to care. She couldn't cope with this revelation right now. She had to ignore it. She had to! Anger swept through her, clearing her mind, giving her the strength to do what she had to do.

"That rock should have bounced off your head," Letitia scolded. "Then there wouldn't have been any damage at all."

She jammed her foot hard against his flesh and pulled with all her might on his arm. His shout of agony echoed across the clearing.

Letitia added another chunk of wood to the fire and glanced anxiously at Adam. She knew she'd yanked his shoulder back into place because he'd told her she'd been successful before he passed out from her brutal efforts at doctoring. He still hadn't regained consciousness. When she lay her hand briefly on his face it felt burning hot.

She dunked a rag into a bucket of water, wrung it out, and placed it on his forehead. His lips moved, but he made no sound. He quieted and lay still, so still, as still as death. No! She couldn't let herself think about that. She racked her brain, trying to think what else she could do for him.

His shoulder was bruised and swollen, but she didn't think the damage could cause his mounting fever. There was only one answer. He'd gotten soaked more than once during the storm. That must be the reason for his illness, an illness she had to fight without medicine.

She saw the remains of their meal. Without thinking of her earlier nausea, she reached for his knife. With the rabbit, and the wild herbs Adam used for seasoning, she could make a broth. That might help. She dropped the ingredients into a pot, filled it with water, added some of their precious salt, and put it on the rock they used for cooking at the center of the fire.

She turned back to Adam. If anything, his fever had mounted while she was working to create the broth. She made a quick trip to the stream to refill the bucket, then knelt by him to sponge his face. She had to bring that fever down.

She wiped her rag carefully across his thickly furred chest. She'd wrapped a bandage around him to support his shoulder, and she had to keep the cloth dry. The golden hair on his body converged into a single vertical line above his navel. She bit back a little moan of fright. What if she'd done irreparable damage wresting his shoulder into place? What if she couldn't break his fever? What if she killed him?

"Stop that," Letitia said, the sound of her voice startlingly loud in the clearing. The fire seemed to be burning lower. The black night pressed in on all sides. She added more wood and checked her still-watery broth. Then she went back to tending Adam. She dampened and wrung out her cloth until her hands were red and sore, but she wouldn't let herself stop sponging him until, at last, his skin felt cooler.

By then the smell of the cooking broth competed with the smoky scent of the wood fire. She rose and stumbled across the clearing to move the pot from the flames. She could do nothing now until he regained consciousness. Exhausted, Letitia curled up against his good side and pulled a blanket over the both of them. She'd take just a short break to let her soup cool, then she'd see if he could take any of the broth.

With a sigh, she shut her eyes, but the memory of the boulders tumbling down the hillside toward Adam seemed to be permanently imprinted on her mind. What an awful country she'd come to—deserts, snakes, bears, earthquakes. Was there no end to the danger?

Adam muttered, tossing his head restlessly.

"What is it?"

Letitia sat up, peering at him in the flickering firelight. He muttered again, but the words were indistinct and she couldn't make them out. He twisted, his good arm flailing about, his legs twisting, his back arching as he struggled to move.

"Be still!"

She grabbed his wrist and tried to ease him back onto the blankets. He resisted her and struggled all the harder. She wrestled with him as he grappled with his own private demons.

Frightened that he'd injure himself further, Letitia pleaded, "Don't fight so."

She wrapped her legs around him and tried to pin his right arm to the ground, but his greater strength kept defeating her. His fevered ranting increased in volume, but the words made no sense. He kept calling for reinforcements and ammunition and repeating, over and over again, "No, no, no!"

When Letitia thought she couldn't fight Adam any longer, he fell back against the blankets, deathly still, his flesh burning hot. She sighed and reached for her rag. She had to get his fever down again.

Exhaustion seemed to be rising up from the ground in waves, battering her, but still she persevered, sponging him repeatedly. She tried to force some of the now-tepid broth between his teeth, but he kept his jaw tightly clenched. She couldn't get him to take the liquid. She dashed her hands at the tears gathering in her eyes and wondered how much longer this ghastly night could continue. He seemed cooler at last, so she lay down by his side again and dozed.

Adam thought he heard the sounds of artillery, the whine of minié balls, the shouting of men. They must be in battle. His shoulder was on fire. The pain from his injury swept through him like a red flame, reducing all sensation to a single white-hot spear in his shoulder.

He concluded he'd been hit and struggled to open his eyes. He had to move. He knew too well what the wounded suffered while they waited to die on the field of battle. If he could get moving, get behind the lines . . .

Adam's eyelids felt as if they'd been glued shut. He concentrated on moving them as he fought to relegate his pain to a remote portion of his consciousness. He felt something stir by his side. That reb he'd fought earlier was back. He must get up. Get up and fight.

At last his eyes opened. He looked at Letitia.

Comprehension swept through him. The war was over. He wasn't the one dying on the battlefield. That had been countless others. Adam clenched his teeth against his memories and tried to focus on what had happened to him.

He'd been standing at the mouth of the cave when the earthquake struck, he could remember that. And he could remember Letitia screaming and the rocks raining down. After that everything seemed blurred and hazy, but he thought he could recall arguing with her about who should put his dislocated shoulder back in place.

He moved tentatively, testing the pain. His head felt as if it were stuffed with wool, and his chest and throat hurt. But it was nothing like the pain in his left arm. It felt as if it'd been ripped from its socket. He grimaced. That comparison wasn't too far from reality.

Letitia stirred. She raised herself on one elbow and gazed at him anxiously. "Adam?"

His voice came out in a croak when he tried to answer. "Y-yes." He moistened his lips with his tongue and tried again. "Yes?"

In the pale gray of predawn, he could barely make out her features. He strained to look at her and saw her hair cascading down her shoulders. The worry etched in her face, and the dark gray shadows under her eyes, made him summon up the necessary strength to reassure her. "You did a good job. My arm feels a lot better."

She reached out to touch his forehead and he steeled

himself not to break down and give in to the motherly gesture.

"Better than what?" Letitia shook her head. "You've still got a fever. I made some broth from what was left of that rabbit. If I warm it up, can you drink some of it?"

He nodded and winced at the agony generated by that small movement.

She returned with a cup and spoon. She folded a blanket, knelt, and helped him lift his head so she could wedge the makeshift pillow behind his shoulders. Moving was a miserable business and, when it was over, he felt pale and as drawn as Letitia looked.

She lifted the spoon to his lips. He reached out with his good hand and grasped her forearm. "I don't need to be fed. You can give me the cup."

"Don't be foolish. You're not strong enough."

He shut his eyes for a moment against the relentless pain, knowing he should agree with her, but he was driven to battle on, as much against Letitia as against his injury. He felt the spoon against his lips and this time his mouth instinctively opened. The soup was warm and tasted surprisingly good.

He watched the spoon approach his mouth again, Letitia's jaw dropping as she unconsciously imitated the gesture he should make. He smiled and the spoon dove in between his teeth.

He dodged the next spoonful and said, "When Swen was little and wouldn't take his food, I used to say, 'Eat like a baby bird. Open your mouth and say ah.'"

She pressed her lips firmly together, but he could tell she was repressing a smile.

"Say 'ah!'" she parroted, smiling at last.

Adam complied.

With the broth in his stomach he did feel a bit better, but the pain in his shoulder gnawed at him relentlessly. He'd dislocated that joint before. He knew only time could cure the swelling and other associated damage.

Letitia resettled him in his blankets. He watched her moving about the fire. Suddenly, he remembered what they'd been arguing about before the earthquake. "How do *you* feel?" he asked.

Surprised, she turned to look at him. "I feel fine. Why shouldn't I?"

"Because yesterday you were sick."

"I told you it was nothing."

He knew it was a weakness, but he let himself be satisfied with her answer. He repressed a sigh and shut his eyes.

She watered Buck, putting the bucket down so the thirsty horse could drink. She moved his rope so he could have fresh grazing and then, soft-footed, she walked back to check Adam. His chest rose and fell with the deep breathing of genuine sleep. She dared to touch his forehead, lightly. He still felt feverish, but not dangerously so.

She looked around the small campsite and wondered where their next meal would come from. She realized she was solely responsible for their survival until Adam recovered.

With a sigh, she reached for the rifle. She'd check the snares and pray they'd caught another rabbit. She knew it would probably make a big difference in the chances for Adam's survival if she could force herself to kill a deer.

For Adam, she could do it. She could do anything

she had to do. Except, she admitted honestly to herself, she didn't have the slightest clue of how to deal with the carcass of deer, should she find one to slay.

She would figure it out, she reassured herself. She picked up his rifle and knife and trudged away from the clearing.

Adam woke feeling much better. His shoulder still hurt like the very devil, but at least the pain was manageable. Grimacing, he raised himself up on his good elbow and called, "Letitia?"

Even as his voice echoed around the clearing he realized she wasn't there. How long had he slept? It'd been dawn when she'd fed him. It was probably mid-morning now, at the earliest. Damn it, she'd tried to escape again and she had a good start on him. He had to find her and bring her back. After her tangle with the bear, didn't she have any sense at all? She was no more equipped to deal with the dangers waiting for her than a defenseless kitten. He had to follow her.

"Damn!" He struggled to his feet. What in the hell had happened to his pants? He saw them folded neatly by the fire, his boots resting nearby. By the time he'd gotten them on, sweat was running down his face. There was no way he could struggle into his shirt.

Buck nickered and Adam realized she hadn't taken his horse. He looked around the clearing. The rifle was gone. He stepped forward.

"Hell and damnation!"

He gritted his teeth as pain shot from his shoulder and raced down his spine. He bent and tugged at his saddle, the effort leaving him gasping.

"So don't saddle Buck," he muttered to himself. "Just get on the horse and go. Letitia needs you."

He staggered toward his gelding. Buck shied away nervously, alarmed by Adam's wavering steps.

"Stand still," he said thickly.

The ground moved under his feet and he wondered if they were having another earthquake. He fell to his knees, his right hand gripping his left arm, as he fought to retain consciousness. He heard a terrible rushing in his ears and then collapsed to the ground, not wondering about anything anymore.

Letitia followed the game trail Adam had led her down the day before, the Enfield rifle weighing heavy in her right hand. Grandmama had insisted they all learn to use a gun the year the war had started. She would have delighted in an opportunity to slay Yankees from the front porch of Bellewood, but she'd never had the chance.

Now, Letitia was thankful she knew how to fire a gun, but she still prayed she wouldn't have to shoot anything, a bear included. The first and second snares were empty and she didn't know whether to be relieved or glad. Adam needed food, and for that matter, so did she. It would be several days before Swen and Billy returned with fresh supplies. Until then she had to rely on herself.

The third snare held a rabbit. She hardened her heart and did what was necessary, relieved beyond words that she seemed to be past the strength-sapping nausea that had plagued her for days. She completed the circuit of the snares and sat down to rest, for just a moment.

She tried to block off her thoughts, but images kept crowding into her mind. Adam leading her away from the Bickles. Adam pulling her back up the ravine. Adam helping her from the tree. Adam just standing there, with his shoulders back and his hands on his hips, the sun gilding his blond hair.

And the most compelling memory of all . . . Adam pulling himself from the pool at the desert oasis and lowering her to the blanket while he showed her the reality of honest passion, showed her how to give comfort and release to a man while receiving the same gifts from him.

She shook her head to clear her thoughts. It wouldn't do to sit there dreaming, she told herself, but she lacked the necessary impetus to stand and return to the cave.

When the rocks had rained down on him, she'd admitted to herself that she loved him. In the middle of such turmoil she couldn't allow herself to think about her revelation, about what her emotions meant. Now she could. Now she had to confront the meaning of what she felt.

What *did* it mean to love him? she wondered. She decided it meant she accepted him, unconditionally. Love meant *he* was the meaning.

She thought of Ruth in the Old Testament. Like all Bible stories it was written to teach a concept. Letitia realized she'd never truly understood the lesson before. Now the verses spoke to her heart, not to her mind: *Entreat me not to leave thee, or to return from following after thee: for whither thou goest, I will go; and where thou lodgest, I will lodge: thy people shall be my people.*

That was what love meant. That was what she felt

for Adam. She'd loved Shelly. He'd been her friend, her almost-brother. His memory would always be precious to her. They'd been children together. Adam, though . . . He was the love of her life.

What could she do about this startling discovery?

She didn't have the full answer, yet. She just knew she couldn't let Adam continue with his plan to ransom her to Papa. Instead of praying to God, asking for someone, something to help her, this time she would have to find her own way. It was up to her to make the blindingly clear emotion she felt for Adam into something more—something more both for them and for their child.

She'd pinned all her hopes, all her future on Papa. That wasn't the answer. She couldn't depend on others anymore. If nothing else, she'd learned she must depend on herself. Perhaps Papa had perished in that terrible second earthquake. Perhaps not. It didn't matter anymore. What mattered was Adam and how she could convince him they belonged together, no matter what.

Suddenly the earth lurched underneath her.

"Oh no!" she moaned. "Not again."

This time the rumbling sound didn't come. In an eerie stillness the ground rose and fell beneath her in quick, jerky bounces. The trees above her swayed as though they were being tossed by a strong wind.

Within seconds the quaking ended. An odd hush settled over the forest, as if everything there held its breath, waiting to see what would happen next.

Absolutely nothing happened.

Encouraged, a bird started to sing. Letitia realized she'd been gone much longer than she'd intended. Adam needed her and the food she carried. Armed with the serenity of the absolute rightness of her love for him, and an abiding trust that she could make things work out for them, she lifted her game and started down the trail leading back to the cave.

She pushed her way past the bushes that screened their clearing and stopped, stunned. Adam lay flat on his face, unmoving, halfway between the fire and Buck's picket line. The rifle and rabbit fell from her hands. All the fine plans she'd made while sitting under the tree scattered like dandelion milkweed floating away on the wind.

"Adam!" She raced to his side and checked the pulse beating at the side of his jaw. She breathed a huge sigh of relief when she felt the steady beating of his heart. Thank God he was still alive, but he felt much warmer than when she'd left him this morning.

Anger swept through her. What had he done to himself, trying to get up? Now, somehow, she'd have to get him back to the safety of his bedroll and then get his fever back down.

She looked at his muscular body and wondered how she'd accomplish all that. Maybe she could drag him, but that wouldn't do his swollen shoulder a bit of good.

Ruthlessly, she shoved her hands under his good side and struggled to roll him over. He flopped onto his back. She brushed her hair away from her damp forehead. He'd have to help her, if she were to move him, that was all there was to it. She bit her lip and slapped his face, hitting him as hard as she dared. He moaned and stirred.

"Adam! Wake up!"

He grunted. "Wha . . . zit?"

"I said, wake up."

He made a strangled sound and his eyes flickered open. "I thought you'd left."

"Why did you get up?" she countered, exasperated. "You're not fit to move."

He swallowed. "Thirsty."

"All right. I'll get you a drink."

She sped to the stream and returned with a full cup of water. She lifted his head and held the drink to his lips. He swallowed almost half of the liquid before he stopped to scowl up at her, comprehension obviously returning to his muddled brain. Uncertain whether to be relieved or not by the alert glint in his eyes, she pressed the cup against his mouth again.

He brushed the mug away. "Where have you been?" he demanded.

She gestured at her pile of game. "I went to check the snares. In case you haven't heard, we're pretty low on supplies around here."

"Damn it, woman. Why didn't you tell me you were going? I thought you'd run away again. Help me stand."

If his bad temper was any indication, he must be feeling better, she thought, as she helped him struggle to his feet. She tried to guide his wavering footsteps back to his bedroll, but he resisted her gentle shove.

He rested his good arm on her shoulder and looked down at her, his blue eyes narrowed, his face stony. "Why did you come back?"

She deliberately chose not to understand him. Now wasn't the right time to tell him what was in her heart. "To pick you up out of the dirt, what else?"

"What else, indeed?" he murmured, his head lowering, his lips a scant inch from hers.

She recognized that gleam in his eyes. She shoved at

his right shoulder. "That, and to get you back into your bed, such as it is."

He moved incautiously and grimaced against the answering thrust of pain. "I give in—for now. But this isn't settled."

Later, after she'd followed Adam's instructions on how to dress and cook a rabbit, she brought him his meal. She speared one of the pieces of meat on a fork and lifted it to his lips. His hand curled around her wrist.

"Give me that." He smiled suddenly, with great charm, his teeth white against his tan and the golden stubble covering the lower half of his face. "Please. I'm feeling better. I can feed myself."

Wordlessly, she let him take the fork from her fingers. His hand fell away and she turned to her own meal.

"I need to know," he said. "Why didn't you take Buck and ride off to your papa? Why did you come back?"

11

"*I won't say* I never considered leaving you," Letitia said. "But what sort of person would I be, going off and abandoning you, injured? I wouldn't do that to a dog."

"Thanks," Adam said wryly.

Silence lengthened between them as taut as a piece of string stretched to the breaking point. She shifted her gaze from his supine position on the blankets to a fist-sized rock resting just beyond her foot. She bent and picked up the stone, rubbing her finger across a bronze-colored streak that snaked down one side.

"I wouldn't have blamed you if you'd gone," Adam said at last. "I've kept you here against your will. You know I don't mean any good toward your papa."

She nodded. Adam could be a hard man at times, but inside that iron armor of his, where he caged his emotions, he was a good man. How could she tell him what she felt for him? She would have to explain some other things first.

"I've been thinking," she said carefully. "Thinking about what Papa is doing. Why he refused to acknowledge me, ransom me. I think I lied to you about Papa sending for me."

"You *think* you lied?"

Letitia wiggled uncomfortably and pitched her stone toward the stream. It fell short. "I didn't think I was lying. Not in the beginning. . . . I didn't think . . . that is, not exactly. . . ."

"Perhaps you could explain." Adam shifted, trying to find a more comfortable position for his shoulder.

"I got a letter from Papa," she said. "I mean I thought the letter came from him. But it could be that Cecily forged it. Both she and Papa use a copperplate script. There was no way Papa could have known when Grandmama died. His letter came the same day as the funeral. When I think about it, it's just too convenient, too much of a coincidence."

"What did the letter say?" Adam asked.

"It said if I ever needed his help, I should just ask."

"Did you write to him, asking for his assistance?"

"No. I just came." Letitia sighed. "Grandmama had arranged events so I had to leave Bellewood. I asked Cecily for help but she refused. I had nowhere to turn. She never liked me, and after Shelly and I were married her dislike of me changed to hatred. I think she forged that letter so I'd decide to leave Kentucky. You know, a lot of people think going to California is like falling off the edge of the earth. Cecily knew once I was gone no one would worry about what happened to me."

"I still don't understand. Why wouldn't he attempt

to rescue you once he got my ransom note?" Adam thumped his fist on the ground. "No man can be so base as to ignore his daughter's existence. Damn it, Ramsey's trying to build a reputation for respectability. It's part and parcel of his desire to build that railroad. Back in Washington they don't know what sort of a son of a bitch he is. It's important that he keeps his scandalous actions out of sight."

"Papa's indifference is the only answer that makes sense," Letitia said. "If he intended to come and rescue me, or at least send his men, you'd think they would have found us by now. I think it was an accident when Jonas and Billy bumped into Papa's men. Especially after that, you'd think they'd come hunting me—hunting you—but they haven't."

Adam cursed long and fluently. "If I didn't have enough reasons to flay that bastard alive before, I certainly do now. As soon as I'm fit, as soon as Swen and Billy get back, we're leaving. But I'm *not* giving up. I will find a way to stop Ramsey. In fact, public disgrace may just be the way."

"How will you do that?"

"I'll make damn sure everyone in the state knows he refused to help you." Adam fell silent, pondering. He pushed his blankets away with his right hand. "That may not work either. Hell, Ramsey's already a disgrace. The powerful people in the state know that and it's not stopping him from building his empire. I've got to think about it."

"Think about this," Letitia countered. "You're never going to achieve what you want by using me."

Adam gazed at her, stunned at the truth of her words. Damn it, she was right. It had been too long. What Ramsey's messenger had told Swen—that Ramsey wouldn't be ransoming Letitia for the document that gave him all that land as a railroad right of way—had to be the truth. Ma must have been right. Ramsey was totally without virtue.

"Letitia, what do you think it means, your papa refusing to acknowledge you?"

She knitted her fingers together. "It means a lot of things. It could mean Papa believes it isn't me you're holding. I wrote him when Shelly died. But the letter I got when Grandmama died was the first time I'd heard from Papa in almost three years. If Cecily forged that letter the way I think she did, then he probably believes I'm still living in Kentucky."

Adam snorted. "Your husband died and your papa never acknowledged the news?"

Letitia ducked her head, staring at her folded hands. "No, he didn't. But how can he know it's me you've got? You told him you have me, but you didn't give him any proof. The last time he saw me I was ten. It makes a lot of sense that he's refusing to pay the ransom."

"Why do you insist on defending that devil?"

"He isn't a devil," Letitia said simply. "I know."

"How can you say that?" Adam asked, scowling. "How can any father take a chance with his daughter's well-being? Even if he doesn't believe we're holding you, he's duty bound to investigate, if for no other reason than to assure himself his daughter is safe back in Kentucky."

Letitia shook her head back and forth. "You're missing one thing. Papa isn't responsible for me. No man is."

"That's wrong. That's very wrong. Every man is responsible for the well-being of his family, and he's

especially responsible for the women in the family."
His lips twisted into a bitter smile. "Why do you think
I took Ramsey on in the first place?"

Letitia gaped at Adam. "I've asked you to explain
so many times. You know I don't understand why you
hate Papa so. Trying to make sense out of this has been
like trying wandering through a thick fog. Tell me,
please tell me why. What did Papa do?"

"Do?" Adam's eyebrows drew together in a frown.
He reckoned she did have a right to know. But if he
showed her the letter, he'd have to explain. Still, she
deserved that, more than deserved that. He glanced
around the clearing. "Where are my saddlebags?"

"By the fire. Do you want me to bring them to
you?"

"Please."

She brought the heavy leather containers to him. He
undid the buckles on the right-hand-side pouch and
fished among the contents. He pulled out a worn piece
of paper and handed it to her. "Read this."

She opened the fragile sheets of paper carefully. *My
dear son,* she read. She scanned the first few lines
swiftly, her eyes widening as she came to the second
paragraph.

There is only one thing in my life left undone.
If you have any feelings left for me you will undertake this task for me. Just recently I learned a
man who calls himself Hunt Ramsey is living on
a rancho near San Diego. He dishonored me
when I was young and vulnerable to his persuasive ways. He condemned me to a life of eternal
sin, and he's the man who destroyed your grandparents and your father.

Letitia finished reading and refolded the letter. Absentmindedly, she ran her palm over the paper, the edge of her index finger tracing one of the creases.

"Well? What do you think now?" Adam demanded. Tongue-tied, she tried to marshall her thoughts. What did she really think? First of all, she thought, how could any woman who truly loved her son send him on such a vengeful mission? Such behavior was in direct contradiction to everything Letitia believed a mother should be, everything she hoped to be for the child she carried.

She remembered Adam telling her about his mother and her harsh life. What had he said about a man always protecting his family, especially the women? Now she understood his strong sense of familial duty and, even more important, his inability to love and trust someone else. But if no one had ever loved him, especially not his mother . . . Could he ever learn to love?

"What you're doing does make sense, in a way. I guess it's because I know you and Swen. I'm sorry your mother was so . . ." Letitia paused. She wanted to say "crazy." "So disturbed at the end."

"Swen and I are doing what any sons would do. Explain what you mean."

"Why are you so determined to injure my papa, Hunt Ramsey?"

"It's all because of what's in that letter. We're going to stop him because he's a greedy son of a—because his quest for power is a threat to democracy in the West—"

"Oh?" Letitia interrupted. "How noble. And kidnapping and extortion are a part of this democracy?"

Adam stared at her for a long moment, his blue eyes

blazing with frustration. Finally, he exhaled. "You're right. I don't really give a good goddamn about all that, not really. What I'm saying is the truth, but that sort of truth normally moves me to contact some friends in Washington to get some action. So Ramsey does get all that land for building his railroad. Maybe it'll be a fair trade. The state does need a southern rail link. You can't deny that. It's Ma's letter—what she says about Ramsey destroying her parents and my pa. . . . What she asks me to do—Ma, who'd never accepted anything from me. That's what's driving me. I couldn't help her while she was living. I had to do what she asked once she was dead."

"I can understand that." Letitia looked away for a moment and then turned back to gaze at him. "If my mother had left me a letter like that . . . well, I do understand why you're doing what you're doing. It's just that . . ."

"That what?"

"That Grandmama tried to manipulate people all her life. She had to be able to control people, even from beyond the grave. Grandmama specifically wrote in her will that I was to inherit nothing from Belle-wood, not even the right to continue living there. That was her revenge, don't you see? She wanted to hurt me because of her own twisted sense of family honor. I can't deny Grandmama hurt me. I always wanted her love, yet I never had it. But the person she truly hurt was herself. She died an old, bitter, unloved woman. I was there when she died, but that didn't matter to her because she didn't want me. She died alone, all alone."

"Just like Ma," Adam said softly.

"Still . . ." Letitia sighed. "Who's to say? In her

own way Grandmama was just as disturbed as your mother."

She stood, her movements abrupt yet decisive. "All this talking hasn't done your fever a bit of good. If you're going to get better, you've got to sleep."

Obediently, Adam shut his eyes. She was probably right. He did need to rest. More important, he needed a chance to think.

Letitia gazed into space. She didn't think she'd ever come across anything as sad as Ingrid McCormick's last letter. Poor Adam. In his determination not to fail his mother again he couldn't see how deranged she'd become.

Somehow, their conversation had gotten out of hand and veered off track as they'd discussed her papa and the fact that he didn't intend to ransom her.

At first, she'd been so sure she could lead their talk around to what she felt in her heart—somehow be able to tell Adam of her love. Instead, as he'd spoken, she'd realized the full truth of her plight. Her wealthy papa had as good as disowned her, which meant all she had to depend on was Clay Jewell's money—less than sixty dollars. Worse, she owed Adam two hundred dollars for rescuing her from the Bickles.

In addition, she literally had no family or friends who could help her in the middle of this benighted wilderness. And her pregnancy complicated the situation beyond comprehension. Of course, she was a widow and she could pretend Shelly had fathered her child, but would anyone believe her? She had no proof she'd been married. In the beginning, Adam hadn't had any idea of her status.

Almost penniless, and pregnant. Letitia stuck her scuffed boots out in front of her and scowled at her toes. She didn't even have a decent dress to wear.

If she told Adam she loved him now, he'd never believe she spoke the truth. Who could fault him? A desperate woman would do anything. She smothered a groan as the full realization of her helplessness hit her.

She couldn't show him her true feelings, not yet. She wouldn't be able to stand his pity. The only thing she had left was her pride. She had to cling to that or she'd be lost, totally lost and completely abandoned. She had to preserve her sense of self. She didn't have anything else. Things were worse, so much worse than when Grandmama had died.

Adam laced his fingers across his chest, trying to think the situation through to its logical end. Why in the world had he ventured out on this crazy quest in the first place? He didn't need to read Ma's letter to recall her words. They were burned into his mind for the rest of his life. *I need you now, Adam, as I've never needed you before.*

He was thirty-three. The deed Ma described must have happened close to thirty years ago. Justice was supposed to come swiftly, not at less than a snail's pace. What made Ma decide he would be the proper person to dispense justice? He didn't want to be a crusader. Ma must have known that.

So why had she selected him to be the recipient of secrets she'd kept his entire lifetime? The answer was obvious. She had no one else, not even God. Clearly, he'd failed Ma just like everyone else in her life. Still,

what good did she expect to achieve by sending him
off to wreak vengeance on her supposed enemy?

He twisted on the hard ground so he could look at
Letitia. She still perched on her rock, one hand cupping her chin as she gazed across the clearing. He had
no idea what she was thinking about, but he had the
answer to his last question.

Letitia had said, "I'm sorry your Ma was so . . .
disturbed at the end." Swen had talked more than once
about how Ma's religion had overpowered everything
else in her life. Now, Adam forced himself to face facts
squarely. Ma had not been a well woman in body or
mind.

She'd accused Ramsey of destroying her parents.
Adam frowned as he tried to pierce the veils of his
memory. He thought he could recall his grandfather.
At least he could picture, in a hazy sort of way, a
kindly old man who'd carved a whole barnyard full of
wooden animals for Adam to play with.

He wasn't sure, but he thought his grandparents
had died in that fire long ago. He recalled his sadness
over the loss of his farm animals and his even deeper
grief over the deaths of the old man who'd made them
and the remote, equally elderly woman he'd called
Mrs.—what was the name? It was the same as Ma's
maiden name—Bjorklund. Except Adam had always
called her Grandma. He remembered the way Pa's
hands shook and his eyes, one blue, one brown, glittered with tears as the fire raged and Ma wailed.

Maybe Ramsey had set the fire. He must have, for
Ma said he'd destroyed her family. But what if he
hadn't? Who could tell after all these years?

His chest contracted as he fought his grief and fury.
Why, Ma? he asked silently.

Maybe her letter . . . Maybe her life with Robert and her illness had affected her perception of the truth. This whole quest had been based on her letter; considering her state of mind when she'd written it, could he trust her accusations?

Even if he could trust her, were revenge and violence the answer? Vanquishing Hunt Ramsey wouldn't bring back Ma or change anything that had happened. Given that, her thirst for vengeance didn't seem to make sense anymore. He didn't believe her hope of everlasting glory depended on him. He hadn't started out on this journey because of that—he'd done it because she'd asked him.

True, Ma hadn't been that far off when she'd branded Ramsey a bad man. He was thoroughly unprincipled, the way he'd refused to come to his daughter's assistance. Ma was right, he had to be stopped. But the place to do that would be in the halls of Congress.

Adam wondered if he should abandon this frontal attack? But what about Letitia? Ramsey didn't want her. Hell, even if he did, he didn't deserve her.

Adam thought of Ma again and realized the only feeling he had left for her was pity. It was the only emotion he could muster on her behalf—that, and regret.

Suddenly, all he knew was that he wanted Letitia, more than anything or anyone else in the world. It'd been a mistake of horrendous proportions when he'd let Ma's letter become the driving force in his life. Since that night at the Bickles' campfire, Letitia had been steadfastly there before him and he'd been too blind and too stupid to see it, or to see her clearly.

Now he saw that she was his future. He groaned,

and his fists knotted together as the full misery of his situation hit him. After all he'd put her through, there was no way in the world she'd ever have him. He had to find a way to correct the grievous harm he'd caused her. It was the only way he could redeem himself now.

12

A *dove, nesting* in one of the trees, called its monotonous "ca-hoo . . . hoo . . . hoo," intruding into Letitia's consciousness. She refused to open her eyes, wishing she could go on sleeping for just a little longer, blessedly unconscious to the reality of life.

She heard a sharp pop, the sound a fire makes when green wood is shoved into the greedy flames. She sat up, leaning back on one elbow, watching Adam carefully place the coffeepot over the embers.

"You shouldn't be up." She tempered her scolding with a smile.

He scowled and then smiled. "Good morning to you, too." He slipped his arm back into his sling. "With luck, Swen and Billy should be back today. They'd better—I just used the last of the coffee."

She cautiously climbed to her feet, wondering if this

would be the day when the awful morning sickness reclaimed her. Everything felt normal, except her aching breasts. She knew her waist must be thickening, but in the loose trousers she wore, who could tell? She made her way to the spring and dashed icy water on her face, gasping as the cold drops stung her skin. She scrubbed at her teeth with her finger and then walked back to the fire, glancing at Adam.

She could sense his moodiness. He'd never been so withdrawn with her before—not when he'd told her he intended to ransom her and not even when they'd fought the night the storm started. This morning she could actually feel him distancing himself from her. What had happened? Did he regret showing her his mother's letter? Did he think he'd revealed too much of himself?

With his free hand, he moved the pot away from the fire, poured a cup of coffee, sipped, and said, "I've been thinking." He swallowed some more coffee, looked at Letitia, and smiled sadly. "There's no way I can say this quest was futile, but it hasn't been worth it. Ramsey's a no-good, there's no doubt about that, but I'm not a one-man army, either. I have to believe what he's done in this life will come back to him. It's hard for me to admit this, but what Ma asked of me is wrong. I'm not the person who'll bring Ramsey down. I'm just a man who wants peace."

"Papa isn't a *bad* man," she countered. "It seems as if we've had this conversation, this argument dozens and dozens of times. He was kind to Mama, he was good to me—"

"You can say that after all that's happened?"

Letitia reached for the pot and poured herself a cup of the coffee. It might be the last, but that was no reason to let Adam drink it all. "That's how I remember him."

Adam sighed. "I think I've misjudged everything. After I told you Ma's story, I thought about it, and what she wanted me to do, all night long. I've come to the conclusion that Ma . . ." He cleared his throat. "I've come to the conclusion that Ma's illness affected her mind, somehow. Maybe Ramsey did all the things she accused him of doing. Maybe he didn't. There's no way for me to tell—it all happened too long ago and in a place too far away for us to ever learn the truth."

Letitia could sense how badly he was hurting. Obviously, he was grieving for his mother and his inability to change her harsh life. Her heart ached with her love for him. "Adam, I'm sorry. I'm so sorry."

He turned away from her, refusing to accept her sympathy. The one person he'd ever really cared for—his mother—had betrayed him from the grave. Yet he couldn't, wouldn't share his grief and his bitter disillusionment. He could only seal it up inside.

Still not looking at her, Adam said, "I've decided it's all over. As soon as Swen and Billy get back, I'll take you to your papa."

"What?" Letitia gasped. "What are you saying?"

Finally, Adam faced her. His lips twisted into a little smile. "I won't actually take you to him. After all I've done, I'm still willing to bet he's out for my hide. But I'll take you as close as I can. It'll be safe—I promise there won't be any bears. I'll leave you just a short distance from the hacienda and you can walk the rest of the way."

Letitia stared at him.

"Oh my God," she whispered, her hand coming up to cover her mouth. He was going to abandon her. He was going to dump her on Papa's doorstep, almost literally, and then ride away out of her life forever.

Tears gathered, and resolutely she blinked them back. What was she going to do? Pregnant and next to penniless, that's what she was. She shrank at the idea of throwing herself on Papa's mercy, but what could she do? Where else could she go?

Memories of her mama sprang unbidden to her mind. Melanie had faced the same dilemma, the same lack of choices. No matter what Clay Jewell had said that day, Letitia knew with a calm certainty that her Mama had loved a man who didn't love her back. In the end, that was what had beaten her down and killed her, not Grandmama.

What would happen to her now? What would happen to her child?

Adam's voice broke into her thoughts. "The least you could do is thank me."

"Thank you?"

"It's what you want, isn't it? All you've ever said to me is that you want to be with Hunt Ramsey. I thought you'd be dancing with joy when I told you I'd take you to him."

Her chin lifted. She couldn't let him see how he'd devastated her. He didn't want her. He'd just proved that. Anger helped to straighten her back and square her shoulders. "You're right. It is what I want. Thank you very much."

"You're welcome." He fairly shouted the words. He stomped away, and then turned back to look at her. "I'm going to move Buck's picket line. He's eaten out most of the grazing around here."

More than anything else in the world, Letitia wanted to find a hole somewhere, crawl into it, and sob out her heart. She looked at the cave, remembered the earthquake, and changed her mind. She didn't want a hole, but she still wanted to sob her heart out. Later, after Adam left her, there'd be plenty of time for that. But she couldn't let him see how deeply she loved him when he cared nothing for her.

She reached for her coffee, sipped, and curled her lip in distaste. Nothing tasted worse than cold coffee.

Adam returned from moving Buck. He reached for the pot and shook it. "Is there any—?" He stilled, holding up a hand as he listened intently. Then he frowned and in one lithe movement reached for his gun.

Letitia froze, her cup scant inches from her lips. If it was Swen and Billy, would Adam be reaching for his gun? What if Papa and his men did appear after all this time? She heard the sound that had first attracted Adam's attention, the clunk of an iron horseshoe on a rock and the jingle of a bridle, the sound coming from the south. He waved her into shelter behind one of the boulders that dotted the small clearing and joined her there.

A bay horse, laden with twin gunnysacks dangling down from each side of the saddle, pushed its way through the trees, its rider throwing up his hand to protect his face. Swen glanced cautiously around the clearing, shoving at the gunnysacks to clear his rifle scabbard. Billy's mare, her rider slumped over her withers, pushed through the trees and stopped, too.

"Adam?" Swen called in a low voice.

"Here." Adam stood and holstered his pistol. "What's happened to Billy? Did you two tangle with Ramsey's men?"

"No. Billy's broke his leg."

Swen dismounted and Adam joined him; together

they eased Billy from his horse. Letitia spread out a blanket near the fire and the three of them edged the youngest Bickle onto the ground.

"What happened?" Adam demanded.

White-lipped, Billy explained. "It happened not more than fifteen minutes ago. We'd stopped to water the horses at that little stream just a little ways from here."

Adam nodded. "I know the place."

Billy continued his story. "When we mounted up, my offside rein broke. I wasn't expecting nothing like that. It spooked my mare and she reared up and dumped me."

Letitia touched his leg gently. "Are you sure it's broken?" She could see the pain clouding his eyes and they way his freckles stood out on his milk white skin. "Maybe it's just sprained. I've heard a sprain sometimes hurts much worse than a break."

"I heard the bone snap when I hit the ground." Billy tried to smile. "It was the damnedest sound I ever heard."

"We're going to have to get Billy to a doctor," Adam decided. "We can splint his leg, but it's going to take a professional to set the break. Sorry, Billy, but we're going to have to get you up on your mare and you're going to have to ride her back to Temecula."

"I know," Billy said. "When we were little and times were hard, Pa used to say, 'It could of been worser. You could of broke your leg.'" He mustered up a grin. "Well, I reckon it's worser."

"We'll get it splinted," Adam said. "That should make it easier. That, and a slug of rum."

Swen glanced at the sling hanging empty from his brother's shoulder.

"What happened to you?" Swen demanded. And then, more eagerly, "Did you tangle with Ramsey?"

"No. Earthquake."

Swen's eyes widened. "We felt a little vibration, but it wasn't much."

"It was here."

Adam reached for the hatchet resting by the wood-pile and handed it to his brother. "Since I'm temporarily one-handed, you go and cut a couple of saplings so we can use them as splints. Sorry, Swen, but you're going to have to be the one to take Billy to the doctor."

"We can't leave you here," Swen protested. "What if Ramsey's men show up? We took a chance splitting up once, but I don't think we should do it twice. You and Letitia had better come with us."

Adam hesitated. "I may have miscalculated, since it doesn't appear as if Ramsey is coming after us the way we planned."

Swen nodded. "I know. I've been worrying about that. But . . . but Ma . . ." He swallowed and tried again. "Ma wanted us to do this for her. How can we let her down? Ramsey has to come."

Adam's lips tightened at Swen's criticism. "You were with her at the end, in fact you probably knew her much better than I ever did. And that being the case, did she strike you as being a woman in her right mind?"

"This is our ma you're talking about," Swen said. "You know what she wanted—how she begged for your help in that letter of hers."

"I know. I know what she wanted. Thing is, I can't stop asking myself if what she wanted is worth it. All that religious mumbo jumbo . . . Worse, I'm afraid in her last illness she fixed her mind on Ramsey for some misguided reason and made up the story that he destroyed my grandparents and my father." His voice rose angrily. "She raised me, Swen, same way as she raised you, but I can't find her faith repeated in me. She believed in life everlasting. I don't."

Letitia felt as if a fist was tightening around her heart. She'd wondered if Adam would ever be capable of love. Now she had her answer. How could he, when he professed to believe in nothing?

Swen started to protest, but Adam held up his hand. "I've seen too many men killed. Hell, I've killed too many myself, to believe in much beyond the fact that when you're dead you're dead and that's all there is to it. And if I believe that then I can't believe in that letter of hers, period."

Letitia sensed his struggle as he tried to reason through his complex emotions so his brother could understand. "I've told Letitia that I'll take her to Ramsey."

Swen started to protest but Adam cut him off. "Don't worry. I won't take any chances. But what I did to Letitia was wrong. The only way I can make amends to her is to do what I should have done when I found her with the Bickles. I'm taking her to Ramsey and that's all there is to it."

Swen shook his head. "In San Francisco, when you showed me Ma's letter, well, it seemed right that I'd decided to come with you. It gave some meaning to my life, too. Ma wanted you to avenge her and I felt like a man when you asked me to help. I . . . oh, hell," Swen swore with a quick glance at Letitia. "I feel like we've quit without really trying. Ma wouldn't have liked that."

"That's what I'm trying to explain." Adam raked

his hand through his hair. "If Ma hadn't been ill for so long, if Robert had been a better husband, if she hadn't lost my pa, if she'd had anything else to cling to besides her religion, she'd never have asked us—me—to do anything like this."

Swen looked disbelievingly at Adam.

"I can barely remember, but I know we, the three of us, my pa, ma, and me, we lived with my grandparents. Ma wasn't so rigid, so strict back then. Before the fire, well . . ." Adam cleared his throat and forced the words out. "Back then I think she loved me."

"I don't have those memories, do I?"

Adam sighed. "No. You don't. And the memories I do have are all vague and shadowy. It's hard for me to sort out the truth. Maybe she never loved any of us. Maybe I just wish she did, maybe I've made up some memories to prove it so. Trust me when I say this, Swen, it's through. It's not worth it."

"But Ramsey—"

"I agree. He deserves to burn in hell for what he's done to Letitia, leaving her with us when he knows nothing about us. But I'm not going to be the man who sends him there, and I don't want you to be that man, either. Letitia wants to go to him and I intend to see she gets what she wants."

Even though she'd believed him last night, Adam's words, spoken out loud to his brother, made his intentions toward her brutally final. She looked down at her folded hands and widened her eyes to keep back her tears. It was all over . . . so awfully over.

Silence filled the clearing. Billy shifted restlessly, clearly uncomfortable. Letitia looked at the two brothers, each with their square chins set, the determined posture of their shoulders identical.

"Look," Adam said. "After I know Letitia's safe, I'll join you and Billy. I've had it with this place. Let's go back to San Francisco. Hell, let's catch a ship and go around the world. I've always wanted to see China."

Letitia's heart contracted in her chest. He was making plans, plans that gave her no hope at all. She'd thought he'd at least stay in California. But now, why, he wouldn't even be in the same country when their baby was born.

"I don't know," Swen said. "I'm going to have to think about this some."

Adam sighed. "Will you at least promise me you won't take Ramsey on single-handed?"

"I don't know about that, either."

"Swedes sure are bullheaded."

"Yeah."

The silence stretched out again, neither of the brothers willing to give an inch. Finally, Adam said softly, "Please. Will you at least promise to think about what I said about Ma. After Letitia is safe with her papa, I'll see what I can do to stop Ramsey's railroad. I've got some influence with our congressmen. But this—this plan isn't working. Even you will agree to that."

Swen inclined his head in a stiff nod. "I reckon you're right about that, at least. What we're trying to do . . . I agree, it isn't working. And you're right. It was wrong to keep Letitia against her will. If she wants to be with Ramsey, that's her choice. But the rest, well, like I said, I'm going to have to think about it."

Adam relaxed. "That's fair. I couldn't ask a man for anything more." He stood up, towering over Letitia. "I reckon we'd better break camp."

She made herself to look up at him. With his actions, with his words, he'd declared their time together over. There was no way to fight the obvious, yet her heart wouldn't acknowledge such an awful finality.

Adam strode across the clearing to pull the sacks from Swen's horse. "We'll split up the supplies. You two get out of here and I'll dismantle the booby traps. We don't want some poor cowboy stumbling into one of them. Then Letitia and I'll leave too. I'll drop her off, but I won't be that far behind you. The important thing right now is to find Billy a doctor."

Swen paused and then said, "And about Ma— maybe you're right. She was awful strict about right and wrong. But at the end, well, I don't think she was seeing things too clearly."

Adam finished dividing up the supplies. He handed Billy the rum bottle and the younger man swallowed gratefully.

"I'm serious about leaving California," Adam told Swen. "If you don't like the idea of China, there's always Europe."

"I haven't really thought that far ahead. I don't know what I want to do." Swen turned to Letitia, looking awkward. "I'm glad Adam decided to take you to your papa. What we did to you was wrong. . . ." Swen cleared his throat and tried again. "I'm sorry we caused you so much grief."

"It's all right," she said softly. If he only knew! Letitia prayed that Adam didn't know what was in her heart. She couldn't bear it if he knew how she felt and he pitied her.

Swen turned away. "I'll get those splints. As soon as Billy's ready, we'll go."

* * *

Letitia walked a few steps behind Adam as he strode up the hill toward their camp. It'd been easier to dismantle the booby traps than to build them, but she could see the effort had cost him some of his strength. When he slipped his left arm back into his sling, she said, "Why don't we wait until tomorrow to leave? You could use the rest."

He stopped and turned to face her. "We need to get out of here today. Swen and Billy will be waiting for me."

She followed Adam into the small clearing. "At least sit down while I get things ready to go." He turned and she could see the strain in his face. "It's okay," she said. "You're doing what I want. Let me help."

It didn't take long to pack up Adam's possessions and douse the fire. Letitia swung around when she was finished, looking at the clearing. Already it seemed abandoned. Only the fire ring proved they'd been there. Soon, that too would be overgrown. Then there would be no proof that anyone had ever occupied the rocky clearing. Sadly, she shook her head and turned to saddle Buck.

She smoothed the blanket from the horse's withers toward his tail and stooped to pick up the heavy saddle. She slipped her left hand under the pommel and reached for the cantle, but the stirrups and the girth which had been crossed over the seat slid to the ground.

She muttered under her breath and rearranged the unwieldy wooden stirrups. Adam had decided it was time to go, so damn it, they'd go. The only problem was, she didn't know how she could bear this final time with him before they parted near Papa's home.

When something is over, Letitia thought, *why can't it just be over and done with? Why does it have to drag on so painfully?*

Adam shouldered her aside. "Let me do that. I'm not totally useless."

"Men!" Letitia huffed. "You never give up, do you?"

"Nope." He swung the saddle onto Buck's back and grimaced with pain.

"Let me do the rest."

He didn't answer her but continued the task without a word.

Adam slapped Buck's shoulder. "Damn it, quit holding your breath."

The horse jerked his head up, exhaling with a heavy snort. Quickly, Adam tightened the cinch. He rubbed his sore shoulder.

"I hope you think you've proved something," Letitia said.

"I proved my collarbone hurts like hell." He tempered his complaint with a smile.

He helped Letitia up onto Buck's rump and then mounted, swinging his leg over the pommel of the saddle rather than the cantle. He guided the gelding away from the clearing, and Letitia clasped her hands around Adam's flat middle, careful not to jar his shoulder. This would be the last time she'd touch him. Soon he'd be on a ship bound for God knew where.

A lump formed in her throat, and she fought the urge to rest her forehead against his broad back. She shut her eyes, savoring the feel of him beneath her hands. Now, perversely, she didn't want this final interlude with him to ever end. She wanted their remaining hours together to last for an eternity. When she felt him tense, she drew back, opening her eyes. At the same time she heard the whine of a bullet speeding past their heads.

"Son of a bitch!" he swore, jamming his spurs into Buck's sides.

The horse bolted. Letitia clung to Adam's waist, trying to see past him to determine what was happening. She could make out three men, charging across the meadow, about to converge on them. They were gaining. She realized Buck, carrying double, could never outdistance the men.

Adam swung the horse to the right, and the gelding dodged behind the outcropping of boulders almost as large as the cabin at the other end of the meadow. He jerked down on the reins, and Buck slid to a stop, Letitia bouncing on his rump. The horse's legs were still plunging up and down as Adam leaped from the saddle and yanked his Enfield rifle from the scabbard while simultaneously pulling her to the ground.

He tugged her behind the dubious shelter of the rock and ripped the sling from his shoulder. "Keep your head *down!*" he ordered.

"What's happening?" she shrieked. "I don't understand—"

"It's Ramsey, damn it! The bastard has had his men out there, waiting, or else they just got lucky. It doesn't matter which, the result is the same."

A bullet smashed into the boulder and chips of stone exploded into the air.

"Keep your head down!" he shouted again.

He moved like lightning, exposing himself as little as possible, as he leapt up and fired at the oncoming horsemen.

She heard the anguished scream of a wounded

horse. Adam swore savagely, his movements blurred by speed as he worked the action to force another bullet into the rifle chamber. He bobbed up, snapping off another shot, and ducked back down, panting. His grim face reflected his fear and the pain his abused body absorbed each time the Enfield kicked against his injured shoulder.

At that moment, what was happening to them took on the hard edge of reality for Letitia. Her stomach knotted with a terrible fear and her mouth felt as dry as a flannel rag. Another bullet hit the rock with the same savage eruption of stone chips. She rolled herself into a tiny ball and tried to burrow into the earth as a fusillade of bullets peppered the air above them.

Adam leaped up and fired again. This time she heard a man scream. Someone shouted, "Jack's killed!"

"Two against one," he muttered. "That's better."

Better than what? she wondered, flinching as another rock fragment flew by. Adam grunted in pain as the chip sliced its way across his back, the split fabric of his shirt crimsoning with blood.

She watched him gather himself, coiling like a spring as he positioned himself to leap up and fire again. She had to so something to stop this madness. She grabbed his arm and yelled, "Adam! Wait!"

"Keep down!" he shouted back, his face a mask of fury and sweat.

"Listen to me," she screamed. "They want me. They don't want you. They're going to kill you—"

"Not if I can help it."

"They will if I don't do something. Stop shooting."

She forced herself to stand. Adam grabbed her and threw her flat on the ground. The impact drove her breath from her lungs and she gasped desperately for air.

"Listen to me, you crazy woman," he shouted. "You are *not* going out there. You do that and those bastards will still blow me full of holes. Unless," his lips curled into a snarl, "that's what you want."

"I don't want you to get killed," she shrieked. "That's just what's going to happen if we—I—don't do something. Won't you listen to reason?"

Another barrage of bullets whistled overhead. Adam gripped his Enfield tightly. "Those men don't intend to listen to reason, now or later. If they valued your life they wouldn't be firing at us the way they are. Can't you understand that?"

He glared at her and the truth of his words sank in.

"If I don't do something fast, they're going to out-flank us and the whole matter will become academic." He fingered the pistol holstered by his thigh. "Whose side are you really on?"

"Yours." She knew she'd just shut the door on her past life. It didn't matter anymore. "If I wasn't before, I am now. Like you said, Papa sent those men and the way they're shooting proves they don't care if they kill me, too." She felt tears rolling down her face. "You're right. You've always told me the truth. Papa is evil."

Adam gently wiped the tears from her cheeks with his thumb and wrapped her right hand around his Army revolver. "For God's sake, don't you dare expose yourself. Just keep firing this thing at regular intervals so they'll think I'm still pinned down."

His mouth descended on hers in a hard, fast kiss. "Don't worry. I'll be back."

13

*Half-kneeling, half-crouching, Adam swift-*ly made his way to where the shelter of the rocks ended. An open space of perhaps twenty feet stretched between the last boulder and the deceptive safety of the forest. He heard Letitia fire his revolver and consciously counted, *One.*

The tall grass of the meadow rippled in the gentle breeze, almost like the swells of the ocean. He threw himself full length on the ground, his Enfield rifle cradled in his arms, and wiggled his way into the dry, inadequate shelter of the vegetation.

His head low, he crawled as swiftly as he could, elbows and knees digging into the earth, his thoughts deliberately focused on what he had to do and not on the woman he'd left holding his heavy Army revolver the way she'd grasp a poisonous snake.

He heard her fire his gun, and then when he still had ten feet to go to the trees she fired it again. *Three,* he counted, forcing himself not to rise and run the last few feet to shelter. Still crawling, he made his way well into the forest before he let himself stand. She fired the Army revolver once more, and the answering barrage of bullets made him swear. Anxiety crowded in, threatening his icy calm.

He swung his Enfield up in his arms as he noise-lessly followed a zigzag course, using every bit of cover to bring him into position behind Ramsey's men. They stood perhaps six feet apart, anonymous men with their hats pulled down low over their foreheads.

Adam raised his rifle to his shoulder, sighting in on the man on the left. He knew this situation could end only in death—either his death or the death of these men. Revulsion tightened his stomach. Ruthlessly, he ignored his conscience, squeezed the trigger, and felt the kick of his Enfield.

All hell broke loose.

The explosion of his adversary's gun almost deaf-ened him. Fragments of the gun barrel flew in every direction, slicing through the trees. Smoke billowed up, hiding Ramsey's men from view. Bits of branches, leaves, and even blood showered down on Adam.

The echo of the explosion continued to ring in his ears even as the smoke cleared and he was able to take in the carnage. The man he'd fired at no longer existed. He'd seen plenty of dead men on the battlefield, and it gave him the detachment necessary to concentrate on the gunman's Winchester, which lay yards away, pieces of its barrel curled toward the blackened wooden stock. The man's companion had been hit by a piece of shrapnel from the exploding gun. He lay on his back, his open, sightless eyes staring up at the sky.

The sickening smell of blood and death filled Adam's nostrils. He forced his shaking legs to obey and made himself walk forward to make sure the second man was truly dead. He stumbled away, the trembling in his hands incongruously mingled with triumphant joy that he still lived. Now that it was truly over he realized just how badly his shoulder hurt and how his sweat stung as it ran into his scrapes and cuts. He'd come back and bury those two later.

Four. He heard the word as clearly as if he'd just spoken it out loud. He'd heard Letitia's last shot a long time ago, just after he'd slithered into the forest.

"Christ!" Adam groaned aloud. He turned and ran, his chest suddenly tight, the meadow suddenly miles long, his legs suddenly heavy and slow, the grass suddenly as thick and resistant as a ten-foot-high stand of chaparral.

At last he rounded the massive boulders. He saw her half-sitting, half-crouching, somehow wedged into a cleft in the side of one of the rocks. "Letitia!"

She looked up at him and smiled weakly. "Adam," she whispered.

"No!" He skidded to a halt beside her, on his knees, his hands reaching for her, searching for the cause of the bright crimson stain on her left side.

"I don't know what happened," she said softly, her eyes dilated with pain. "Something just slammed into me."

"Ricochet," he said. "Move your hand. Let me see."

"Nooo."

"Yes." Swearing steadily, he moved her onto her

back as gently as he could, steeling himself to ignore her short gasps of pain. He reached for her wrist, shocked by the fragile slimness of her bones. She'd always seemed so indomitable to him, so full of life, and now . . . His fingers tightened on her soft flesh and he felt the hard, rapid beat of her blood and, thankfully, not the faint threadiness he'd felt so often among the dying on the battlefield.

He forced himself to inspect her wound dispassionately. The almost-spent bullet had hit her side just above her hip and plowed its way up her side toward her rib cage. There was no exit wound, but he could see the lump of lead distending her skin. That meant that if she were to survive, he'd have to dig that bullet out of her.

He whipped his bandanna from his neck, folded it into a pad, and pressed it into position over the bloody wound. He freed the tails of her shirt and tied his makeshift bandage into place.

"I'm going to pick you up now," he said, his low, even voice at odds with the gut-clenching panic building inside him. "I'll try not to hurt you too much."

She nodded, her hands knotting at her sides. She couldn't contain a small grunt of pain as he lifted her. Each step he took jarred her. She bit her lip and held back the cries that wanted to escape. Buck stepped forward to meet them, his head cocked to one side as he stepped daintily to avoid the reins trailing from his bridle. The horse fell into step behind Adam and they both paced their slow, careful way across the meadow to the cabin.

He kicked the door wide and maneuvered her through the small opening. She couldn't keep back a small moan as he settled her on the hard bunk. She

watched him kindle a fire and steeled herself to endure
the surgery she knew he had to perform.

"I'll be back," he said.

As the flames took hold, the light brightened the
cabin and she could plainly make out the wooden
poles supporting the sod roof. She concentrated on one
twisted piece, trying to distance her thoughts from her
side, which felt as if it were on fire.

Adam returned and, even though she still stared
fiercely at that piece of bent roof support, her ears
couldn't block out his preparations. She heard the hiss
of boiling water and the clatter of metal objects in a
basin. His footsteps thudded on the earthen floor and
her view of the inside of the cabin roof was blocked by
his grim face.

He held a tin cup. "Let's get some of this into you,"
he said. "It'll help."

Gently, he slid his arm under her shoulders and
with exquisite carefulness raised her so she could
drink. She gasped and tried to twist away as the rum
burned down her throat.

"Easy." He held her closer and lifted the cup to her
lips again. "Try it once more."

Artfully, he coaxed the rum down her throat. When
he lowered her back to the bunk, she couldn't even
focus on her piece of twisted wood anymore. Vaguely,
she realized he'd removed her bandage. The touch of
tepid water as he bathed her side soothed the burning.

"If I'm to do this, you can't move," he said, his
ragged breathing reflecting his strain. "Do you understand? There's no one to hold you and you have to
stay still so I can get the bullet out."

Stay still while he cut into her? "I can't do it," she
whimpered. "I can't."

"The only alternative is to tie you down. Please—" His voice broke. "Please, Letitia, don't make me do that to you. Help me."

His desperation cut through the fog clouding her senses. Somehow she'd find the strength to do what he asked. "Okay," she whispered through stiff lips.

He grasped her hands and wrapped her fingers around the posts supporting the head of the bunk. "Hang on to these," he instructed.

She fingered the rough wooden supports.

He traced the curve of her cheek with his fingers. His face, and even his eyes, all seemed to be the same shade of pasty gray. She tried to find a way to reassure him, but her thick tongue couldn't put voice to her thoughts.

"I'm going to do it now."

His words didn't make any sense, but the hellish torment of his knife jerked her back to full consciousness. Her body arched, as tight as a bowstring, as she fought to remain still for him. She grabbed the poles with all her strength, her sweaty palms slipping on the rough wood. She hung on tightly, forcing herself to still the scream of pure agony building inside her chest.

It seemed to go on forever. Why did her body insist on clinging to consciousness? Why didn't she faint? How could she go on enduring the unendurable?

"Thank God!" Adam gasped.

The metallic clatter of an object rattling around in the basin penetrated the red haze that held her captive. Once again she felt the tender relief of cool water on her tortured flesh. She dared to breathe again. Was it over?

He unwrapped her stiff fingers from the poles and

gently lowered her arms to her sides. "Letitia?" he said urgently. "Are you there?"

"Umph." She moistened her lips and tried again. "A-Adam?"

"Shh. It's finished."

He brushed her hair away from her forehead, and she realized she was bathed in sweat. Yet her hands and her feet were cold and she felt clammy.

"How do you feel?"

The fear in his words registered somewhere in her woolly brain. She had to reassure him. "I . . . I feel . . . fine."

"Little liar."

She sensed rather than saw his smile.

"How bad is the pain?"

She focused on his lined, drawn face and all her brave resolve washed away. "It h-hurts."

Again he lifted the cup of rum to her lips. "Try to drink this. It'll take off the edge."

"No." Feebly, she batted at his hand. "If I do . . . if I fall . . . asleep . . . I may never wake up . . . again."

"Rum won't kill you. You need rest now more than anything else." He held the cup against her lips again. "I promise you, you'll wake up again."

Comforted, she obediently sipped. The harsh bite of the liquor seemed dulled, and a gray fog pressed down, driving her away into nothingness. She struggled to make her way back but the effort of trying defeated her.

From somewhere she heard him say, "You're safe now. Don't fight it. Rest, Letitia, just rest."

* * *

He watched the frown etched across her forehead slowly dissolve. Her breathing evened out and he pulled the blanket up to her chin.

The shakes hit him then. He turned away, hunching his shoulders and twisting his hands into fists, trying to still the tremors sweeping through his body. He felt exactly as he had during the last months of the war—as if he were falling apart, scattering into a thousand bits of cowardice.

Blindly, he stumbled the few steps it took to reach the cabin wall and clung to the uneven logs, fighting to regain control. He squeezed his eyes tightly shut and concentrated fiercely on simply hanging on. Somehow, he had to find the strength to ride out the storm raging inside him.

It seemed an eternity, perhaps it took only a few minutes, but at last he managed to gain some control. He forced himself to abandon the support of the rough wall and face the interior of the cabin again.

Deeply ashamed by his breakdown, he stumbled across the cabin to check Letitia. She was sleeping. He didn't dare touch her in case he might disturb her. His tired gaze fell on the basin and wearily he gathered up the tools he'd used during his rough surgery. They needed to be cleaned.

Outside, he performed the necessary chores. As he dried his knife, the vivid memory of what he'd done with that blade flooded through his mind. Her perfect body . . . her silken flesh . . .

Adam's stomach clenched and heaved as his body tried to rid itself of his terrible guilt and sickness. Revenge had done her no good. From now on, he vowed, no matter what, Letitia would always come first.

* * *

Adam shoved another chunk of wood into the fire and squatted down on his heels. The sun had gone down perhaps thirty minutes ago. He didn't feel like eating. His shoulder ached. Hell, it more than ached, it just plain downright hurt. There was still some rum in the bottle and he looked at it longingly. He couldn't find any relief in that bottle. Letitia needed it, just as she needed him.

He watched her face in the flickering light from the fire, noting the lines that pain had etched on her pale skin. Her thick brown hair was fanned out across the blanket he'd rolled up to serve as a pillow and she lay stiffly, even in sleep unable to relax.

He saw her tongue flick out, unconsciously licking her lips. From experience, he knew she must be thirsty. He reached for a spoon and carefully trailed tiny drops of water across her lower lip. Her mouth parted and her tongue gathered up the moisture. He repeated the delicate maneuver three more times before her head turned away and she gave a petulant little sigh.

He rested his hand on her forehead, silently swearing at the fever he could feel building. He'd done his best with the crude tools he had available, but he had nothing to fight the infection he feared would follow her gunshot wound.

Her head moved restlessly and her eyelids flickered. He froze, praying she wouldn't regain full consciousness just yet. At least while she was out she wouldn't feel the pain. She seemed to sink deeper into sleep, but he couldn't relax. What if she never woke again?

Her head tossed against the pillow, and her legs and arms pushed against the confining blankets he'd wrapped around her. She muttered, and he strained to catch her words but he couldn't make any sense out of what she said. He tested her forehead again and found it much warmer. He knew only one cure for fever. As she'd done for him the night of the earthquake, he reached for a rag and a bucket of cool water and started to sponge her down.

He worked doggedly, even as fatigue made his head spin. It was his quest for vengeance that had brought this pain and danger to her. Now he had to save her. He wouldn't, couldn't give up.

She thrashed against the blankets and the bunk. He considered tying her down, but he couldn't make himself subject her to that terrible degradation. In desperation, he sat on her legs. If she kept struggling like that, she'd rip open his inexpert stitches. Her muttering grew louder until she said clearly, "Papa?"

Adam's jaw clenched. He bit back sudden, boiling anger. How could she call for that snake? How could she still care for him?

"Papa?" she repeated anxiously. "Papa? Where are you?"

Adam paused, the dripping rag hanging from his hand. How could he quiet her, reassure her?

Her eyes snapped open and she gazed at him. "Papa? Please don't leave me."

Adam realized that although she appeared conscious, she wasn't. She was trapped in a fever-induced dream, calling for a man who didn't care if she lived or died.

He swallowed hard. She deserved so much and received nothing. He wanted to say, "It's Adam." He wanted to be the one she called for. But she didn't need him. She needed . . . Huskily he said, "I'm here, Letitia. It's Papa."

She nodded and he thought she whispered, "Good." With a little sigh she seemed to relax but her fragile white skin felt just as hot under his hand.

He sponged her face and trailed the cold, wet rag across the burning flesh of her upper arms and breasts. Her nipples puckered against the icy liquid, but he felt no response. Her wonderful body, her satiny skin had been ravaged. Perhaps her life was ending. If he'd done as she'd begged, taken her to Ramsey, none of this would have happened.

What would have happened? Adam's stomach twisted at the thought of her in her papa's clutches. Today had proved no good could have come from that. And yet, had he treated her any better?

Consciousness seemed to come back in stages. She realized her mouth felt dry. Her head buzzed and throbbed. It felt as if a storm raged inside her brain, the lightning lancing down her forehead behind her eyes.

She moved and pain ripped up her side. Memory returned with all the force of the bullet that had pierced her flesh. She remembered Adam leaving her, going to do battle against Papa's men. Her hand still seemed to feel the kick of the revolver and the amazement she'd experienced when she felt something rip into her body.

Her eyelids felt as if they were glued shut, yet she managed to lift them. What had happened next? In the dim, predawn gloom, she struggled to focus her eyes. Adam's worried face swam into her limited field of vision. She licked her dry lips and tried to speak, but only managed a weak croak.

"Shhh. Don't try to talk," he said.

She swallowed, disregarded his command, and forced out the words, "A-are you okay?"

He smiled tenderly, but she couldn't keep her eyes open. The pain tore at her and her thoughts turned inward. Her hands clenched into fists, and she forced herself to lie still and endure. She could do nothing else.

"Letitia? Are you still with me?"

She nodded.

"Don't try to fight it," he advised. "The first time you wake up is always the worst. Try to take it easy. Try to go back to sleep."

He heard her sigh and sensed her body relaxing as she obeyed his advice. He felt a rush of relief and let his tight muscles loosen, too. He checked her forehead and swore under his breath. Her fever burned just as high as before.

Carefully, he moved from the bunk, his shoulder so sore and tight he groaned aloud at the pain. Bleary-eyed, he stumbled around the small cabin, building up the fire, starting the coffee. He made his way outside, blinking against the early morning brightness. He drew fresh water from the barrel and deliberately tipped the bucket over his head.

The shock of his icy bath restored him to a measure of alertness. He took stock of his supplies in his mind, trying to figure out what he could concoct that would serve as invalid fare for Letitia.

She had to eat—she had to regain her strength. Broth had helped him; perhaps it would work for her, too. He returned to the cabin and assembled the ingredients for soup in a pot. With a cup of coffee cooling on the table, he returned to the task of sponging her.

Letitia twisted away from the cool cloth; she seemed much closer to consciousness than she'd been the night before. He paused, wondering what he should do. She needed to sleep. Then she wouldn't feel the pain. But he had to break her fever. Hardening his heart, he applied the rag to her flesh over and over again.

"Stop!" Letitia cried. "Please stop."

"I can't," he said. "I have to do this."

"Nooo." Her knees curled up, her body twisted, and her lips peeled back as she rolled from side to side. "No!"

He tried to still her frantic movements, feeling as panic-stricken as she sounded. He checked her bandage, but no blood seeped down her side. "What is it? What's wrong?"

"Oh! Don't let this happen to me! The baby—my baby!"

"Baby?" He grabbed her shoulders and pressed her back against the bunk. "What baby? Letitia, what's going on?"

She moaned in response, tears streaking down her cheeks.

Was she delirious? Had she lost Shelly and a baby, too? Adam groaned aloud. There was so much he didn't know about her. She'd told him very little about her life. A baby? It just didn't make any sense . . . unless . . . what if . . . ?

Horrified, he glanced downward and, as if on cue, a red tide started to seep from between her legs.

*   *   *

Adam pulled a fresh blanket over Letitia and she stared up at him, more than physical pain shining from her huge, tearful eyes. He reached for the bottle of rum and ruthlessly forced her to drink the last of it, even though she sputtered and complained.

"You have to sleep," he commanded. "For a while, at least, the liquor will help you forget."

He rested his hand briefly on her forehead. Instinctively, she turned, her cheek nesting in the curve of his palm, seeking comfort. He brushed her sweat-darkened hair away from her face. "Sleep now," he whispered.

Mutely, she nodded, her lids obediently closing, too fuddled by the drink to disobey him. He held her hand, watching her until her body finally relaxed and her breathing grew deep and heavy. He tested her forehead, wondering if it did in fact feel cooler or if it was just his imagination.

Thank God he'd been able to stanch the flow of blood. He shuddered, remembering just how much blood there'd been. How could she still live when she'd lost so much? What could he do to help her? What if, through ignorance, he had done the wrong thing?

The walls of the cabin pressed in on him, the air heavy with the scent of all that had taken place within the small room. He felt as if he'd choke to death if he didn't get away from the hated place.

He couldn't leave her. She needed him. He forced himself to stay in his chair, his brooding gaze focusing on the empty rum bottle, finally unable to deny the horror of the past twenty-four hours.

A baby. He'd never even known about it, and now it was gone. A sob tore at his chest and his head dropped down, resting in the palms of his hands. He sobbed heavily, as a man unaccustomed to tears cries.

The storm within him embarrassed him dreadfully, yet he couldn't stop, couldn't find the strength to control himself as he felt pain worse than anything he'd ever before endured rip his guts to shreds. Finally, he leaned back, exhausted, his tired, red-rimmed eyes searching the cabin walls as if he could find, written in the rough logs, the answer for what had happened.

Ultimately, it was Ramsey who'd done this. He had to pay.

Adam's thoughts shied away from the idea that Letitia might be dying. He couldn't face that—not now, not ever. Whether she survived or not, because she'd lost their child, the outcome for Ramsey would be the same. Adam's head bowed as he faced the necessity of yet another death. He looked down at his hands, red and chapped, nicked, and scarred.

Death seemed to have filled his life to the exclusion of all else since he'd returned to fight for the North. Was the loss of the baby God's way of paying him back for all he'd done? Memories of the grim God who'd ruled his mother's life crowded into Adam's mind. He shuddered in reaction. He'd convinced himself he didn't believe in anything—didn't believe in God. Was this God's revenge? Perhaps it was.

Adam found himself on his knees, praying silently, pleading with God to spare Letitia. *Don't let her die,* he asked. *God help me, I love her. I've never been able to love anyone—until now—she's my life. Don't take her away from me—not yet, please.*

His entreaties seemed to bang against a brick wall. He felt alone, frightened, and abandoned as he'd never felt before. Nothing could help, nothing made any difference anymore—not even his love for her. He was trapped in the inexorable outcome of his fate as surely as any doomed Greek hero. He couldn't even control Letitia's fate; he could only battle to save her.

He pulled the blankets more tightly around her shoulders and carefully stretched out next to her, his arms gathering her so he could cradle her against his right shoulder.

"Please," he whispered desperately.

Nothing else could be done. He could only wait.

14

It was midafternoon when Letitia woke. Her head still ached and her teeth felt furred by the rum Adam had forced her to drink. She continued to catalog her various aches and pains—her side hurt like the very devil, but this time it wasn't so intolerable. What was intolerable was the knowledge that she'd lost her baby. Her body felt different . . . empty. Stony-faced, she gazed up at the roof supports, her grief too deep for tears.

The back of her neck and her shoulders were damp with her perspiration, and so were the blankets Adam had piled around her. She pushed at them, feeling trapped by the woolly cocoon and the confines of the small cabin. She wanted to get up, go outside, and fill her lungs with fresh air.

Carefully, she turned her head, looking for him. He

was stretched out beside her, asleep. Her movement must have disturbed him, for he struggled to a sitting position, one hand rubbing the rough bristles on his cheeks.

"How do you feel?" he asked hesitantly.

She could only stare at him, her chest tightening with the tears she still couldn't shed.

"It's late afternoon. You've been asleep since last evening," he said. "Would you like a drink?"

Her face felt as if it would crack if she even whispered a single word. She could only nod.

He tended her, taking care of her personal needs and replacing her blankets with fresh ones. The new coverings smelled of clean air, and she inhaled their scent gratefully. It helped for a brief moment to abolish the closeness of the cabin.

Once she was fed, her face and hands clean, and dressed in Adam's spare shirt, she shut her eyes, more tired than she believed possible. She slipped across the borderland of sleep, her dreams wild, confusing, and disjointed. Once, during the night, she roused enough to realize Adam was again sponging her down. With the strange lucidity of fever, she knew she must be ill, but she couldn't rouse herself to worry.

She woke to sunlight and the clammy dampness of sweaty blankets. This time she felt clearheaded but still painfully sore. Her stomach grumbled, letting her know that at least one portion of her body was functioning normally.

Adam was stretched out on a blanket on the dirt floor. He looked exhausted, his lined face revealing every second of the tension he'd endured. The shadows under his eyes looked like bruises, and his fast-growing beard couldn't disguise the gauntness of his cheeks.

She knew she owed her life to him. Mixed in with her anguish over the loss of her baby she felt the contradictory softening of her love for him swelling in her chest. That, at least, hadn't changed, would never change. But would he want to still leave this valley, never looking back, never thinking about Hunt Ramsey again?

Somehow, Letitia didn't think he would. In fact, she didn't think she could simply ride away either. All her life she'd clung to the idea that her papa cared for her. But how could he? He'd sent his gunmen, and she'd lost her baby.

Her baby—Adam's baby—was gone. The words marched round and round in her mind, irrefutable, irreversible, inescapable.

The sound of him climbing to his feet broke into her thoughts. He bent over her and brushed her hair away from her face. "Letitia?"

"Yes."

She watched his face soften with relief. Suddenly, she knew she couldn't bear to lie on the hard bunk a second longer. She had to get out of the cabin, had to be out in the sunlight, away from this horrible place, away from the smell of death.

She struggled to sit, but he held her back. "You'll hurt yourself. Lie still."

"I can't. I can't. Please, Adam, get me out of here." Panic-stricken, she pushed his arms, not feeling the stabs of pain in her abused body. She only knew she had to be free, had to get away from the walls closing in on her.

She gasped for air. "I can't breathe."

He understood and scooped her up, blankets and all, and carried her outdoors. He sat on the bench, still cradling her in his arms. Gratefully, she gulped in the fresh air. She turned her face to the sun and felt warmed by its rays. Adam's arms tightened around her, and she even felt a measure of security.

"Better?" he asked.

"Yes." She ducked her head, ashamed. "Adam, I don't think I can bear to go back in there."

"I understand." He laid his rough cheek next to hers. "I can scarcely bear it myself, but we have nowhere else to go until you're stronger." In a low, ragged voice, he said, "Why didn't you tell me about the baby?"

For the first time it occurred to her he'd lost something precious, too. She bit her lip, searching for the words to make him understand. "At first, well, I couldn't. And then . . ." Her voice broke. "I can't change anything now."

"No," he agreed. "But it doesn't make it any easier."

"Nothing can help grief."

"They say time is a great healer. I don't think I believe that."

As badly as she was hurting, she had to find a way to help him. "Time changes grief. It doesn't make it any better . . . it just changes it. I've found that out. It makes the unbearable somehow bearable. The baby, our baby, was a promise we didn't get to keep. We're going to have to live with that. We can't do anything else."

Adam fell silent. Finally he straightened and said, "We can do something."

"What?"

"When I realized those bastards had shot you, I was glad I'd killed one of them—glad the other two had died. I've never felt that way before. I've always felt that killing took away a part of me. Then, when you were losing the baby, well, I realized some other things, too."

She twisted in his arms so she could gaze up at him, trying to read the raw emotions in his dark blue eyes. She'd never understood before that a man could feel sorrow as deeply as a woman did. The loss of the baby ate at him exactly the same way it ate at her. He was quiet for a long time, lost in his thoughts. Finally, she prompted, "What did you realize?"

"I've realized even if Ma didn't know what she was doing, she was right. Ramsey must be stopped. For a while, I thought I'd have to be the man to do it after all."

Letitia struggled in Adam's arms. "No. Oh, no."

He looked down at her. "It's okay. I've come to realize I'm not the man who'll stop him. It took a long time for me to see this, but what I've been doing is wrong, all wrong. No one, not even Ma, gave me the right to go after Ramsey. What's an even greater wrong is the way I used you. None of what you went through would have happened, except for me."

She considered his words carefully. "Part of me agrees with you."

He held her closely but he didn't say anything.

"Except," she added, "I've learned I have to stand up for what I think is right or else I'll be just as weak as I was back in Kentucky. What happened isn't your fault. It isn't your mother's and it isn't Papa's. It just happened. It can't be changed. We can't go back."

He didn't reply.

She looked at him for a long time, and when she spoke her low voice held more conviction than any emotional plea. "I've said what I felt I had to say. I'm ashamed to admit part of me doesn't agree. Part of me wants to hurt Papa as he's hurt us. I know it's madness, but I'm having a hard time caring about right and wrong. But everything's said and done, it can't be changed. You're no more responsible than anyone else."

He pulled her closer. "Thank you. I promise you, even though I'm not the man who'll do it, Ramsey'll be brought to justice. The fact that you're alive proves there is justice in this world. I swear to God, you'll never regret trusting me."

He swallowed, and she realized he was nervous. *What now?* she wondered. She didn't think she could bear anything else.

He cleared his throat, and asked again. "Letitia, why didn't you tell me about the baby?"

"How could I? You said you were taking me to Papa. You said it was what I wanted. But all I could see was that you didn't want me."

His arms tightened around her. "*Never* say that! *Don't even think it.* I want you so much. It seems as if I've always wanted you. God help me, I wanted for you what you said you wanted, and I thought that was Ramsey."

"I only wanted you," Letitia confessed. "But I didn't know how to tell you."

"It's taken me a while to figure it out, too long, in fact," he said. "Taking care of you the last few days . . . well, it has sort of clarified things for me. I know now that I want to make my life count for something positive, something good. And, more important, I know now that I can only do that if you're by my side. I promise I'll spend the rest of my life telling you this. I love you. Will you marry me?"

"Oh!" Letitia gasped, a dawning joy building inside her. "Oh!"

"So, what do you say? Will you be my wife?" He smiled, his whimsical grin taking years off his tired face.

"I say yes." She gazed at him, her own smile parting her lips. Miraculously, her burdens had just been halved. "Of course I'll marry you, because I love you, too. That's why I was going to let you take me to Papa. I love you too much to force anything on you."

"My gentle sweetheart." His lips brushed her forehead. "So indomitable, so brave, so lovable."

His lips claimed hers. His gentle kiss promised so much, more than desire, more than companionship, more than caring; his kiss promised a lifetime of sharing the good times and the bad. His kiss promised his commitment to marriage in the best and purest sense.

She nestled her head into the curve of his shoulder. His work-roughened hand brushed her tousled hair away from her face. "As soon as you can travel," he said, "we'll stick to our original plan to meet Swen and Billy. Then," his hands held onto her as he made his vow, "then we'll be married. And, after that, we'll look for a place to settle. It's mighty pretty country up north of Santa Barbara. Do you think you would like to be a real rancher's wife?" He smiled with almost boyish enthusiasm. "I'd like to raise some cattle . . ." He paused. "And some children. But if it's not what you want—"

"It sounds like heaven," Letitia said. "I can't wait."

*　　*　　*

She watched Adam knot the gunnysack containing what was left of their supplies to Buck's saddle. The horse stamped, his long, full tail switching at a tormenting fly. Carefully, Adam lifted her onto the saddle, placing her so both her legs hung down on Buck's near side. Adam mounted and pulled her close across his thighs. Secure in his arms she felt a fleeting sensation of happiness.

Guiltily, she squelched that small sensation of joy. Her lost baby would always be a tragic reminder of what might have been. If only she could come to terms with the awful finality of what had happened to her and to her child.

Adam reined the horse in and turned him so they could look back into the small valley.

"I learned a long time ago," he said, "that it doesn't hurt to look back. What's important is to know when something is over. I'll never miss this place." His arms tightened around her. "Too much has happened. But I'll always say it was worth it because now I have you."

"So will I," Letitia said softly. "So will I."

He bent his head and she stared up at him, so close she could make out every line on his newly shaven cheeks and gaze into his clear blue eyes. He kissed her briefly before he lifted Buck's reins, the signal for the horse to move out. The gelding obediently stepped forward and then stopped, his sides shaking as he neighed at something only he could sense.

A pack of a dozen riders swept out of the trees at the base of the slope leading from the meadow's entrance. Adam swore and in one easy movement placed Letitia on the ground and reached for his gun. "Run for those rocks again," he ordered.

She'd only stumbled a few steps when the rider in the lead pulled his horse to a sliding halt and yelled, "Please! Miss Ramsey, wait, please!" Instinctively, she half turned, her flight arrested by the sight of the rider lifting his hands in a gesture of peace.

"Adam McCormick," the man shouted. "Hunt Ramsey has sent us to tell you he wants to talk to you."

"The time for talking is past," Adam yelled back. "I have nothing to say to Ramsey."

"You have his daughter."

"According to Ramsey, he has no daughter."

Still keeping his hands in the air, the man continued to shout. "We're here on a peaceable mission. Look, I can't keep yelling like this."

"I can," Adam hollered back.

"I'm coming up so we can talk sensibly. Don't shoot."

The man spurred his horse forward. Adam didn't know whether to appreciate the stranger's bravery or not. Sure, he could gun down Ramsey's man, but Adam knew that would be his last living act, for the rest of that gang wouldn't remain even halfway peaceable if their leader was killed.

The man pulled his horse to a halt six feet away. Adam leveled his Enfield at the rider's midriff and gazed at him thoughtfully. The leader was perhaps forty and had a rugged air of command.

"What is it you've got to say that's so important?" Adam asked.

"Remember me? I'm Bill Kennedy," the man replied. "Ramsey's foreman. Maybe the woman with you is the boss's daughter. Maybe she isn't. I don't know about that. What I do know is Mr. Ramsey's decided he'd like to see her and find out for himself who she is. Mr. Ramsey has instructed me to inform you that you'll be suitably rewarded for helping us deliver her to him."

"How can I be sure of that?"

Kennedy shifted his weight in his saddle and shoved his hat back, revealing red hair and a sunburned, freckled face. "I'm instructed to tell you that you have Mr. Ramsey's word on it."

Adam straightened his shoulders and snorted derisively.

"Look," Kennedy said, "you don't have much of a choice, McCormick. I reckon you can either go peaceably or we can make things very unpleasant for you. If Mr. Ramsey weren't a man of his word we would have just swept in here, gunned you down, and taken his daughter."

"You could try," Adam offered.

Kennedy's pale blue eyes narrowed. "I don't try, mister, I just do. And you're trying me something awful right now."

"Good."

Kennedy leaned back in his saddle and laughed. "By God, you do think you're something, don't you?"

"Ever hear of the Ingrid?"

"It's a gold mine—one of the biggest."

"She's mine." Adam crossed his hands over the saddle horn. "I wouldn't recommend you mess with me, Kennedy. I can afford as many hired guns as Ramsey."

Kennedy coughed, covering his confusion. "That may be so. I don't suppose you'd say it if you couldn't prove it. And then again, maybe you would. Desperate men do some crazy things. But it doesn't matter much in the long run. Besides, Mr. Ramsey won't take kindly to losing me, if you want my opinion—"

"I don't."

Kennedy gathered up his reins. "Look, mister, you're lucky Ramsey's decided to do it your way and you're damn lucky I've decided to do what the boss told me to do."

Adam gazed at the men grouped at the bottom of the hill and then looked levelly at Kennedy. "You've made your point. Let's ride."

"After you hand over your guns."

Adam wanted to debate the point with the foreman, but he knew he'd never win. If he were in Kennedy's place, he'd do exactly the same. His mind spun furiously, trying to find a way to keep from relinquishing his guns, but he couldn't find a satisfactory solution. He'd promised Letitia that he was through with all thoughts of vengeance, but damn it, it was hard to hand his rifle and pistol over to the smug Irishman.

"Which way's it going to be?" Kennedy asked.

Adam shrugged and handed over his guns.

With Letitia securely in his arms again, feeling naked and vulnerable without his Enfield, Adam spoke in a low voice, for her ears only. "Beats me how we're going to get out of this one."

"Me, too." Her voice quavered. "Oh, Adam. Will this never end?"

"Yeah, it'll end." But he didn't want to tell her what he thought would happen once they stepped, unarmed, into the rattlesnake's den.

The cavalcade made its way steadily south and west. Adam insisted on frequent rest stops. Letitia was grateful for the brief respites, for she was still sore, even though his arms cradled her from the worst of the jolts. Eventually, in a daze, her head dropped wearily against his shoulder.

Kennedy reined his horse back until he was riding beside his captives. "What's wrong with her?" he asked.

If Kennedy knew his men had tangled with Adam and been killed . . . Adam decided it would be better if the foreman didn't know that right now. For if he did, Adam reckoned his chances of survival would evaporate like a drop of water in the desert at high noon. He considered his words carefully. "Mr. Ramsey's daughter has been ill."

"We'll never make it to the rancho today unless we speed up the pace." Kennedy glanced at Letitia. "And it's obvious she can't go any faster if she's gonna be in any sort of shape. We'll have to stop. Mr. Ramsey won't like that."

Letitia breathed a sigh of relief as Kennedy's words penetrated her numbed brain. The mountain pine trees had long since been replaced by chaparral and oaks when he called a halt by a small stream that meandered through a stand of cottonwoods.

"We're on Ramsey land," Kennedy informed Adam. "But it's still a couple of hours to the hacienda. We'll stop here for the night. In case you decide to do something stupid, I figure I should let you know we'll be watching you pretty damn close. Mr. Ramsey wants you and your lady friend alive. Just how alive depends . . ." Kennedy cracked his knuckles. "Depends on just how smart you are."

Adam fixed a place for Letitia to rest and she braced her back against the trunk of the slender tree, thinking. What would she say to Papa when she finally saw him again? Greet him and then say, "It's nice to see you again. Excuse me, but I must be going now"?

From Adam's grim face she knew he expected something awful to happen to them. Kennedy had been threatening him, but that wasn't the reason. Adam wasn't the type of man to be cowed by threats. He had killed their attackers—but no one could send him to jail for that. She would testify that those men had attacked them and that Adam had acted in self-defense.

He walked over to the fire and returned with a plate of food. He handed it to her and she pushed a fork at the unappetizing mess, longing for fresh vegetables. Or a peach . . . a ripe peach, the juice filling her mouth, running inelegantly down her chin, and . . .

Adam sat down next to her, shielding her from the other men. All her worries crowded her mind.

"What will you do when we see Papa?"

He shook his head and said softly, "I don't know. I honestly just don't know." He glanced down at his empty holster and laughed mirthlessly. "Wait for a sign from heaven, I reckon."

She placed her untouched food on the ground. "Please. Can we get out of this without any more killing?"

"It's out of my hands now."

He stared into the dusky gloom, thinking about the events that had led him to this final frustration. There was so much Ma hadn't told him over the years. There was so much she hadn't said in that letter of hers. He'd spent his life running away from those gaps. He clenched his jaw, trying to put aside all the questions boiling around in his brain. He had no answers and not even a whisper of a plan for what he'd do tomorrow when he finally confronted Hunt Ramsey.

Adam didn't have a lot of hope about how that confrontation would turn out. How could he protect Letitia? He'd killed Ramsey's men—retribution was sure to be unpleasantly fast once the event was discovered.

He glanced at her, barely able to make out her exhausted face in the deepening gloom. What a hell of a life for a gently bred girl. She deserved to be sheltered in a fancy house and waited on hand and foot by willing servants. He'd done this to her. Every time he reached for happiness—

His jaw firmed. By God, this time he'd win. Nothing, no one would take Letitia away from him now that he'd discovered his love. He wasn't finished yet.

He stretched out beside her, dozing fitfully, too attuned to danger to let himself relax fully. Then, unbidden, like a snake, the dream wove its way into his brain. Again, he suffered through the fire, the death of his grandparents, Ma's hysteria, and Pa's misery. Pa's strange eyes, one blue, one brown, dominated the dream. "Pa," Adam shouted. "Wait, Pa. Come back!"

"Adam! Wake up, Adam."

Letitia's concerned voice penetrated his dream. Fathoms deep, he struggled to swim back to consciousness.

His eyes snapped open and he gazed up at her worried face, softly lit by the fire burning nearby. The images of the dream still burned vividly in his mind.

He sat up and buried his face in his hands. *Why tonight?* he wondered.

Her arms crept around his shoulders and he hugged her tightly, comforted by her unspoken love, sympathy, and understanding.

* * *

Midmorning found the little band riding across a tree-shaded stream and into the valley that held Hunt Ramsey's rancho. Freshly plowed fields lay warm and brown as the group rode up the lane toward an impressive adobe home. A man, just a hair under six feet, stood waiting for them, his face shaded by a wide-brimmed Mexican sombrero.

Adam pulled Buck to a halt. Letitia stared down at the stranger, trying to remember. He didn't look familiar, dressed as he was in the clothes of a Spanish grandee. Could this be her papa? It'd been so long, ten years too long. Nothing seemed to trigger a special memory, but she had to know if this man was Papa. She wiggled in Adam's arms.

"I can't tell," she whispered worriedly. "I don't know who he is. What if he isn't Papa?"

Adam grinned crookedly. "Then we're in for one hell of a lot of trouble. You'll have to go see."

"All right." She slipped from his arms and walked toward the man.

Kennedy signaled his men. They spurred their horses and surrounded Adam, cutting him off from Letitia and Ramsey as neatly as a cowboy separates a single calf from a herd.

Isolated on the hard-packed clay in front of the hacienda, she swung around, forgetting about her papa, intent only on finding a way to return to Adam.

"Letitia?" Ramsey called loudly. "Is that you, child?"

Distracted, she twisted back to look at him again. In her childhood, only Papa had pronounced her name with that flat, harsh Northern accent.

He was the one in charge, not Kennedy. He was the one who could free Adam. She clenched her hands into fists and waited to see what Papa would do next.

Ramsey nodded at Kennedy, and the band of men began to herd Adam away.

"No!" She shrieked. "No!" She tried to run after them, but Ramsey grabbed her arm and held her back. She spun around in his grasp, finally close enough to see his face, see his eyes clearly. She had no doubts any longer. "Papa, don't! Adam has helped me. It's you— it's your men who—"

"I know what I, what my men, have done." Ramsey said harshly. "I'll deal with McCormick later. But you come first."

Uncertain what to do, Letitia swayed in the bright sunlight. She fought her sudden dizziness. It was up to her to save them. She couldn't faint now.

Dazed, she couldn't find the strength to fight Ramsey as he guided her through the front door of the hacienda. The massive building was actually a hollow square with a lush, tropical garden growing in the center. But her impression of huge, exotic plants was brief, for he steered her into one of the rooms next to the tunnellike opening that led back into the outside world.

It was a cold room. Tiled floors and massive dark furniture did little to counteract the chill of the morning. The tiny windows that opened to the north weren't large enough to accommodate much of the spring sunshine.

Ramsey helped Letitia to one of the chairs, poured some wine into a silver goblet, and handed it to her. "Drink," he said. "It will give you the strength to tell me what you're doing here when you should be in Kentucky."

"But your letter . . ." she faltered.

"Drink," he ordered.

She sipped the heavy red liquid, involuntarily grimacing at the bitter taste. She felt as if her throat were closing, but she sipped again, knowing she needed the wine's false strength. She looked at Papa closely, trying to decide what sort of man he'd become since she'd seen him last.

"How . . ." Ramsey paused. "How tired you look, my dear. I apologize that I was unable to free you from that scoundrel sooner." He crossed the room to pour himself some wine.

"Adam's no scoundrel. If I look 'tired,' as you so tactfully put it, it's due to your men. Did you know they attacked us? They didn't stop to find out who we were, they just started firing their guns. One of them shot me."

Ramsey's hand jerked, splashing the red liquid. His lips hardened when he spoke. "I will take care of it. Thank God you're alive." He turned, holding another goblet in his hand. "I'm afraid I'm not as strong as the man you knew in your childhood. Did you feel the earthquake?"

Letitia nodded.

Ramsey shrugged his shoulders, the fluid movement reinforcing the image of a Spanish nobleman. "I regret to admit that I suffered a spasm to my heart. Much worse, one of our dams was seriously damaged. Kennedy disobeyed my orders and called in all the men I had searching for you and put them to work repairing the harm nature wreaked on my land."

Ramsey crossed to a chair. "When I found out what

he'd done, I ordered him to start the search for you once again. It appears as if he has disobeyed my orders by allowing my men to fire upon you. Kennedy shall not have the opportunity to make another such error in judgment."

He sipped at his wine. "Which brings us to the crux of the matter. As delighted as I am to see you, my dear, why did you come here?"

She sighed. Here was the confirmation she didn't need. Cecily must have forged the letter to get her daughter-in-law out of Kentucky. How could Letitia explain?

"Things have changed at Bellewood," she said. "I was led to believe you had written, asking me to join you."

Ramsey considered the contents of his goblet. "Which I should have done when I learned that Shelly was dead. Cecily, a conniving bitch if there ever was one, and your grandmother are cut from the same piece of cloth. Yet I can't believe the old witch could ever be convinced to dispose of your services and give you your freedom."

"Grandmama's dead."

He laughed, but the sound had no mirth. "I'll bet dying came as a great shock to the old harridan. So Cecily must have been the one who forged a letter that purported to be from me. I can guess what was in the letter—'Come to California, daughter. I'll give you a home.' She must have been desperate to get rid of you. Why does she hate you so?"

"I married Shelly. That was enough."

Ramsey placed his fingertips together to form a tent. "The joke is that it appears as if Cecily has done us a favor." He straightened his hands. "I know what it's

like to be an outcast among that Sinclair tribe. You
could be an asset to me, Letitia."

"The situation has changed since I left Kentucky,"
she said. "I'm going to marry Adam."

"What?" Ramsey stood and paced about the small
room. He stopped by the decanter and refilled his
glass. "From all reports, he's just a drifter, a no-good.
You needed me all those years ago. Certainly you need
my help now, and I'm glad to give it to you." He
swirled the wine in his goblet, gazing down at the tiny
whirlpool. "It will be pleasant to have a daughter
again."

The silence lengthened. Nervously, she shifted her
position in her chair.

"In fact," Ramsey said, "in time, I'll even find you a
husband."

"I don't need you to do any of those things," she
protested. "I've found my life."

"McCormick's a user. He'll use you and leave you,
probably with a passel of howling brats."

Letitia flinched. "He's the one I want," she said
flatly, fighting the waves of exhaustion threatening to
swamp her. "When I left Kentucky, I thought I needed
someone to look after me. That's what happens to
poor   relations.   They're   dependent." Her   hand
clenched around her wine goblet. "I'll never be a poor
relation again. With Adam, I'll be his wife."

"On that miserable dirt hill of a ranch." Ramsey
returned to his seat. "I tried that once, many years ago,
and I and my—. But it was no good. Then we lost
what little we had left to a fire and it finished us. That
isn't the life for you. It isn't the life for anyone."

"It's the life I want!"

Ramsey shook his head back and forth. "You're

tired. I can see you've been ill. You're still young—how can you know what you want? When you've regained your strength we'll talk again. Trust me. You need a bath, a bed to sleep in. Any decisions that need to be made, I'll make them for you."

"But Adam—"

"I realize you think you're telling the truth about what happened at that ranch of his. But you've got to realize you've been his captive. That does strange things to one's outlook."

She tried to interrupt, but he went on.

"I'll see McCormick," he said. "In fact, he looks familiar. I'm sure I've met him before. I'll talk to him. I can promise no more than that."

"But—"

Ramsey stood and pulled a bell rope. "Consuela will show you where you can rest. There's nothing more to be said. I will let you know what I've decided after I've spoken with McCormick."

15

From his position on the dirt floor Adam stared at the barred door of the small adobe shed Kennedy used as a jail cell. A mound of sacks, obviously containing rotting potatoes, scented the air most unpleasantly.

Adam's lips peeled back from his teeth in a grimace. He hadn't had a chance to do anything when Letitia walked up to her papa. He'd tried to go to her, but Kennedy and his men had swiftly made any attempt at resistance impossible. Worse, Adam knew his aborted bid for mastery of the situation had directly led to his incarceration in this smelly hole.

He strained at the ropes binding his wrists behind his back. His shoulder responded with a savage jab of pain.

"Damn!" He tried to find a way to sit that would

ease his arms yet enable him to free his hands. Such a position just didn't exist. He set his teeth against the trail of fire running from his fingers to his neck, and continued to strain against the ropes.

Panting, he tried to distract himself from his misery by finding some glimmer of hope that would make the situation appear to be a little less desperate. He didn't succeed at that, either.

The image of Letitia walking up to Ramsey filled his mind. *Please*, Adam thought, *let me see her again*. Something about her papa tugged at his mind. He'd seen Ramsey before, somewhere. There was something about the set of his shoulders, the tilt of his head. *Where?* Adam thought. When? maybe he was the one who had set that fire all those years ago.

He had to see him again, he promised himself. And it would be up to him to make sure the circumstances were in his favor.

He outlined his plan of action. All he had to do was free himself, locate a weapon, rescue Letitia, elude Kennedy and his men, and get away. He continued to strain at the ropes.

Without warning, the door swung open. Kennedy pointed his rifle at Adam's stomach and ordered, "On your feet, drifter. Mr. Ramsey wants to see you."

"Fine." Adam rolled to his knees and struggled to his feet. "I want to see Ramsey, too."

Kennedy guided Adam across the open space between the barn, the low adobe outbuildings, and the hacienda. Once inside the garden courtyard, he yanked his captive to a halt and cut the ropes binding Adam's wrists. "Mr. Ramsey said to untie you."

Gratefully Adam massaged his tender wrists and flexed his sore shoulders.

"I'm warning you," Kennedy continued, "don't try anything. Mr. Ramsey has a gun and he'll use it, if need be."

He swung the rifle he carried to prod Adam in the small of his back. The foreman gestured with his other hand at the open door to Ramsey's office. "In there."

Adam stepped into the room, his dusty boots noisy on the dull orange tiles. Ramsey looked up at his visitor, his face clearly illuminated by the midday sunlight flooding into the room.

Adam moved forward, eager to finally confront his enemy. In midstride he paused, staring at Letitia's papa. Damn, but the man was familiar. Where had he seen him before? Something about Ramsey's face, something about his eyes, tugged at Adam's memory.

A deep foreboding clenched at his stomach. This was wrong—very wrong. He moved closer, searching his adversary's face for confirmation. It couldn't be possible. He couldn't be seeing what he saw. It had to be an illusion. He took another step forward, unable to deny the truth any longer.

Each of Ramsey's eyes was a different color, one blue, one brown.

Adam threw up his hands like a boxer defending against an illegal punch. Suddenly, he was again experiencing the flames and the smoke of his dream, his few memories of a man who had to be his father, all mixed in with his recollection of his pa's odd eye coloring. "No!" he exclaimed.

To keep more words from slipping out, he bit, hard, into his lower lip. His hands clenched and unclenched by his sides as the words of his mother's letter and his few memories of his father ran through his mind. Now, at last he understood why Ma . . .

"You're my father." The words came out half-disbelievingly, half-despairingly, filled with a lifetime of hurt, pain, and fury.

Ramsey stared back at Adam. "What?"

Suddenly, the words in Ma's letter took on new meaning. The odds of two men having the same peculiar eye coloring were just too slim. Adam knew the truth, and it couldn't be denied.

"My mother's name was Ingrid . . . Ingrid Bjorklund," he said softly.

Ramsey paled a little. "No. It can't be. . . ."

Undaunted, Adam went on. "You were married to her, weren't you?"

"I . . . Yes, but I . . . she . . ."

With awful finality, Adam said, "And she gave you a son. Me."

All the color drained from Ramsey's face. He groped for a chair, collapsing onto the leather seat. "How?"

"Ma sent me after you," Adam said. "She changed my last name and her own when she remarried. She led me to assume you were dead. Even so, I didn't know who you were, didn't have any idea that you were alive, but she did."

"Are you trying to tell me that you're my *son?*"

"No! It takes more than blood to create the ties that bind two men together." Adam spat out the words, his fury building. "It appears as if you did father me . . . And Ma, *she* sent me after you, told me to destroy you!"

Ramsey passed a shaking hand over his face. "Adam," he began. "Adam, my son. I never dreamed. How can I make you understand?"

"Don't try. I'll never understand."

"Perhaps you're right. When I left you were too young to understand."

"I understand more than you think."

Ramsey uttered a harsh, bitter sound, one that could never qualify as a laugh. "You? You were barely able to walk when it happened—you've only had Ingrid's side of the story. Did she tell you how our crops failed and I lost our farm? We moved in with her parents. . . . Did she tell you about the fire . . . ?"

Adam could sense his dread of that night repeated in the older man. "I remember the fire," he said.

Ramsey shook his head, forcing himself to continue. "I got you and Ingrid out of the burning building. She wanted me to go back for her parents, but I couldn't. The whole house was ablaze by then. I never could have rescued them and I'd only have killed myself if I'd tried. But Ingrid never forgave me. . . ."

Ramsey's voice trailed off into silence as he recalled the past. Finally, he said, "Did she tell you I wanted to go west and make a new start? Did she tell you she refused to go? She threatened to kill herself, and you too, if I made her obey me."

"You could have stayed."

At last Adam understood his mother's fierce determination to keep her second husband. If she hadn't he would've walked out on her, too.

"If I'd stayed, perhaps I could have found work," Ramsey said. "More than likely, though, we all would have starved. I heard of work in Kentucky, and I found a job as an overseer on a plantation. It was owned by the Sinclair family, who called their place Bellewood. When I could, I sent for Ingrid and you. But she still wouldn't come."

Ramsey paused. "The old lady, Honoria Sinclair,

liked me—she didn't know I was a married man. And, I . . . ah . . . when Melanie Sinclair needed me . . . needed a man to marry her . . ."

His words trailed off, and he shrugged. "It wasn't an easy decision, but still I wrote Ingrid one last time, offering her a final chance. If she refused, I'd lose my son." He spread his hands wide. "A man has to look to the future. Ingrid made her choice—what more could I do? I married Melanie and stayed at Bellewood for ten years. Later, I looked for you, but it was as if you and your mother had fallen off the face of the earth. No matter how hard I tried that was the end of it . . . until today."

Adam had no words. Ramsey's brief story explained more than Ma had ever told her son. A woman's place was with her husband. . . . But when a woman wouldn't, couldn't do what her husband wanted, then what? Still, Adam knew he couldn't easily relinquish a lifetime of pain and anger in the space of a few minutes.

"You said Ingrid sent you to destroy me." Ramsey's flat voice made his words a statement, not a question.

Adam nodded.

"Well, it looks as if she succeeded. Everyone in California knows of my wish for an heir."

Adam nodded again. It was common knowledge that Ramsey's wife, Theresa, had presented him with two stillborn daughters and then died in childbirth along with her third child, a son. Adam knew Ma, and knew her rigid way of looking at things. She probably thought Adam would declare himself and then walk out on Ramsey, just as his father had walked out on his wife and son all those years ago.

But this man was his father. And, damn it, after

hearing his side of the story, Adam did feel something besides fury. Sympathy, perhaps. What hell it must have been trying to satisfy Ma, and still, Ramsey had tried to keep his family together. His story had the unvarnished ring of truth. Most likely, it'd been Ma's rigidity, her inability to bend, more than the circumstances of her life, that had made her so bitter and unyielding.

He was through with doing what Ma wanted. He remembered how he'd promised himself he was through with revenge. Ramsey wasn't an enemy. If he was anything, he was Letitia's papa. Adam recalled how he'd promised Letitia—

The truth of the situation suddenly hit him with all the unexpectedness of a foul hit below his belt. Ramsey was Letitia's papa. He'd been named to Melanie, Letitia's mother. That meant, God in heaven, it could only mean that he and Letitia . . . that they were brother and sister. Letitia! His sister!

Ramsey's voice broke into Adam's thoughts.

"What's wrong? You look . . . Are you ill?"

Adam tried to swallow back the bile swelling in his throat. "You're Letitia's *father?*"

"I . . . ah . . ." Ramsey sighed. "How do I say this? Letitia is a dear child and I do care for her. But Melanie, her mother, was enceinte when I married her. I hate to say this bluntly, but she was carrying another man's child and that child is Letitia."

Adam exhaled, his breath gushing out of him in relief. So she was illegitimate. So what? It didn't matter, not to him, although it did explain a lot about her reticence, her strength under adversity. He'd thought —what he'd been thinking was too awful to be contemplated.

Ramsey continued his story. "I was the overseer at Bellewood. In the normal course of events, old Mrs. Sinclair wouldn't have even allowed me to look at her daughter. But she needed to cover up the scandal. None of those tight-assed Kentuckians would accept a bastard in their family, though. From the day she was born, Letitia's grandmama gave her hell. I felt sorry for the poor little mite and tried to do what I could for her. But my title 'papa' is a courtesy one only, I fear."

"Thank God," Adam whispered.

"Letitia told me she is engaged to you. Is that wise?" Ramsey moved to a chair and motioned Adam into another.

Still weak-kneed, Adam took a chair. "It's what we both want," he said, "with or without your blessing."

"Be reasonable . . ." Ramsey leaned forward in his chair. "Son."

"I'm not—"

"You can be if you wish." Ramsey lowered his voice, his tone persuasive. "I've prospered greatly in California. Like me, you're obviously a determined man. With you, my son, at my side, there's no telling what the two of us could accomplish."

"I know what I want to accomplish," Adam said. "I want Letitia at my side. I don't wish to offend you, but I don't want to be at yours. I know how you and your associates are plotting to increase your wealth through a railroad. Letitia and I, we're through with plotting, we're through with dancing to someone else's tune."

Ramsey brushed his hand across his eyes. "Ingrid has turned you against me. The woman is dead—has been dead to me for almost thirty years. I feared the same fate had befallen you. Don't let her poison continue to spread."

"I'm not." Adam shifted uncomfortably in his chair. "I have a good idea of what it is you're doing. I don't like the monopoly you're creating with your plans for a railroad. I don't like the people you associate with and I especially don't like the way men of your stamp grind the less fortunate under your heel. You must understand, I don't want any part of it. My future and Letitia's doesn't lie with you. We'll be making our own future. You and Ma, neither of you have anything to do with this decision."

Ramsey massaged the muscles just above his heart. "I must find a way to make you change your mind. I can't lose my son again."

Adam stood. "If you understood me, if you truly understood what it means to have a son, as I hope to do one day, you'd understand your flesh and blood is not another puppet to control. When you can accept that, when you can accept me, and Letitia, for what we are, without making any demands on us, then you'll understand what it means to have a son, and a daughter."

"No, wait." Ramsey heaved himself to his feet, one hand braced on the arm of his chair to keep himself upright.

Feeling a tug of regret for what could never be, Adam turned and walked away. At the door, he turned back to face Ramsey. "You and Ma, you're both cut from the same cloth. You're both manipulators. No wonder you couldn't weather tragedy together. Letitia and I will be leaving now."

"You must give me a chance," Ramsey demanded. "You must . . ." He choked suddenly, and beads of sweat popped out on his forehead. He swayed, one hand clawing at his chest. His strangely colored eyes seemed to roll up into his head and he collapsed, falling heavily to the dark Turkish carpet that covered the tile floor.

"What now?" Adam dropped to his knees by Ramsey's side. It wasn't fair. Why couldn't he and Letitia just get away from this quagmire? Adam thought as he loosened the older man's collar and felt for his pulse. Ramsey was still alive, but obviously he'd suffered some sort of fit.

Reluctantly, Adam realized that he couldn't just take Letitia and leave her papa lying there on the floor. He might be dying. Worse, Adam accepted that the man had fathered an ungrateful louse of a son so full of pride that he wouldn't even try to meet his father halfway, a son who'd more than likely caused his father's fit.

"Damn!" Adam gritted his teeth and tugged Ramsey's limp body from the floor. He wasn't a lightweight, and Adam staggered a few steps until he got the body balanced over his still-aching shoulder. He maneuvered Ramsey through the door, shouting for help. They'd have to get him into bed, send someone for a doctor—

"Hey! Stop, you damned drifter!" Kennedy rushed across the patio, his pistol sliding from its holster. "What have you done to Mr. Ramsey?"

"I didn't do anything to him. He suffered some sort of fit. He's alive, but he's going to need medical help."

Kennedy tipped his hat back with his free hand and wiped his forehead. "Oh, hell. It's his heart. He's had a couple of these attacks before. His bedroom's just along here. Follow me."

Adam fell into step behind Kennedy, who was hollering at the top of his lungs, "Consuela! Consuela, get over here right now!"

Despite her bulk, the heavyset woman fairly flew across the patio, dodging around the leafy banana plants and citrus trees to reach Ramsey's side. Letitia followed, only a few steps behind the housekeeper.

"*Aye de mios.* The poor señor." Consuela led the way into the bedroom. She stripped the coverings back from the bed. "Put him here."

Gratefully, Adam eased Ramsey down on the mattress and stepped out onto the covered walkway that edged the patio. Letitia followed him.

"What happened?" She looked up at him, her lovely eyes wide and frightened. "Is Papa . . . ?"

Adam shook his head, understanding what she couldn't say. "No. He isn't dead. It's his heart. Kennedy said Ramsey's had these fits before. They're sending for the doctor. He's a tough old—. There's no reason he won't live through this attack, too."

Letitia wrung her hands. "Papa told me the reason he didn't respond sooner to your ransom note was because he'd had a spasm. There was something wrong with Grandma's heart, too. That's how she died."

Adam drew her close, more to comfort himself than her. "Ramsey'll be all right," he muttered. He had no idea if his words were true or not, but he sensed they were what Letitia needed to hear. "Not that he deserves it after the way he treated you."

"Papa explained," Letitia said, her voice low. "He explained about those men who shot at us. They weren't supposed to do that. They were supposed to bring us back, like Kennedy and his men did. I . . . if it's possible, I'd like to stay with Papa, at least until he's better."

Adam sighed. "I know. We can't go, not yet."

She looked up at him. "What happened?'

"How well you know me." He smiled tenderly at her, and then his expression sobered. "This is going to sound fantastic, but I've discovered why Ma set me on your papa's trail. Before she married Robert, she was married to Ramsey. I'm his son."

Letitia gaped in astonishment. "I don't understand."

"I'd always assumed my father was dead," Adam said. "As religious as Ma was, I was certain she'd never enter into a bigamous marriage. But she did just that when she married Robert. Things got so twisted around in her brain that she ended up blaming Ramsey for all that had happened to her."

"And the shock of discovering you're his son caused Papa's spasm?"

"Not exactly. The shock of the discovery almost gave me an attack, though." He looked down at her. "You little wretch, with you calling him 'papa' every step of the way, what do you think I thought when he confirmed my parentage?"

"Oh!" Letitia's hand flew to her mouth. "It's not true. He isn't my father . . . he's just . . . I didn't tell you, Adam, because it's so shameful—"

His hands captured hers. "Your illegitimacy is not shameful. Never think that. You have no responsibility for what your parents did or what your Grandmama thought. That's what Ramsey and I fought about. He's a wily old bastard, another one of those who have to control everyone and everything. I refuse to be a part of that. I was leaving to get you when he collapsed."

Inwardly, Letitia felt the last vestiges of her old inadequacy slip away. What had happened to her in

Kentucky didn't matter to Adam, and she knew, without a doubt, that it never would. For one horrified moment, she contemplated what might have been if she'd indeed been Papa's daughter, as she'd thought for all those years. For the first time in her life, since the day Grandmama revealed the truth, Letitia blessed her illegitimacy. For without it, loving Adam would have been impossible, and he would have been lost to her forever. That was simply too awful to contemplate.

Kennedy walked out of Ramsey's room. "Consuela says she thinks he's dying this time."

"Oh, no," Letitia groaned. Adam had said Papa would be all right. What had happened?

The foreman fingered his gun. "Three of my men are missing. They were out looking for you and they haven't come back."

She turned to face the foreman. "It was self-defense. They shot at us. Papa said they weren't supposed to do that. They were supposed to bring us to him, like you did."

Kennedy trained his gun on Adam. "Jack, Miguel, and Paco had their orders, although I do have to admit Miguel and Paco are—were—a couple of hotheads. Even so, McCormick, you'd have shot me if you dared. And, to my way of thinking, if Mr. Ramsey dies, you'll be responsible for that, too. I don't know what's going on, but it'll be smartest if I keep you locked up for the time being."

"What do you mean?" Letitia edged closer to Adam's side. "He's done nothing."

"That's not the way I see it." The foreman jabbed his pistol into Adam's ribs. "You're going back into the shed until I hear differently from Mr. Ramsey."

"Don't do anything rash, Kennedy. Letitia tells me Ramsey's had several of these fits. Anything could have brought this last one on."

Kennedy poked the pistol again. "Jack, Miguel, and Paco?"

"Letitia told you the truth. They attacked us. It was self-defense. In a trial it will be my word against yours. No jury will convict on that."

"We'll see about that." Kennedy shoved Adam back a step. "And until we do, you'll be safe in the shed."

"No!" Letitia protested. They couldn't have come so far, have gone through so much, only to be torn apart again, especially when Papa might be dying. "Mr. Kennedy, please." Letitia reached for his arm and he shook her off.

"Don't distract me, miss. If Mr. Ramsey lives, we'll let him sort this out. If he doesn't, well, I don't know what we'll do. We'll cross that bridge if we come to it."

Adam looked at Letitia and she read his expression as clearly as if he'd spoken to her. If he could have, he'd have said to her, "Don't argue with the man holding the gun. Go around him, find a way to outsmart him."

Clearly, it was up to her to find a way out of this new dilemma. Kennedy wouldn't listen to either of them, and Consuela said she thought Papa was dying. What could she do?

Consuela joined the little group on the patio. She raised her eyebrows at Kennedy's gun but directed her attention to Letitia. "Miss Ramsey, you'd better go to your Papa now."

Undecided, Letitia looked from Adam to the foreman and then to the housekeeper. "What do you mean?"

Consuela shrugged her shoulders. "The señor, he is a very ill man."

"Go to him," Adam said gently. "Both of us should be with him now, but we haven't much hope of convincing Kennedy of that." He smiled grimly. "I'll be safe enough in that shed."

"I can't," Letitia said, speaking what was in her heart. "My place isn't with Papa, it's with you, Adam."

"I know, sweetheart," he said. "I feel the same way. But Ramsey needs you more than I do." He glanced at Kennedy. "I'll be safe enough. Kennedy's only doing his job as he sees it. When your papa rouses, tell him what's happened—he's the one in charge here. He'll tell Kennedy to free me and it'll all be over."

"All right. I don't think it's the right thing to do, but if you think so . . ."

"I do." He smiled at her, his expression as tender as a caress.

Letitia watched the two men walk away, her last glimpse of Adam, his broad-shouldered silhouette as he disappeared through the tunnellike opening that led to the front of the hacienda.

She joined Consuela in Ramsey's bedroom, crossing the room to his side, taking one of his hands in hers. "Papa," she said urgently. "You have to wake up. I need you. Adam needs you."

"Letitia," Ramsey breathed weakly.

"God be praised." Consuela fell to her knees and crossed herself. "The señor speaks."

Letitia sighed in relief and her fingers tightened around Ramsey's dry, cold hand. With him conscious, there was a simple way out of this horrible situation after all. "Kennedy is taking Adam away. He says Adam is responsible for killing those men I told you about. Kennedy says—"

"Hush!" Consuela struggled to her feet. "The señor is ill. Do not bother him with this. Later, when he is better."

"No." Ramsey struggled to rise. "No harm must come to my . . ." He collapsed back against his pillows, unconscious again.

"Now see what you have done!" Consuela turned on Letitia in a fury. "Between the two of you, you will kill my señor. Get out of here!"

Aghast, Letitia retreated only as far as the door while she watched the housekeeper attend to Papa. What if Consuela was right? What if Papa was dying? What if Kennedy really thought Adam had murdered those men? Had this been her only chance to save him? Had she failed?

No. She couldn't let herself think such terrible thoughts. Consuela had to be wrong. Papa had to wake up again, he had to tell Kennedy to free Adam. Letitia feared Adam was correct—the foreman wouldn't listen to any other authority.

Her thoughts whirled as she feared she'd killed Papa with her driving urgency to have Adam back at her side. Anxiety gnawed at her as she tried to fix on a ironclad reason to convince Kennedy to free Adam.

"Don't die, Papa," she whispered. "Oh please, God, don't let him die. Not now. Not when we've come so far."

She realized she was praying, not only for Adam's deliverance, but for Papa's as well. He'd been kind to her all those years ago in Kentucky, and in his own way, he'd been kind to her today. She truly believed he wanted the best for her. It would be cruel beyond words if he were to die now, especially when he'd finally been reunited with his only real child.

After a while, her strength gave out and she slid down to the floor. She silently cursed her bodily weakness. Why did everything depend on her when she wasn't able to cope, physically or mentally? She rested her back and shoulders against the wall and waited, knowing it was the only thing she could do now, hating every second as it dragged along.

There was only one chair in the room, the one Consuela sat in. Letitia didn't dare leave to search for another. What if Papa woke while she was gone? She had to be there to speak to him again. This time it would be up to her to not shock him senseless, yet still have him order Adam released.

Adam watched as Kennedy swung the shed door open and motioned his captive inside. The scent of rotting potatoes wafted out into the bright spring air. Adam wrinkled his nose in distaste. A dark-haired man rhythmically hammered at the gate beside the barn, and the sound rang in the midday stillness.

Maybe he shouldn't have agreed with the foreman. Adam admitted to himself he hadn't been thinking too clearly, but that wasn't too hard to understand, considering what he'd learned this morning. He hadn't even had time to sort out his feelings for Ramsey—for his *father*.

This shed wasn't the place to do it, Adam decided suddenly. He should be with Letitia, and yes, damn it, he should be with his father. Especially at a time like this, a son's place was with the man who'd sired him.

"Look, Kennedy," Adam did his best to sound level-headed and reasonable. "I'm not about to leave this place without Letitia, and we both know she won't go anywhere until Ramsey's better. This isn't the right way to solve the problem."

Kennedy slid his gun back into its holster. "Until the boss comes around, I reckon this is the safest place for you. With Jack, Miguel, and Paco dead, I don't know what else to do." He pulled a length of rope free from his belt. "I'm sorry about this, but I'm going to have to tie you up. That shed isn't all that secure."

"You don't have to do this."

"Yeah, I know. But I'm going to do it anyway." Kennedy brandished his rope. "Put your hands behind you."

With an exasperated sound, Adam complied. At the moment, he couldn't think of an easier way out of the situation. Experimentally, he flexed his wrists in their bindings. Kennedy hadn't tied his knots very tight. Adam knew it wouldn't take him very long to work his way out of the rope. He wondered if Kennedy had done it deliberately.

The dark-haired man tossed his hammer to the ground and walked toward the shed.

Distracted by the movement, Kennedy swung to face the cowboy. "Ramon," he called. "That corral needs to be fixed today."

"I need to talk to you!" Ramon shouted.

"Make it fast, then."

Ramon paused a few feet away. "Did you find out what happened to my brothers? Miguel and Paco, they went out with Jack and they still haven't returned. Did you see any sign of them?"

Kennedy shoved his hat back and rubbed his hand down the side of his face before he pulled the brim back into place. "I'm sorry," he said. "They're dead."

"What?"

Adam watched the cowboy pale, the mark of a knife cut clearly visible as his skin tightened over the long, curving scar. Ramon stepped closer, his hands knotting into fists. At six feet plus his height seemed to give him an advantage, and Adam stepped back a pace. He tugged impotently at the rope binding his wrists. He needed his hands free, now! Damn, he knew he shouldn't have cooperated. He should have just slugged Kennedy and gone back to Letitia.

"I don't believe this." Ramon grabbed Kennedy's shoulder and shook it. "What happened? Who killed them?"

Kennedy stood his ground. "Hey, just take it easy. The boss's daughter, she said your brothers and Jack attacked them. Everybody knows you Gomez boys have a tendency to go off half-cocked. From what I hear, they got what they deserved. You know I gave strict orders about using guns if Miss Ramsey was nearby. The boss would kill me if anything happened to her."

"Wait a minute. If Miss Ramsey says my brothers attacked her, then this man must have been there, too, because she was with him when you found her." Ramon's brown eyes narrowed dangerously. "And that makes me think he killed my brothers." He advanced menacingly.

Adam remembered his gut-clenching horror of the battle and its horrible aftermath. He could justify to himself what he'd done, but he couldn't deny his part. It had to be faced. If Swen had been killed, even in a fair fight, Adam knew how he'd be feeling.

He stepped forward. "I did what I had to do to save Miss Ramsey and myself. We were fired on first. I didn't have any choice."

"That's what you say," Ramon taunted. "Miguel and Paco are dead, they can't defend themselves!"

Kennedy tried to intervene. "I've already told McCormick there'll be a trial."

"Ha! What kind of trial," Ramon demanded, "when we only have the word of this drifter and that of a woman?"

The cowboy swung away, and then turned back, his movements blindingly fast, as his fist swung out and hit Kennedy square on his chin. The foreman went down like a felled ox, his hat falling from his head and rolling away. Ramon stepped forward to check his handiwork.

Adam frantically worked at the rope binding his wrists, pain from his injured shoulder shooting like a red lick of fire across his back.

Ramon kicked Kennedy in his side. There wasn't any response.

"Look out!" Adam shouted.

The cowboy glanced up instinctively. His hands still imprisoned, Adam launched himself headfirst toward the other man. His shoulder butted into Ramon's stomach. The cowboy grunted in pain, collapsing under the force of the surprise attack. Adam couldn't stop himself from following his adversary to the ground. He tried to get his weight fully on Ramon's torso and endeavored to wrap his feet around the cowboy's thrashing legs.

Ramon swore. He twisted lithely and freed his fists. Adam tried to counter by butting his head into Ramon's chin. The cowboy hit at his attacker repeatedly, first at Adam's chest and then at his face. One of Ramon's punches connected with Adam's temple. Darkness threatened to engulf him. He felt himself going limp and fought to remain conscious.

Hearing returned first, the sound of something being dragged across the hard earth. He blinked and saw Kennedy's flaccid legs disappearing into the shed. Ramon emerged into the sunlight, secured the wooden door, and trained a pistol on his foe. The knowledge that the cowboy had Kennedy's gun drove Adam to redouble his efforts to free himself from the rope securing his hands.

"You'll pay for what you did to my brothers." Ramon swore, his voice low, his words thick with his fury. "I know how the courts work in this land. Me, Miguel, and Paco, we are *Californios,* we are worthless. It is up to me to make you pay for what you have done. It is up to me to avenge my brothers' deaths."

Ramon poked the gun in Adam's side. "Get up, get moving, you murderer."

Adam staggered to his feet, his head pounding, his shoulder throbbing savagely. He stepped back from the pressure of the gun's barrel. Ramon's hand was steady, his eyes hard and full of purpose. He didn't look like a man who'd listen to reason.

The cowboy poked his captive again, herding him toward a low adobe building standing behind the barn.

"It is almost noon," Ramon explained. "There will be plenty of my *compadres* waiting for their meal. But they will forget about their food when I tell them what has happened to us. They will know what has to be done."

About a dozen men loitered outside the adobe shed. Adam recognized a few who had ridden with Kennedy to escort him and Letitia. Adam figured he could reason with them. They had to realize that Ramsey didn't want the man they'd captured killed. The men formed into a group, waiting as Ramon marched his prisoner closer. When they were less than six feet away, Ramon ordered, "Stop."

Adam ignored the command and launched himself into the middle of the group. He knew Ramon would never fire his gun; the odds of hitting an innocent bystander were too great.

Adam hit the ground face-first, the hard clay abrading his left cheek. He tried to roll, but with his hands tied behind him he succeeded only in driving his injured shoulder into the ground. Pain swept through him, and he temporarily lost interest in what was happening around him.

He felt rough hands dragging him to his feet and he shook his head, trying to clear his brain, trying to focus his thoughts, trying to seize on a way to regain his freedom.

"Listen to me, all of you," Ramon shouted. "This man, he murdered Jack and my brothers, Miguel and Paco."

An angry muttering ran through the crowd and the men formed a circle around Ramon and Adam.

"It is true," Ramon continued. "He has admitted it."

"It was self-defense," Adam shot back. "I had no choice. Those three, they fired first. It was them or me and—" No. He couldn't bring Letitia into this. She was safely in the house. Who knew what Ramon would do if he mentioned her?

"He is lying," Ramon countered. "It is up to us to avenge the deaths of three of our own."

"What do you mean?" one of the men asked.

Ramon fingered his gun, pointing it at Adam. "I could shoot you, right now, like a mad dog. That is what you deserve. You didn't give my brothers a chance—" Ramon spat. "But we are not animals. We will give you justice."

"Justice?" Adam countered. He looked at the angry faces of the men circling him and his heart fell. Clearly, no one in this group was a lover of fair play.

"Justice!" Ramon exclaimed. "We will have real justice, not like what we get from the local law." He turned to the men, seeking support. "Remember how that judge released the *Americano* who raped José's sister? 'No evidence,' he said. But we have the evidence, right here before us. This McCormick, he has admitted he murdered my brothers!"

Adam jerked harder at the rope and finally tugged his left wrist free. His hands came up, clenched into fists as he crouched in a fighter's stance. He whirled around, searching the line of men for an opening. The hard, implacable faces surrounding him sent a shaft of fear twisting into his gut.

"And what do you do with a murderer?" Ramon shouted.

"You hang him," someone shouted back.

An angry, feral growl ran through the crowd as more and more of them shouted, "Hang him! Hang him!"

* * *

Adam stared between the ears of the swaybacked roan gelding they'd mounted him on. The horse's age was reflected in the gray hairs wreathing his muzzle, and Adam could only surmise that Ramon had selected the quietest mount in the barn to assist him in his horrible deed. The cowboy must have known he needed a horse who would stand quietly until someone whipped him into action.

The roan's bone-jarring trot vibrated up through Adam's spine, and his shoulder throbbed furiously with every jounce. Once again his hands were confined behind his back, but this time the knots cruelly tight.

He could see the stand of oak trees lining the creek they'd crossed this morning on the way to Ramsey's ranch. It made sense that the men had elected to do their terrible act away from the house and the outbuildings.

They believed they were executing a murderer and they wouldn't want to perform that grim deed in the place where they lived and slept, worked and played.

He tried to force his thoughts away from the dread building in his gut. Even in battle he'd felt he was in control of his actions. At times like that, life or death, a higher authority made the choices, not man. He'd never faced death this way, so hopelessly. He promised himself he would find a way to carry on, to not give up.

He focused his thoughts on Letitia, blocking out everything but his memories of her and all the ways her presence delighted him.

A shout broke his concentration. The man leading the roan jerked the horse to stillness. "It's Kennedy!" someone yelled. "He's following us!"

Adam exhaled. He'd been in some close calls before,

but never one as close as this. His lips tightened as he watched the foreman spurring his horse to greater speed. These men worked for Kennedy, Adam thought, they'd listen to him. He sighed again, gratified and astonished by this last-minute turn of events. *McCormick,* he told himself, *you are one damn lucky so-and-so.*

Ramon reined his horse around to face the foreman, and Adam sensed the Californios' unease. He wouldn't want to be in Ramon's boots when the foreman lit into the cowboy.

Ramon pulled his rifle free, lifted the gun to his shoulder, and fired quickly. Horrified, Adam watched the foreman throw his arms up into the air and crash to the ground while his riderless horse galloped away.

Adam's hopes of a moment ago dissolved faster than a drop of water in the midday sun.

"You've killed him!" someone shouted.

This can't be happening, Adam thought wildly. With Kennedy gone, there wasn't much hope left.

Ramon reined his horse around to face the men. He leveled his gun at the group. "Who's next?" he demanded. "Who's too weak-livered to do what has to be done?"

Letitia had lost track of time. Fatigue had taken over and she'd dozed exhaustedly. Dimly, over her disjointed thoughts and dreams, the sounds of a commotion outside the hacienda filtered into the patio.

The foreman, Kennedy, stumbled into the room. A long red gash streaked across his forehead, the surrounding flesh bruised and almost as purple as the lump on his chin.

Letitia leaped to her feet and grabbed the swaying man. Consuela joined her, and they guided his wavering footsteps to the chair. He collapsed onto the seat, groaning.

"What happened?" Letitia demanded, her stomach clenching with dread. "Adam?"

"I fell off my horse when they shot at me." Kennedy carefully touched his injured temple. "That doesn't matter. They've taken him down to the creek."

"Who have they taken? What's going on?" Letitia demanded. Fear drove her, but still she handled the man gently, turning him so she could see the injury to his forehead. "What's going on?"

"There isn't much time." Kennedy gasped. "One of my men, Ramon . . . he discovered that his two brothers were killed when they attacked you, back up there in the mountains. He's convinced the rest of the men that McCormick is responsible. They're taking him down to the creek to lynch him."

"No!" Letitia cried.

Consuela's words cut across Letitia's agonized moan. "How do you know this? Why didn't you stop them?"

"I tried." Chagrined, Kennedy lowered his head and he mumbled. "Ramon surprised me. He knocked me out and locked me in the shed." Kennedy looked up. "By the time I came to and got out of there it was too late. They were gone. They'd left old Alfredo behind and he told me what had happened. I grabbed a horse and rode after them." Gingerly, he fingered the wound on his forehead. "That's when I got this."

Letitia braced her shaking hands on the wall beside the chair where Kennedy sat. She knew she shouldn't have let Adam out of her sight. She turned to face the foreman. "How long ago did this happen?" she demanded.

"Not long," Kennedy said. "If we're quick, maybe we can get back there in time. But we've got to bring Mr. Ramsey, too. He's the only one that mob will listen to. He's our only chance to save McCormick."

Letitia covered the few feet to Papa's bed. Trying to calm the sick quaking of her stomach, she touched his face. "Papa, can you hear me? It's urgent. You must wake up."

Consuela shoved Letitia to the side. "Let me do this. I know how to rouse the señor."

Wringing her hands together, Letitia stepped back. Kennedy heaved himself out of his chair and touched her shoulder.

"I'm sorry about this, miss. I tried to stop them. When I took McCormick away I was doing what I honestly thought best."

"Sorry!" Letitia rounded on him, her anger superseding the panic building in her chest. "If you'd just left Adam here with me, with Papa, none of this would have happened. They're killing him, and you're sorry!"

"Alfredo's bringing the buckboard around to the front of the house." Awkwardly, Kennedy patted Letitia's hand. "I think we can make it."

Would they? Letitia wondered. How could they? How long had it been since they'd shot Kennedy? Adam might already be dead. She heard the sounds of Ramsey stirring as Consuela brought him back to consciousness.

"Señor," Consuela's voice was low and soothing. "You must be strong now. Adam McCormick needs you."

Ramsey coughed and struggled to sit. "My son? What has happened to Adam?"

Letitia sensed Kennedy's start of surprise. "McCormick is the boss's son? Oh, shit!"

"Señor, you must calm yourself if you are to do what must be done," Consuela ordered her employer. Swiftly, yet dispassionately, she outlined Kennedy's story.

Still pale, Ramsey swept the bed covers aside and tried to sit up. Letitia braced his shoulders, fearing his sudden movement would make him pass out again.

"Give me my pants," Ramsey growled.

Wordlessly, Consuela helped her employer into his trousers. She reached for his boots, but he waved them away.

"There's no time." He stood and thrust the front of his nightshirt into his pants, his color visibly improving by the second. "Let's go."

The buckboard was waiting outside the door, and Alfredo was standing by the horse's head with a driving whip in his hand. Between them, Letitia and Consuela helped Ramsey into the passenger seat. Kennedy joined them, mounting his gray, a new pistol gripped in his hand.

"Follow me!" he shouted.

Letitia ran around the back of the buckboard and climbed up into the driver's seat. Consuela heaved her bulk into the back, telling no one in particular, "You're not going without me."

Letitia grabbed the reins, took the whip from Alfredo, and braced her feet against the dashboard. "Hang on tight, Papa," she warned as she shook the reins and yelled "Get up!" at the horse. She lashed at him with the whip to drive the chestnut into a wild gallop.

Please, God, she prayed. *Don't let us be too late.*

Adam forced himself to watch Ramon emotionlessly as he ordered the men into action. They discussed which tree to use, weighing the merits of various limbs.

"I saw a man hung once," one of them commented, "and the branch wasn't strong enough. It took three tries before they found one good enough to hold the fellow and break his neck."

Adam bit down, hard, on the soft tissue inside his mouth. It was enough to muster the courage to survive this ordeal once. How could he manage three times?

Survive? his thoughts mocked him. Yes, damn it, he would find a way to outsmart that loudmouthed cowboy. It wasn't over yet. He squared his shoulders, forcing himself to ignore Ramon as he leaned over from his horse to drop the noose around his captive's throat. *This can't be the end*, Adam thought. Not now, not when he'd found the love of his life. She'd given him meaning and purpose. *I love you, Letitia*, he pledged.

That thought galvanized him to fight once again.

"Listen to me, all of you!" he shouted.

"Be quiet," Ramon said. "No one wants to hear you, not now."

"A condemned man deserves the right to speak," Adam pointed out. "It's the custom."

"He's right," one of the men said. "We owe it to him to hear what he has to say."

"No one will believe you," Ramon taunted.

"I'm a dead man, near as not—" Adam started.

"You're a dead man, period," the cowboy interrupted.

"Let him speak," someone else said.

Adam tried again. "What I'm telling you is the truth. There were four people that day who knew the facts, and I'm the only one left to tell the story. Those three men, the ones you call Jack, Miguel, and Paco. They jumped me. They fired first. I admit it, I killed one, Jack, I think, but it was self-defense. The other two, it was an accident. I won't lie, I would've killed them if I could have. Except one of them was using a rifle. I don't know what went wrong, but it exploded in his hands and it killed him and the other man. Their blood isn't on my hands."

"Miguel never did clean that rifle of his," a man muttered. "I told him often enough he was heading for trouble."

"No! Do not listen to him!" Ramon shouted. "He is telling lies, lies only a desperate man would tell. He has admitted the killing. That is good enough for me."

Ramon leaned over and tightened the knot. The pieces of hemp on the rope bit into Adam's throat like tiny needles. At least he'd tried to convince this mob of his innocence. He shut his eyes, and thought, *Letitia, my love. Letitia!*

Ramon spurred his horse away. "It is time."

The blasting percussion of a gunshot snapped Adam's eyes open. Scarcely able to believe what he saw, he watched as Kennedy, brandishing his pistol, charged into the knot of men clustered around the tree. Immediately behind him a buckboard, driven by Letitia, rattled through the trees, lurching wildly over felled tree limbs and rocks.

Letitia sawed at the reins, endeavoring to bring the

panicked horse under control. She saw Adam, mounted on a roan, his hands tied behind him, the noose around his neck, and a measure of the fear twisting her stomach into knots eased. He still lived. They'd made it!

One of the men ran to the carriage horse's head, trying to bring it under control. She lashed at him with the whip. "Get out of my way!" she screamed. "Don't try to stop me!"

"Nor me." Ramsey attempted to stand upright in the still-swaying buckboard. He settled for half-crouching, one hand clutching the arm rest for balance. "That man is my son. Do you hear me? Adam's my son! Touch one hair of his head and I'll see that every single one of you burns in hell!"

Ramon reached for his pistol. Horrified, Letitia watched helplessly. She realized that the man who'd been standing behind Adam's roan had switched his attention to Ramon's horse. He used his quirt to lash at the bay, and it bolted. A shot rang out and Letitia cringed. A branch crashed to the ground, and the roan danced nervously. The quick-thinking man with the switch darted to the roan's head, quieting the horse.

Fifty feet from the group, Ramon regained control of his mount. He swung his horse around and shouted, "This is not the end. Someday, somehow, justice will be served." He spurred his horse ruthlessly and the bay galloped away, soon disappearing into the trees.

Kennedy pointed at the men. "You three," he ordered. "Mount up and go after Ramon. He can't get away with what he's done today."

Until that moment, Letitia hadn't realized she was holding her breath. Gratefully, she released it. Her attention fully centered on Adam, she made her way through the mob. As one, the men backed away from her nervously. The man with the quirt reached up to cut the bindings that held Adam's hands behind his back. He grimaced and rotated his shoulders before he removed the rope from around his throat.

Giddy with relief, she lifted her hands to him. "Adam . . . Thank God . . . Are you all right?"

In a rush, he came down off the horse and swept her into his embrace. A whimsical smile tugged at his mouth. "I've been around the world. I've been in a war. I've done just about everything a man could or should do, and more than a few things a man shouldn't do. Hell, I just barely missed my own lynching. There's only one thing left that I want, and that one thing is you." He stroked the line of her cheek, his fingers tracing the tender curve of her lips.

She turned her face into his palm, glorying in his gentle, loving touch.

"Sweetheart, words cannot describe all the ways that I love you. Perhaps this can." Ignoring everyone around them, he lowered his lips to hers.

In the midst of the blazing embrace, Letitia finally understood him, understood all the complex nuances that made up the man who was the center of her world. She felt oddly maternal and protective and at the same time wanton and completely giddy with desire as she responded to him.

Swen watched Adam and Letitia as they stood in front of the minister. The black suit Adam wore strained across his back as he squared his shoulders and gazed lovingly down at his bride. To Swen, it seemed strange to see Letitia wearing a dress. It hugged her tightly, emphasizing her tiny waist before it belled out and ended in a short, graceful train.

He'd thought all was lost when Adam hadn't caught up with them. Swen had left Billy with the doctor and returned to the cave, only to find the place deserted. He recalled how gut-clenching fear had dogged every step of his journey to Ramsey's ranch to pick up their trail. It'd been a welcome anticlimax to find Adam and Letitia planning their wedding while Ramsey benignly watched the two, agreeing to all their plans.

"You may kiss the bride." The minister's voice intruded into Swen's thoughts.

As he watched Adam sweep Letitia into a tender embrace, Swen's lips tightened and his eyes misted. If he didn't watch out, he'd be crying like Consuela. Clearly, Adam and his trusting, steadfast woman had found their happy ending. An odd longing lumped in his throat. They'd found each other, he realized, but what had he found?

The answer in his mind surprised him. He wasn't a little brother or a son anymore. He was a man. It was time for him to find his own life, his own happy ending.

ONE GOOD MAN by Terri Herrington

From the author of *Her Father's Daughter*, comes a dramatic story of a woman who sets out to seduce and ruin the one good man she's ever found. Jilted and desperate for money, Clea Sands lets herself be bought by a woman who wants grounds to sue her wealthy husband for adultery. But when Clea falls in love with him, she realizes she can't possibly destroy his life—not for any price.

PRETTY BIRDS OF PASSAGE by Roslynn Griffith

Beautiful Aurelia Kincaid returned to Chicago from Italy nursing a broken heart, and ready to embark on a new career. Soon danger stalked Aurelia at every turn when a vicious murderer, mesmerized by her striking looks, decided she was his next victim—and he would preserve her beauty forever. As the threads of horror tightened, Aurelia reached out for the safety of one man's arms. But had she unwittingly fallen into the murderer's trap? A historical romance filled with intrigue and murder.

FAN THE FLAME by Susanne Elizabeth

The romantic adventures of a feisty heroine who met her match in a fearless lawman. When Marshal Max Barrett arrived at the Washington Territory ranch to escort Samantha James to her aunt's house in Utah, little did he know what he was getting himself into.

A BED OF SPICES by Barbara Samuel

Set in Europe in 1348, a moving story of star-crossed lovers determined to let nothing come between them. "With her unique and lyrical style, Barbara Samuel touches every emotion. The quiet brilliance of her story lingered in my mind long after the book was closed."—Susan Wiggs, author of *The Mist and the Magic*.

THE WEDDING by Elizabeth Bevarly

A delightful and humorous romance in the tradition of the movie *Father of the Bride*. Emma Hammelmann and Taylor Rowan are getting married. But before wedding bells ring, Emma must confront not only the inevitable clash of their families but her own second thoughts—especially when she discovers that Taylor's best man is in love with her.

SWEET AMITY'S FIRE by Lee Scofield

The wonderful, heartwarming story of a mail-order bride and the husband who didn't order her. "Lee Scofield makes a delightful debut with this winning tale . . . *Sweet Amity's Fire* is sweet indeed."—Mary Jo Putney, bestselling author of *Thunder and Roses*.

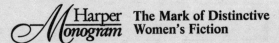

Harper Monogram — **The Mark of Distinctive Women's Fiction**

ANALISE
Analise Caldwell was the reigning belle of New Orleans. Disguised as a Confederate soldier, Union major Mark Schaeffer captured the Rebel beauty's heart as part of his mission. Stunned by his deception, Analise swore never to yield to the caresses of this Yankee spy...until he delivered an ultimatum.

ROSEWOOD
Millicent Hayes had lived all her life amid the lush woodland of Emmetsville, Texas. Bound by her duty to her crippled brother, the dark-haired innocent had never known desire...until a handsome stranger moved in next door.

BONDS OF LOVE
Katherine Devereaux was a willful, defiant beauty who had yet to meet her match in any man—until the winds of war swept the Union innocent into the arms of Confederate Captain Matthew Hampton.

LIGHT AND SHADOW
The day nobleman Jason Somerville broke into her rooms and swept her away to his ancestral estate, Carolyn Mabry began living a dangerous charade. Posing as her twin sister, Jason's wife, Carolyn thought she was helping her gentle twin. Instead she found herself drawn to the man she had so seductively deceived.

CRYSTAL HEART
A seductive beauty, Lady Lettice Kenton swore never to give her heart to any man—until she met the rugged American rebel Charles Murdock. Together on a ship bound for America, they shared a perfect passion, but danger awaited them on the shores of Boston Harbor.